AN AIR OF DECEIT
A HOLLOW'S GLENN COVEN MYSTERY
KRISTEN KING

Silverster & Eve Publishing

Contents

REMEMBRANCE TEA

1 1/2 cups water

2 springs fresh rosemary (leaves only)

2 springs fresh sage (crumpled leaves only)

1/4 of a lemon

Bring the water to a boil. Place the herbs inside a sachet or a tea strainer and immerse in the water. Let steep for three to four minutes while closing the eyes and chanting the incantation,

Ancestors of the light, come into my sight.

Do this incantation three times and squeeze the lemon into the tea at the end. Sip the tea, peering into the steam of the cup to remember your ancestors again.

CHAPTER 1

The sky shifted to a darker hue. Clouds puffed up and drew nearer, looming over the shop as Autumn peered out the front window, uncertain of what the day would bring. She knew this weather was foreboding, even though she loved the smell of rain in the air and the crispness it brought. Some uneasiness hung in the wind and made her think she would need to draw upon the strength of her ancestors to make it past that evening.

Autumn gently positioned the curtain back neatly in the storefront window, patting down the fabric and ensuring the bottom laid nicely to frame her new fall display. She returned to the counter just as her cousin, Simone, walked in.

"Morning," Simone said with a sigh as she wrestled her black messenger bag off over her head and shimmied out of her matching black, vegan leather jacket. "I was up late last night going over some of my design class submissions, so I'm kinda sluggish today. Plus, it looks like a storm is brewing out there."

"Yeah, I can feel the pressure in the air. This one is bringing some unusual energy along with it, so let's be on our toes today. I wanna be ready with some candles and my pendulum, just in case we need them," Autumn said hurriedly as she whisked up a few items from the tables of the shop.

She put some red and black taper candles, cinnamon sticks, and a black tourmaline crystal into a wicker basket and carefully placed the basket behind the counter where she could reach for its contents at a moment's notice.

"There," she said with a bit of a smile. "It makes me feel better knowing I've got these in my back pocket today. Something tells me I'll be using them," Autumn hinted. Even coming into the shop this morning, she could sense the change in energy, and the whispers she heard occasionally seemed stronger than ever today.

They were whispers of what seemed like caution. "Watch for the bearded man arriving in tandem." But what it meant, she could not yet say. The voices only gave her a head start at what may need her attention. They acted almost like guardians, steering her away from harm and through whatever storm seemed to come. Somehow, they knew she always headed into the eye of a storm instead of away from it, as most people would.

The voices always carried on the wind to her. She started hearing them a few years prior, but her grandmother had warned her that the voices were coming. Autumn was a hereditary witch, after all. So the idea of strange whispers directing her didn't give her much pause. She knew from a very early age that her gifts would manifest one by one when needed, and that's precisely what happened. She was just grateful to have her grandmother, aunt, and cousin around to provide insight.

Her grandmother was the backbone of her family. Autumn's mother had decided years back to travel extensively and perfect her gifts as a healer. She wanted to help as many people as possible and travel to places where many were in need. Autumn understood the importance of that calling, and even though she missed her mother terribly, she took so much comfort in the many years spent by her grandmother's side.

Now, she enjoyed running the cozy paper craft shop on Main Street, Parchment and Pine, in their tiny mountain town of Hollow's Glenn. It was where she provided just the right messages for customers who needed a bit of comfort, joy, and support in their lives. Autumn's insightful messages blended perfectly with Simone's design sense to create the most beautifully cozy product collections for their patrons. They carried handcrafted journals, wrapping supplies, paper lanterns and calendars, and even comforting items such as flannel blankets, hand-poured beeswax candles, and of course, a large variety of their gran's teas on hand to keep the customers warm while they found something special to bring home.

Autumn always knew she would remain in Hollow's Glenn, and opening up her store here felt like her one true calling. As soon as she saw the shop, she knew it was made for her. She had been walking down Main Street with her cousin, Simone, when a little voice told her to look left. It was the first time she had heard the voices, and it led her to find a vacant little shop across the street that would soon become the cozy little paper shop she ran today.

Even when she was little, Autumn loved being a homebody. It was the very thing that warmed her heart and made her aura warm to an earthy shade of green, her favorite. Of course, running through the evergreens that lined her grandmother's mountain cottage was a close second in her mind. The beauty of the forest, especially on fall evenings, would always enchant her, almost as if it would sing in her ear of all the magic she possessed. The forest was her second home, and it enthralled her from the very beginning.

Yet now she devoted herself to the shop, along with her partner and cousin, Simone. Together Autumn and Simone enjoyed delivering comfort to the vacationers and locals alike, sending each one away with a bit of magic in a bound linen notebook or a bag of teas and providing a metaphorical warm hug with each cozy item taken home. It was the perfect way to spend the days practicing the girls' gifts and enjoying their favorite things.

Autumn and Simone kept the shop feeling very warm and inviting every season of the year. On this fall morning, Simone headed over to the fireplace at the back of the shop and began throwing a couple of logs on to make a fire. The smell of the burning cedar wood carried through the entire store, bringing the girls back to their childhood of late-night bonfires by their grandmother's cottage. It was nostalgic and soothing, perfect for the stormy morning's uneasiness.

"How crazy is this weather?" a voice cut through the quiet shop along with the ringing of the bell, signaling the shop had a visitor. Both girls looked up from their tasks to see Simone's mother, Josephine, tumbling in with an enormous umbrella and a bundle of herbs in her hand. Josephine ran the local bath shop and had a knack for innately knowing what type of self-care someone needed in order to recharge. She had a lot of water energy in her, and her intuition was always spot-on. Josephine had passed much of that same water energy onto Simone.

"Aunt Jo, what's your gut telling you about today? These clouds are making me worried, and you know I love a good storm, but I can tell from the dark shades of purple that something is off today," Autumn nervously questioned her aunt. "My guides are even piping up a bit this morning."

"Really? What did they say?" Simone asked inquisitively, brushing a few strands of her dark shoulder-length bob out of her eyes to see Autumn better.

"Oh, sweetie, let Autumn be. It's okay if she doesn't wanna share, but she is right. My intuition is hinting at a tumultuous time. The rain is coming, and we're all just going to have to ride out whatever this storm brings, so let's not get too far ahead of ourselves now. Try to stay in the moment today and not lean into any worry or stress. I know it's easier said than done, but it's best to do what you can to stay grounded and centered." Jo went over to the counter and grabbed Autumn and Simone for a big hug. "I love you girls, and we MacKinnon women don't easily roll over in any weather! So let's prepare for anything and try to enjoy the day."

"Yeah, you're right, Aunt Jo. I know those voices try to look out for me, though. That's one thing I have learned over the last several years. So when I heard them this morning, I didn't wanna dismiss them," Autumn replied.

"Oh yeah, definitely don't dismiss them! They've always sounded to me like they're your best allies aside from us. So if you do wanna share, we can help you sort out what they said," Simone suggested with a bit of a smile and excitement in her eyes. She loved adding a little drama to any day, and Autumn knew her cousin would always be there to spice things up.

"Autumn, it's okay. You can tell us when and if you're ready," Jo tried to soften the persuasion.

"No, it's okay. I heard them this morning as I was heading into the shop. They mentioned something about a bearded man arriving in tandem, whatever that means. But it made me pause and realize I needed to be on the lookout today. Those clouds added on top of the whispers, make me think there's something very eerie in the air. I don't wanna leave myself unguarded today," Autumn confessed as she stretched out her forearms onto the shop counter and looked back and forth at both women as if to search for what to do next.

They all looked at each other with worry in their eyes, and then Jo chimed in, "Well, it sounds like you've got a message that'll give you a leg up for the day. All you can do now is grab some protection candles, slather them with a few drops of clove oil, and keep your fire going for the day. Keep the energy clear as best you can in here, and don't fret. The more stable you can keep your energy, the better." Aunt Jo was well-versed in the power of energy. Water was a powerful force that could set off many emotions, so she learned early on how to harness her energy and protect it from whatever was happening around her.

As Jo discussed what to do, the lights flickered a bit, and they all stopped for a moment. The girls pulled out the candles Autumn had gathered in a basket earlier. They placed a few drops of essential oils on the wax, spread it evenly over the candles, and placed them in taper holders on the countertop. Simone lit them, and the aroma of cinnamon and cloves swirled in the air.

"Now, I need to go open up the bath shop, but call me if you need me at all today. Trust your intuition, girls, and stay inside here at the Pine while the storm passes. Those voices of yours will keep you safe, Autumn. I know that to be true as well. Simone, look out for your cousin, and hopefully I'll see you both for a beautiful fall feast tonight at my house." Jo returned to the shop's front door, grabbed her umbrella and herb bundle, and headed down Main Street.

Just as she walked out the door, a thunderclap shook the store and both girls right along with it. Simone whipped around to Autumn, emphatically drew her arms out to her sides, and exclaimed, "Well, I don't know about you, but I'm officially freaked out about what's in store for us today!"

Always the dramatic one, Simone drew a bit of a laugh from Autumn and a head nod of agreement. It was time to open the shop, but Autumn couldn't help thinking that whatever news was on the wind today, it wouldn't be the last time she would call on the whispers for help and her cousin to back her.

CHAPTER 2

Autumn went to the back room of the shop, pulled her long, auburn hair back into a loose bun, slathered on a quick layer of peach lip gloss, and rifled through her music playlist. She wanted some jazz with a lot of soothing piano sounds for today. It would make the perfect ambiance for a somber day. As soon as she found something and hit play, the slow start of the piano keys accompanied a clattering on the roof. It must have started to rain, and that was her cue to make the shop more inviting to passers-by.

She noticed Simone already gathering supplies in the back to label their latest beeswax candles for the season. She lined up twenty glass jars on the countertop behind the register and strung out the twine, their shop-designed kraft paper labels, cinnamon sticks, and springs of pine from the florist next door to bundle the candles.

Autumn made her way to the front window and peered over the paper-constructed garlands and fall wreaths in the display. As she focused on the raindrops hitting the windowpane, she was soon distracted by an orange tabby cat jumping right up onto the outside window ledge. It had a tufted white collar and looked right up at her with emerald green eyes as if to ask permission to ride out the storm under the shop awning.

She looked at the cat curiously and smiled. Autumn never saw this cat around town before, which was unusual because she knew most animals around Hollow's Glenn. And yet, this tabby seemed to be a couple of years old, but with no owner she knew. Perhaps it had wandered over from a nearby town and gotten too far from home in the storm.

The wind howled now, and she decided it would be best to bring the cat into the back room while the storm subsided. She could probably keep it cozy in one of the shop blankets on the office floor. There was a dutch door back there, so the cat wouldn't disturb any customers coming in for the day.

Autumn called to Simone, "Hey, I spotted a new furry friend outside the front window. I think I'll grab him and bring him into the office so he doesn't get drenched in this weather."

Stretching her neck to look out the window from the back, Simone responded, "Aw, he's adorable! I wonder where that little cutie came from. I'll help you get him inside."

The two girls headed out the door and snatched up the cat just in time before the wind started belting the storefront with rain coming down sideways. They took the tabby to the backroom, found some spare blankets from their last shipment of goods, and got the cat into a makeshift bed all his own. From his circling, it seemed like that was exactly what he'd intended when he'd hopped onto the window of Parchment and Pine.

No sooner had Autumn gone out to grab the cat and get him snuggled inside, than the bell at the front of the shop rang. Simone was first to lead the way as she called out, "Come on in and get warmed up," when she looked up and realized who was standing in the doorway. A man with dark brown hair and a short-trimmed beard carried a messenger bag atop his soaked half-zip sweater. He followed behind a woman all too familiar to the girls, Aunt Jo.

Jo coaxed him into the shop from under her umbrella. Putting it aside, she brushed off the wetness from her cheeks and introduced the man that came in with her, in tandem.

"Oh, girls, sorry to charge in so suddenly from the storm, but I needed to bring James over before it got much worse outside." Her words sounded rushed and flustered, which wasn't typical for Josephine.

"Mom, what's going on, and who is James?" Simone questioned.

Autumn stood right behind Simone now with a questioning look of her own. They walked up to the front to help the two out of their wet jackets and into the coziness of the store.

Autumn stared at the man, unsure of what to do next. He seemed to be the one the voices had warned her about. But why was he with Aunt Jo?

"James, this is my daughter, Simone, and her cousin, Autumn. James is my friend Sorcha's son. They live on the outskirts of town, and Sorcha's known of my special...gift for intuiting what people need for years. She sent James over for some help with a dream he's been having, and I wanted to bring him here so you could hear it for yourselves." Josephine had some seriousness in her voice now and looked at the girls with hints of dismay.

James caught Autumn's eye, and the two of them seemed unable to detach from one another. It was as if she captivated him with her energy, and it was all he could do to stay focused on the conversation.

"Okay, so what's this dream about, and what does it have to do with us?" Simone was always direct and had no qualms about digging right into what most people would delicately breach.

"Simone, Autumn," James nodded at them as they gestured for him to sit on one of the bar stools at the counter.

"I came to your mother this morning on the advice of mine. I've been having some strange dreams, and I've always felt my dreams were sending me messages, but I haven't been able to decipher them. But this one has been coming to me for some time now. When I dreamt it again last night, it seemed to be more urgent than usual, so I talked to my mother about it. After our chat, she insisted I see Jo and explain everything to her." His voice was calm, even while relaying this experience that seemed to have jarred him greatly.

"This dream has been awakening me in the middle of the night, and I can't seem to shake it." As he was talking, his eyes continued to linger increasingly on Autumn. He had a look of being completely mesmerized with her, and his words would trail off until he was quickly brought back on topic by Simone.

"So, tell us more about it. There's obviously something that has you and my mother flustered, so let's have it," Simone prodded, making James shift his gaze away from Autumn for the time being.

"Well, I don't know exactly. The dream is about me walking through a dark wood, stepping on branches that snap under my feet. It's late in the day, but I can make out a cottage ahead of me. As I walk toward the cottage and up the steps of the porch, I notice a distinct smell of eucalyptus. It's intense, and it burns my nostrils. I reach for the doorknob to go inside the cabin, and as I open it, a white owl flaps out, just barely missing my face and flying over my head out into the woods." He glances over at Autumn as he relays this.

"The inside of the cabin is strangely dark and cold, and as I place one foot in front of the other, I see something glistening on the floor. It's a locket of some sort, and while it appears to be glowing with brilliant green light, it's also empty inside. But as soon as I step forward to retrieve it, someone comes out of the shadows to face me." James stopped for a moment to glance over at Jo. She nodded as if to tell him to proceed with his story, and he looked back at Autumn.

"Go ahead. You can tell us what you saw," Autumn spoke intently with a deep sense of compassion for him.

"I saw you." James sat there with his eyes firmly on Autumn now. "You spoke to me and told me to find you. You said you must be the one to unlock the elements and protect the heritage passed down through generations."

Autumn narrowed her eyes and gave James a confused look. "I came to you and said this?" She knew her mother was a dream walker, but she had never experienced it herself. How could she have come to someone she had never met before with a message she knew nothing about?

Suddenly, the eerie feeling she had felt earlier in the day set in again. A pit started forming in her stomach, and she didn't know how to respond.

"Autumn, sweetie, I should have questioned the voices you heard earlier in the day. I wanted to keep you grounded and not add to your stress, but now I see that there's something meant for you to uncover. Our family needs this message right now, and you are the key," her aunt said with dismay in her tone.

"Wow, this is intense. How about before we go down any crazy rabbit holes with this, we go sit in the back where we can all have a moment to think and discuss," Simone rationalized. She loved the excitement of a good mystery and knew her cousin did, too, but Simone could tell Autumn felt taken aback by this.

Autumn looked down at the counter, as if searching for some kind of answer right before her. The voices foretold James's coming, but the reasoning was still unclear. She had to make sense of all of this, but right now, this dream was bringing up many questions.

The doorbell rang again, and a few drenched customers strolled in, hoping for a warm cup of tea as they perused the shelves. Simone moved around the counter toward them and hinted to her mother to bring Autumn and James into the hearth room opposite the shop counter for more privacy.

Jo nodded in agreement and motioned for them to make their way toward the now roaring fire as it crackled in the back. As Autumn and James settled into the two wingback chairs beside the fireplace, Jo unraveled the sashes on the curtains that framed either side of the hearth room. She brought the heavy fabric to a close and told her daughter she would take care of the back while Simone catered to the front customers.

Jo grabbed a tufted ottoman from beside one of the wingback chairs and slid it closer to Autumn. Hugging the back of her long, flowy skirt with her hands, she sat down and looked at them both.

"Now, how can we piece this all together?" Jo asked.

The three of them stared at one another, not knowing where to begin. Then Autumn had a thought. "The woods and cottage sound an awful lot like my grandmother's house. I grew up in that house and continue to live and care for my grandmother there. Aunt Jo, do you think the dream takes place in Gran's cottage?"

Shaking her head, Jo crossed her legs and put her elbows on her knees as she leaned in. "Yes, sweet girl, I do, and I'm afraid that you're about to come face to face with a destiny that's had you in its sights for quite some time."

CHAPTER 3

After James and Aunt Jo left the shop, Autumn realized she was pretty shaken by their conversation. She didn't know what to think of the dream and how she was involved in whatever strange happenings were to come.

All she knew was that, somehow, she felt comfortable with James. The voices had told her to watch for him, but she didn't feel she should be worried about being around him. It was almost as if it was the message he carried portending something ominous yet necessary, and she was more curious than afraid.

Like her aunt said, there was a destiny waiting for her in all of this, and while she felt apprehensive about finding out what it might be, she always had the curiosity of a cat and wanted to know all she could. This dream of James's was no different.

It was time to go to Gran and receive some guidance from the winds. After all, Gran had taught her not to be afraid of the messages carried to her. She would know what the next step needed to be. Plus, Autumn wanted nothing more than one of her warm hugs and to cozy up next to the cottage fire.

Tidying up the counter, she looked back toward Simone, who stood in the back office wrapping some new handmade journals that the girls had made especially for the season. "I can't sit with this dream any longer. I'm gonna close up for the day and head home to Gran's before it gets much later."

Simone came over to her with a concerned look and nodded. "Okay, but don't forget my mom is making Equinox dinner tonight. Gran should already have prepared something, so hurry over after you two gather whatever you need to understand the dream. We can help with preparations, and this will be the perfect evening to sort out some answers." Simone replied as she displayed the new journals neatly on an open shelf.

"Right. Gran will know what to do, and we'll bring everything we need, plus whatever she's cooking on the stove. I have a feeling it'll be something with apples that's just perfect for this evening, and I know Aunt Jo will have the patio table waiting for us in back under the light of the moon. So we won't keep you both waiting," Autumn said with a smile.

"Good. Oh, and Autumn, I know you're already worrying and playing this dream over a thousand times in your head, so just relax, and we'll get everything sorted out together tonight, okay? It is, after all, the start of the season of the witch. And that's our specialty in this family," Simone slyly said as she raised both eyebrows.

"All right, I get it. You're in your element, and you're embracing your inner witch. When do you not do that, though?" Autumn laughed as she flipped the sign to "closed" at the front door. She blew out the candles scattered about the shop on the countertop, shelves, and tables and grabbed her coat and bag.

"Just lock the back door as you leave, okay? I'll meet you at Aunt Jo's," Autumn waved to Simone as she walked out. She stopped, pulled the door shut behind her, and thought for a moment. Simone was right. She had been replaying the dream and worrying all day. Yet, the worry seemed to come from an unnerving sense that everything was about to change forever, for better or worse. It felt like she needed to prepare for something she had never known before, but for what, she wasn't sure.

Autumn's brown faux suede backpack felt heavier on her shoulder this evening than it did most of the time. She couldn't remember what she could have put in it to make it so weighed down. She pulled the bag up a little higher onto her shoulder as she wandered down the street to the Forest Brew bakery and coffee shop. Autumn needed to pick up the order she placed for some fresh pumpkin bread loaves. She hadn't had time to bake anything properly for this evening's annual Equinox family dinner, although she knew Gran and Aunt Jo would mostly take care of all that. The least she could do, though, was to bring a special treat from the local bakery that they'd all enjoy.

The leaves rustled and swept across the sidewalk as Autumn walked down Main Street, and she could feel a change in the winds. It had always been one of her gifts to sense the changes in the air, but this night made her uneasy. She wasn't sure if the change in season was bringing something ominous or whether it was just the voices that she'd heard that were making her imagination come to life.

As she headed into the Forest Brew, she shrugged off her hesitations and put on a smile for Ms. Newbury, the older lady who ran the coffee shop. "Hi, Mrs. Newbury. Just popping in to grab my order," Autumn said as she approached the counter.

"Ah, yes. Hello, Autumn. How are you this evening? The storm we had today was quite something! Did your shop hold up okay?" Mrs. Newbury was always in tune with what was happening in town, especially with the weather affecting the mountain region.

"Oh, yeah. It definitely rattled the shop, but we managed all right. How about you? Was anything damaged that you know of?" Autumn was concerned that maybe that was the feeling she had had this evening… a sense that the town was unsettled and perhaps damaged by the storm.

"Oh no, we seem to be all right, thankfully. The lights flickered a bit which put off a few customers, but you probably had the same thing down at your shop," she replied.

"Yep, the lights were going crazy, but I'm just glad we didn't lose power. So I guess it could have been much worse than it was," Autumn was relieved, but still confused about what might have given her this uneasy feeling.

"All right then, I've got your two loaves of pumpkin bread right here, nice and warm from the oven. And please tell your gran that I'll be ringing her about some of her new tea blends for fall. I've gotta start stocking the new flavors now that the season is turning," Mrs. Newbury remembered as she rang up the bread loaves and bagged them up for Autumn.

"Yes, I will definitely tell her. We're doing our special Equinox meal tonight, so I'll be sure to let her know while we're enjoying this bread of yours. Thank you, Mrs. Newbury." Autumn said as she grabbed the bread bags, and placed them carefully in her backpack, before heading out.

She needed to head back home to Gran's house first to pick her up before they headed over to Aunt Jo's for dinner. It was just a half-mile walk through the neighborhood streets of town before she'd get to the little cottage on the edge of the woods where she and Gran lived together.

Autumn grew up there and had walked to and from town since she was little. The cottage was her heart and soul and the woods next door, her sanctuary. When Autumn's mother left town to follow her own gifts connected to the energy of the earth, Autumn had been quite young. Her gran and Aunt Jo promised to look after her and raise her according to the family traditions while her mother accepted the role of healer around the region. Autumn saw her occasionally as the seasons brought her back to Hollow's Glenn, but it wasn't the regular contact she had always longed for.

She had family here, though, with Gran, Aunt Jo, and Simone. They were always there for her, taught her to connect with the land, water, and sky, and be open to the gifts that flowed within her. Autumn was grateful for them and couldn't think of anything better than to be raised with those three strong women by her side.

The light shifted around her as she slowly approached the walkway up to Gran's cottage. The clouds slowly moved overhead, and she felt a chill overtake her. She adjusted her backpack and looked up at the sky with concern. What could possibly be going on today?

Autumn walked up the steps while looking around her as if to see if anything was out of place. "Gran, the strangest thing happened today, and I wanna talk it over with you tonight," Autumn shouted as she pushed the front door open. But the room was quiet, and her eyes shifted over to a still figure lying lifeless on the living room sofa.

"Gran!" Autumn rushed over to her grandmother's side, dropping her bag to the floor as she went.

"Oh no, Gran. Can you hear me?" Autumn's voice shook as she grabbed Gran's wrist and checked her pulse, but there was none to be found. She touched Gran's face with her palm, but there was no response. Autumn looked around her for some sign of what was going on, but all she could feel was a tenseness in her own chest.

She didn't understand. Gran was perfectly healthy for her age. She had no signs of any issue, and Autumn had left the house this morning with Gran completely happy and up and about as usual. What had happened, and how long had she been like this?

When Autumn couldn't wake her, she closed her eyes tightly and tuned into the energy of the room. She sensed Gran's energy still hovering there as if it was waiting for something, but it wasn't the same lively energy she had always felt around her. It was less constrained, but it still seemed like it was waiting to be freed from one last thing.

Autumn whispered an intention under her breath, "Air of wisdom, reveal the truth to me and set us free." She opened the palms of her hands and turned them upward as if to receive something.

Gran's energy moved around her, and shimmering specs of golden light emerged as if tiny little fireflies were dotting the living room. They gathered around the coffee table in front of where Gran was lying on the sofa. The table had a teacup resting on a crystal agate coaster, and Autumn noticed something strange inside the teacup. A bit of water sat in the cup's bottom along with a long metal tea strainer that seemed to be full of already steeped herbs.

The strange thing was that Gran never liked to use tea strainers. They always left little bits of loose tea leaves floating in the water, which bothered her. For as long as Autumn could remember, Gran kept empty tea bags handy in her kitchen, and she filled the individual bags with her own special blend of herbs, depending on her mood for the day. Autumn occasionally used the metal tea strainer as it was quicker and didn't bother her as much, but Gran would never have used it if she was making tea for herself.

Confused but focused, Autumn followed the shimmering lights around the room. She knew she had to stay with them while Gran's energy remained. No matter how sad it made her, deep down Autumn knew there was nothing an ambulance could do for her Gran. She had already left her body.

Autumn moved toward the bookcases along the back wall as the lights directed her. They swirled along the floor in big circular motions as Autumn bent down to pick up a few books strewn around on the wooden floorboards. A few of Gran's journals were lying there, along with a copy of a meditation book and some energy-channeling guides that Autumn had seen Gran pull out from time to time. It didn't quite make sense why they were all lying here in a pile unless someone else had been here and made this mess. Gran kept her home neat, so even if she searched for something, it would have been unlikely for her to have left a mess like this.

As Autumn contemplated this, the lights moved toward the kitchen. They stopped before Gran's tea cabinet and hovered there while Autumn caught up. She opened the glass cabinet doors of the tall wooden hutch as the lights swirled around inside the shelves.

Autumn furiously darted her eyes around the shelves, trying to find what the lights were pointing out. Everything was in its proper place, and she didn't see any cups missing or disorganized like the bookcase. She brought her eyes up to a higher shelf for a moment and kept her gaze there as she took in the shelf's contents.

The teapots with their respective teacups sat lined up nicely in a row. However, there was one that wasn't the way it was supposed to be positioned. One teapot and one teacup had their handles sticking out to the left, and the teapot spout pointed to the back of the cabinet. There was no way Gran would have put them away like that. She was always adamant about putting the teaware away facing in the same direction and never pointing directly to the front or back to invite good energy into the space.

Autumn grew increasingly nervous looking around the room to find out-of-place items. There was no way that Gran had been here alone. Someone was here with her, and that meant someone else already knew, or perhaps intended all along, that Gran was dead.

Tears streamed down Autumn's face as she covered her mouth in a cry and perused the room. She took a deep breath to calm herself down, and the lights swirled around her as if in a warm, gentle hug. She knew her gran was trying to comfort her and be by her side even in Gran's last moments. Autumn smiled at the thought of that, and she returned to kneel by her grandmother's side.

With her hands hovering over Gran's body and her eyes closed, she spoke the words that she heard Gran say as a child for circumstances like this. "You are one with air. You are one with fire. You are one with water. You are one with earth. Allow this spirit to return to the elements and merge her energy with beauty and love. As I say it, so shall it be."

Autumn opened her eyes and rotated her hands in a semi-circular motion so that her palms were now facing upward. The shimmering lights enveloped Autumn's hands and then swirled above her grandmother's body higher into the air.

"I release you to be one with the elements." And with that, the lights shimmered upward and dissipated in the air. Autumn knelt beside her grandmother's body, knowing that she was truly now gone.

But as she felt the warmth leave the room, some kind of pull drew her to Gran's body. That's when Autumn noticed the glow of Gran's locket. A light was shining from inside of it, and the voices that called to Autumn now came from the necklace.

"You are the key," the voices said as emerald light glowed around the edges of the locket.

Autumn bent over and opened the locket around her grandmother's neck to find a small antique key inside. She remembered seeing Gran use the key from time to time to open the wardrobe cabinet that stood in the living room behind the wall of the front door. It's where Gran said she kept all the family's special items. Yet, whenever Autumn peered into it, the cabinet seemed to be mostly empty aside from a few flannel tartans and some old journals. She never understood what Gran meant by the family's special items.

She made her way over to the wardrobe, carefully placing the key inside the lock and opening it gently. On the wardrobe floor, she found a large wooden box with carvings of the sun and moon on the lid with emerald light streaming out from around the edges, just like the necklace around

Gran's neck. Autumn hunched over to slide the latch open and reveal what was inside, and laid on a bed of her family's tartan MacKinnon plaid sat a hard-bound book that looked ancient yet as beautiful as new.

She opened the first pages of the book to read, "MacKinnon Book of Spells. For the Keepers of the Elements." As she read them aloud, more words appeared on the first page. "We are the earth, air, fire, and water of these lands. Ours is the chosen bloodline to honor and protect what remains here, just as in the place of our family's origin."

Autumn felt the energy seeping off the pages while she read the words, and her body tingled as if she were taking on the energy from it. She closed her eyes along with the book and gently hugged it close to her chest as a few more tears fell on her cheeks.

She looked over at her gran, and her eyes welled up with tears. Autumn knew she needed to step outside for some fresh air before she could wrap her head around calling an ambulance and the police. She moved toward the door, placed the book on the tiny stand where Gran left her energy-clearing crystals and keys, and pulled down her soft evergreen-colored cape from the wall hook. Gran had given it to her for her sixteenth birthday, along with a note about how she was transforming into the witch she was meant to be.

With a deep breath, Autumn enveloped herself in the flowing cape, grabbed the Book of Spells, and flung the door open to peer out into the night.

CHAPTER 4

She blew out of her grandmother's cottage like a storm's wind carried her. Wrapping the hood of her cape over her long auburn locks, she forcefully descended the steps onto the wooded path to the forest surrounding the property. The energy began taking root inside her, and she needed to get into the sanctuary of the woods to think for a moment.

She placed one foot in front of the other, letting her long cape trail behind her through the fallen leaves while sweeping the branches along the path. A developing urge for release built inside of her, welling up from her feet through her body and into her throat. She breathed out a deep sigh and, in one swoop, let out a wafted breath that seemed to mix with the outside air and instantly sent a sweeping tornado around her. She realized that with that gust of wind, she had also levitated herself to a few inches above the ground.

Autumn felt lighter and free hovering there, yet somehow she knew everything was different. It was as if now she carried a great deal more responsibility than ever before. This was the first time her gifts had acted this powerfully and manifested in such a way as to affect her physical body. She took a calming breath and slowly lowered to the ground again. There was so much going on inside her head, and she just needed to get grounded for a few minutes to think things through.

Autumn walked a little further into the woods to a small clearing encircled by aspen trees. She stood in the center of the circle and turned clockwise, chanting, "Energies of the wood, be with me now. Give me the strength to be who I must."

With those words, some emerald green shimmering lights similar to the ones in her grandmother's house appeared on the forest floor beneath the aspens. They rose up and slowly approached her in the center of the clearing. The lights flitted around like fireflies and swirled around her like the tornado of wind she created on the path. The energies of the earth and the sky encircled her, and the whispers on the wind softly came to her.

"You are the chosen one. The four points witch."

She sucked in a breath and felt the spell book under her arm glow once more. Autumn brought herself down to the ground and laid on the earth as the lights continued to glow around her. She placed the book on her chest and straightened her arms and legs before looking at the sky. The aspen trees left an opening at the top of the clearing so that she could see the stars between them. The earth and air comforted her as Autumn felt the energy of this new responsibility take hold.

Placing her hands on the earth below her, she nervously set the intention to honor her grandmother and all of her ancestors by claiming the gifts that were now bestowed on her. Without realizing what that truly entailed or how she could live up to it all, she thanked the energies of the woods and picked herself up off the ground. The lights slowly made their way back under the aspen trees and seemed to dissolve away.

Autumn looked at the path back through the woods to Gran's cottage and knew that whatever she was facing, she would do it with Aunt Jo and Simone by her side. So many questions were still unanswered, but now was not the time for that. She had to take care of Gran now and put her necklace, the key, and the MacKinnon Book of Spells away safely before anyone else stepped foot in the house. As she walked back along the path, she knew exactly where that would be, but when she returned, someone was already waiting for her—James.

Autumn pulled the hood down from her head and stared at him from the path. She wasn't sure what to think of him coming here. After all, he told her of the dream where he found her at the cottage in the woods, but she hadn't put that together again until just now. She wasn't sure what to make of him, but his energy felt warm and comforting. All the while she, Aunt Jo, and Simone had spoken with him in the shop, James had an overwhelming sense of home to her, even though she had just met him.

Autumn moved closer to him so she could make out his face better in the dark. "What are you doing here?" she asked.

"I couldn't shake my dream, and after talking with you today, I needed to know that you were okay. So I remembered you thought the dream was about your grandmother's house, and I asked my mother to give me directions," James relayed honestly. "I just needed to know you were all right."

She shook her head at him and said, "No, everything is not all right. I found my grandmother inside. She passed sometime today, and I wasn't here. She's gone." Autumn looked up into his eyes as they stood on the porch, desperately hoping they would relieve the other's worry.

"I was taking a moment to understand what might have happened and process it, but now I need to call for the ambulance. I need to find out what happened." She paused as she looked out to the woods as the winds howled, "And I think I'm meant to have you here by my side."

Autumn looked at him, unsure of why she accepted him being here. All she knew was that he felt like the song of a red bird on a winter's day, which soothed her. His dream had foretold their meeting, and she was more inclined than ever to pay attention to her intuition and the messages given to her.

"Will you wait here a moment while I check on Gran and get my phone?" she asked.

"Of course, whatever you need." James found an Adirondack chair lined with a plaid flannel blanket on the porch, and he nestled himself inside the chair to wait expectantly for her to return.

He felt strangely drawn to her and wanted to see where this was leading. His mother had always told him that his dreams would lead to his destiny, but he was never exactly sure what that meant or how it would transpire. He would help Autumn in any way he could, though. After all, she captivated him with her emerald green eyes and the jasmine scent that somehow filled his dreams of her and gave him a longing for the beautiful days that lay ahead.

CHAPTER 5

Autumn threw her cape over the hook inside, grabbed her phone from the backpack she had thrown on the floor when she arrived, and started dialing. She figured she would have just a few minutes after she called for the ambulance before they arrived with the police. That would be her chance to say one last goodbye and gather the book and key along with Gran's necklace.

She started dialing, her fingers shaking as she hit the numbers. This all seemed so surreal, playing out almost like a movie in her mind. Somehow she thought maybe she'd awaken from a dream tomorrow, just as James had when he envisioned this all. Yet, she knew deep down that she couldn't hide from the reality in front of her now.

As the phone immediately picked up, someone on the other end spoke, "911, what's your emergency?"

"Yes, I'm at my grandmother's house and found her unresponsive. She has no pulse, and she's stopped breathing. Please send someone. Also..." she trailed off for a moment. "I think there may have been foul play." Autumn could feel a lump rising in her throat. How could anyone do this to Gran? She was a revered member of the community, and while tough at times, she had a big heart.

"Miss, just stay where you are. We're sending an ambulance and a squad car to your address now. I have it coming up in the system. You can stay on the line with me if you'd like if you feel you may be in danger," the voice on the other end said.

"No, I'm all right. I'm here with a friend now, so we'll stay together until the ambulance arrives. Thank you." Autumn hung up the phone and shook off the sadness filling her once again. She had only a few minutes to conceal the family heirlooms.

First, she walked over to Gran, rested her hands on her heart for a moment, and then carefully removed the locket that Gran had worn for as long as she could remember. It chose Autumn now to be the bearer of the key and whatever came along with it. She tucked the locket carefully into a zipper pocket of her backpack and went over to the wardrobe.

She would have to conceal the spell book in the wardrobe once again, just as Gran had done for years. The only problem was that Autumn didn't know the spell to keep it hidden. She placed the book back into the carved wooden box, peeking outside the front window to ensure James wasn't peering in on her. Closing the lid with the latch, Autumn stepped back and raised her hands again.

"Elements of these lands, I call on you to conceal the ancestral contents of this cabinet. Protect and keep them for only those with pure intentions and the bloodline of the four points. As I say it, so shall it be." With her words, the wooden box glowed around the edges, and then suddenly, it was gone again. Amazed that it worked, Autumn recomposed herself, locked the cabinet door with the antique key that had appeared, and placed it carefully into Gran's locket in her bag.

She would get more answers from Aunt Jo later tonight, but for now, all she wanted was to sit on the porch with James and wait. She walked out and sat next to him in an Adirondack chair, just as she noticed the orange tabby from this morning wandering up the walkway toward the house.

Autumn wrapped herself up in a flannel blanket and peered down from the porch at the cat. "It's the cat I saw this morning in the storm. What are you doing all the way over here?"

James looked past the stair rail on the porch to see the tabby making his way over. "Huh, maybe he had the same idea I did about lending you some support right now." James turned his gaze to Autumn.

"Thank you, by the way," she said as she met his eyes.

"For what?" James responded.

"For warning me. For coming tonight, and for not asking questions. I think I needed your energy here to ground me. Strangely, I don't think anyone else could have done that for me. Even though I've barely just met you, I feel like we've known each other our whole lives. Does that sound crazy?" Autumn looked over at him and his eyes met hers.

"No, I feel the same way," James sat for a moment looking out at the walk leading up to the cottage. "I'm sorry, by the way. About your grandmother. And I'm sorry that this was what the dream was about."

"Thank you. But I feel like we're just scratching the surface of what your dream was really about."

James looked up at her, squinting with curiosity.

"Let's call my Aunt Jo," Autumn said matter-of-factly. And with that, the ambulance turned the corner to the cottage road with sirens blaring. Both of them rose, preparing for whatever was to come.

As the paramedics attended to Gran inside, two police cars pulled up along the front road. Autumn knew the officers well; this was a small town, and her family had been acquainted with everyone for years. She had even grown up with several of the local police officers.

"Chief Walsh," Autumn said as the officers approached the house.

"Evening, Autumn. I heard the message you called in. What's going on?" Walsh said as he walked up the porch stairs with one of his officers. He looked over at James and gave him a nod.

"I found Gran inside as I was coming home this evening. We intended to go over to Aunt Jo's for the Equinox tonight, but when I came inside, I found her lying lifeless on the sofa." Tears started forming in Autumn's eyes as she relayed the story.

"Okay, is there anyone else here with you now besides..." His voice trailed off inquisitively as he looked over at James.

"Oh, I'm James. I'm a friend of the family, and I knew Autumn would be here. So I stopped by to talk with her."

"I see. All right, Autumn, why don't you walk inside with me and tell me what led you to think there may have been some kind of foul play." He put his arm around her and guided her into the front door.

As they walked inside, they found the paramedics lifting Gran onto a stretcher. She looked peaceful even in this state, which was pretty telling of the energy Gran always possessed within her. She was a strong but compassionate soul, and her incredible power came from the wisdom in her heart. That would always be clear in her body, mind, and spirit, no matter where they were.

Autumn began explaining to the Chief what she found when she heard Aunt Jo yelling on the front porch. Autumn spun around to find her and Simone barreling through the door.

"Sorry, Chief. I couldn't hold them back," one of his officers replied.

Waving him off, Walsh replied, "It's okay, Adam. Don't worry about it. They're family." With a sigh, Walsh looked at Aunt Jo with sorry eyes. "I'm sorry, Jo. She's gone."

Aunt Jo looked from him to the body lying on the stretcher. She ran over to Gran and threw herself over her body. Autumn could hear the muffled crying as Aunt Jo hugged Gran tight as if never wanting to let her go. "How did this happen?" Jo sobbed.

"Autumn seems to think maybe this wasn't exactly natural causes." Walsh looked over at Autumn, giving her a nod to continue with what she had found.

She trusted Chief Walsh, but she knew there may be others in the room that would talk in town. There seemed to be a strange energy around the house right now, and she didn't want anyone else taking what they had heard and spreading it around.

"Chief, can we just talk between us and the family?" Autumn hesitated as the paramedics were still preparing Gran to be taken to the hospital. She wanted everyone cleared out before what she had to say.

As if he inherently knew there were some things better kept quiet, Chief Walsh escorted the paramedics to the door and waved for one of his other officers to come inside. James watched through the front door as Walsh brought in another officer, and the paramedics took Gran out. He peered inside and caught Autumn's eye. With a questioning look, James seemed to ask if she was all right there. Autumn nodded her head at him and gave a bit of a smile.

Walsh closed the front door back up and introduced the officer. "Ladies, you remember my son, Ben. He'll be working closely with me over the next year as I'm planning to retire soon. Since he's been in the force for a while now, I'm going to entrust him with the station. Whatever you need to say, you can say it in front of him as well. Jo, you and I go back a long way, and I know your family has some... shall we say, strong connections to this land. If there are things you need to discuss, we can do it now." Walsh looked at Aunt Jo, as if to request permission to hear the things Autumn needed to say.

Aunt Jo nodded, turning toward Autumn. "He's right, dear. We can trust the Chief, and I'm confident Ben will be just like his father. We're

Hollow's Glenn people through and through, and we need to lean on each other. That's what Gran would have wanted. So just tell us exactly what happened." Aunt Jo walked over to Simone and wrapped her arm around her as she listened intently for Autumn's response.

"Okay, I came home and ran inside to tell Gran about the storm and all today." Autumn stopped and glanced at Aunt Jo. She wasn't sure if she should really say anything to Chief Walsh about how James's dream was involved, but Aunt Jo looked to confirm that it was okay. "James, the one on the front porch, had a strange dream about meeting me here at the cottage, so I wanted to relay that to Gran. When I came in, I found her lying on the sofa, unresponsive. I ran over to her to see what was wrong, but she wasn't breathing and had no pulse."

She glanced at Aunt Jo again as she continued, "I could feel that she was still here but no longer truly with us." She stopped to get a sense of what Chief Walsh was thinking.

"All right, so what made you suspicious instead of thinking that she just had a heart attack or something? There must have been something out of the ordinary." The Chief looked at her inquisitively.

"Yes," Autumn hesitated and mainly stuck to the facts from here on out. "I found this teacup on the table with a strainer for the tea, something Gran would never have done. There's no way she would use a strainer unless she was politely doing it to accommodate someone else because she absolutely hated tea leaves floating around in her tea."

"That's true. We could never get her to use the strainer. It always had to be a tea bag that she carefully put together herself," Simone chimed in. Now she leaned in closer to hear Autumn's story.

"After I saw that, I started looking around the room to see what else may be out of place. So I found the bookcase was a complete mess. There are books all over the floor, and Gran always kept things neat even if she had been looking for something." Autumn used an adamant tone in her voice now, the one she used when sticking to her guns to win an argument. She always was good about speaking her mind when it really meant something to her.

"Nothing appeared to be missing from the bookshelves, but it definitely seems like someone was going through them in a hurry. I just don't know why. And then there's the kitchen. I realized the teaware isn't how Gran arranged it. The handles are going in the wrong direction, and the teapot's spout on top is pointing toward the back. Gran liked to keep the tea cabinet arranged just so, and even if she had someone over for tea, she would have put everything back neatly." Autumn had her arms crossed over her chest now with a worried look on her face.

Simone hugged her as Aunt Jo approached Chief Walsh. "So what do you think, Ian?" Jo had concern in her voice, but her intuition told her that the Chief would always have their best interests at heart. She did have quite a fondness for him for as long as she could remember.

"I haven't decided yet, but I wanna follow through with all that Autumn is saying. Let's not touch anything else in here until I've had my officers give it a proper look-through. We'll collect any evidence that we can and get back to you." Putting his hand on Jo's arm, he eased his tone, "I'll also have the coroner do an autopsy to see about the cause of death if you're all right with it. Just give me the go-ahead and we can do that." He was clear about the next steps, but his compassion was also evident. Autumn suspected that he knew how sensitive Aunt Jo could get and that their relationship was more than it appeared on the surface.

They all agreed, and Aunt Jo went over to wrap the girls up in a hug as Chief Walsh and his son flagged the other officers down to come into the house.

James knocked on the front door. "Is it all right if I come in or did you want me to stay any longer? I wasn't sure what you needed, but an officer already got my statement."

"Oh, James. Why don't you walk us all to our cars now," Aunt Jo said as she turned to wave goodbye to the Chief. "Autumn is going to stay at our house for the next few days," she said, looking over at her. "And I won't take 'no' for an answer. Autumn, why don't you grab a few things you need if it's all right with Chief Walsh, and we'll meet you at the car."

Autumn nodded, and Aunt Jo and Simone pushed James out the front door along with them. "James, how did you end up here?" Jo asked as they walked down the steps and out to the cars.

"I just couldn't shake my dream. I kept seeing Autumn's face looking up at me in the cottage, and I had the sense that she needed me to be here," he said, shaking his head back and forth. "Turns out, she actually wanted me here. She said she needed some grounding and was coming out of the woods when I got here. I saw the shimmering lights through the trees as I approached the house, but I didn't see her appear until I walked up closer. Honestly, I didn't know what to expect, but I had to follow what I was feeling."

"Oh, dear boy. I don't know what she needed from you tonight, but something called you here, and I'm very grateful that you stayed. Remind me to thank your mother for sending you our way." Jo squeezed her arms around him and let a few tears fall down her cheeks again. "Well, here comes Autumn with her bag. Let's all just get home tonight and rest, shall we? Tomorrow we'll be able to think straight and make sense of all of this."

Everyone agreed as Autumn approached the cars looking right at James. "I don't know what to say except that it's been some night, and I'd like to talk to you more in the next few days if that's all right."

He smiled at her, took her hand in his, and kissed it. "Get some sleep. I have a feeling I'll know exactly when you're ready to talk." And with a nod, he walked back to his car to head home for the night.

"His aura is powerful, and there's definitely some kind of cord connecting you two," Simone broke the silence with her directness. "He's very deep and earthy, but that can be a good thing. I feel like Gran would have approved of him."

Aunt Jo sighed, "We'll talk about James later. Come back to our house, and we'll have a bite to eat. The moon will pour its light over us tonight and give us the wisdom we need from our ancestors. And maybe Gran will, too."

CHAPTER 6

Autumn put her overnight bag and backpack down on the bench Aunt Jo had lining the side wall of the stairs. She flopped onto the bench cushion and rubbed her face in her hands. This had been one of the hardest days she'd ever had. Her grandmother meant so much to her, having raised Autumn since she was in elementary school. She didn't know how she was going to get through her passing.

"Come in the kitchen, dear. Let's salvage what we have left of this night. Gran would have wanted it that way," Aunt Jo said as she wiped her hands with a kitchen towel. Autumn almost forgot about the feast they had planned for this evening. Aunt Jo must have been preparing for weeks as the Equinox marked the beginning of the witch's season. As a water witch, connecting with the fall season ran deep in her veins, almost as if it gave her energy for the rest of the year.

Autumn pulled off her ankle boots and unzipped the pocket of her bag. She slowly pulled out the loaves of pumpkin bread and the necklace she had removed from Gran before they took her away and then wearily slid into the kitchen to find Aunt Jo and Simone.

"Aunt Jo, I didn't say everything that happened in front of Chief Walsh."

"Of course you didn't, dear. I know you held back. Come, grab a dish, and meet us in the back garden. It's getting late, and the moon will shed some light on the answers we seek."

Aunt Jo took after Gran in how they were always so wise. Yet, Jo was much more intuitive than Gran. She led with her heart and always wore it on her sleeve. Gran was wise with the wisdom of many lifetimes, and it showed in the way she approached life with insight and grace.

In the backyard of the two-story craftsman home, maple trees and tall grasses lined the perimeter to create a cozy private garden. Aunt Jo tended to all of it herself. Edison bulb lights ran between the trees and over the trellis that hung above a beautifully laid garden table set for tonight's feast. The three of them sat around the table as the full harvest moon shined its light down around them.

"All right, my darlings. We lost a loved one tonight," Jo said as they held each other's hands around the table. "Gran was the head of this family, and I know we are all heartbroken, but she is not lost to us. Her energy is forever in our blood and in these lands. I know her spirit will come back to us whenever we need it. But now we need to be strong for each other and find our way forward."

"Aunt Jo," Autumn pulled the locket out of her hand and held it in her palm in the middle of the table for both of them to see. Immediately, the edges of the locket appeared to be glowing again as if something shined brightly inside of it.

Jo and Simone gasped as they saw it and eyed Autumn for a moment. "It was calling to me somehow when I found Gran. The light was shining inside of it, and when I opened it, I found a small key."

"You are the key we've waited for all these years," Jo said as though she was putting the pieces together to a puzzle that had baffled them for years. "I suspected, but when nothing happened, I let it go. I spoke with your mother about it at one point. Even though I thought she suspected it too, she worried that this kind of responsibility would be too much for you to handle. So she never mentioned it again. I know she's always been concerned for the path you might lead."

"Wait, what are you talking about, Mom?" Simone looked confused as her gaze moved between Jo and Autumn. "This is Gran's locket. What does it have to do with Autumn? Gran wore this every day, and it's never glowed like this. Are you saying that it's glowing because of something Autumn did? Or now that Gran is gone?"

"Well, in a way, yes. This locket activates our ancestral abilities and our connection to these lands. Gran was the bearer of the locket because she was the matriarch of this family. It was her responsibility to carry it forward until a new four-points witch would make herself known in our bloodline."

"It called to me. As if it needed me to retrieve it and find the key within it, the necklace whispered to me," Autumn said in a low voice.

"Perhaps it knew that its keeper was in danger and that it was time for the true owner to claim it." Jo looked into Autumn's eyes, put her hand on her arm, and asked, "Did you feel Gran's energy as it called to you?"

"Yeah, I did, and that's not all." Autumn recalled the shimmering lights, and as the thought crossed her mind, tiny emerald green specs appeared under the garden's maple trees.

Simone turned her head to find a flurry of them headed straight for the table, buzzing around them. "It's Gran. I can feel her here with us. Her energy is wispy and quick, but it's definitely her. She's bringing me a memory of when we were little and made crescent moon cookies in her kitchen for the Equinox." The usual guard that Simone had up seemed to lift, and she allowed the lights to encapsulate her with shimmers of green. "She wants us to feel comforted and loved rather than worried for her."

"That's exactly how I felt when I saw them at the cottage," Autumn said as she let one light land on her hand like a butterfly.

"You saw these lights when you were at Gran's tonight?" Aunt Jo wondered.

"Yeah, and it seemed to be Gran, too. They showed me all the things I told Chief Walsh about. She wanted me to know, and the lights guided me to everything I needed to see." The three of them watched in awe as the lights danced around the table for a little while. Then, they rose up to encircle the moon before coming back down through the maple trees and disappearing into the night.

"Well, this confirms it, then. We can't ignore what Gran is trying to tell us. Something was going on in her house tonight, and we need to find out what. And you, Autumn, are the linchpin. Our family's gifts are much more than we've even related to you both over the years. The elements are just waiting to be awakened within us so that we may protect these lands and bind the four elements together once again. It sounds like Autumn is the beginning of this awakening."

"Mom, you can't say something like that and just drop it. You're gonna have to tell us more about our elements and what this necklace entails. For starters, what do you mean when you say we need to bind the four elements together again?" Simone, always the blunt one, cut right to the chase. She knew, just as much as Autumn did, that they were each more inclined to connect with one element, and their gifts correlated with those. However, her mother and Gran had been keeping a bit more to themselves about their family.

"Jo, Simone is right. It's time for us to know whatever you and Gran may not have told us all these years. If this is some kind of awakening, then we're all right in the middle of it. And as nervous as that makes me feel, I also know that I want to honor Gran and continue with whatever she was doing for our family and our town." Autumn was doing her best to acknowledge what her heart was telling her, but also respect the wisdom from her grandmother. She was raised to favor her wise woman sensibilities, but for her, that also came with letting her feelings in, too.

Sitting up straighter and looking between both of them, Jo adjusted the rings on her fingers and said, "You're right, girls. It appears you're ready now, and the elements have chosen you to carry our family prophecy forward. Simone, I know you can usually feel the ancestors and any spirits around us. You are so intuitive, and you have the strength of raging waters. But I just watched you sense something much deeper than a spirit. You were engaging with their energy, bringing memories and emotions up along with Gran, and as you were doing it, I saw the water begin to rise and create tides in your water glass. You've never done that before."

Simone looked at her mother with surprise. "I did that?"

"Yes, you did. Which means something has shifted within you and heightened your gifts. And you, Autumn, have been called by the necklace. I imagine Gran's key appeared to you as well," Aunt Jo turned to her and gave a sly smile.

"You're right. It appeared in the locket, and I remembered Gran using it on her wardrobe before. So I opened it to find many things I had never seen before. It was as if they appeared from nothing, or maybe they stayed hidden until truly needed." Autumn ran her eyes back and forth across the table, looking for an answer.

"Our family heirlooms do conceal themselves in that cabinet. The MacKinnon Book of Spells, the staff of our elders, a mountain hag stone, and a burning ember from the bark of the Eternal Tree. There are more items in there as well that Gran kept safe, but these are the ones that come to mind. She was our family keeper as our matriarch, so it wasn't just about holding onto the necklace. The necklace holds the key, but in order to activate it and make it appear, the chosen four points witch of our family must be present and hold the right intentions." Jo placed her hand over Autumn's, and tears welled in her eyes.

"My dear child, I can't believe you have finally activated the key after all these years. But now, it all makes sense. The voices you've been hearing have been getting stronger. Your paper messages for the shop have been coming faster and more intensely than usual. And now, the lights. Those may be Gran, but you're bringing them to us on the wind. You're calling her to us without even realizing it. And your energy has activated the air. But I don't think that's all." Aunt Jo stopped for a moment while she thought.

"What do you mean, that's not all? Did something else happen? I mean, this is all already pretty intense, so what else could there possibly be?" Simone flailed her hands around while she spoke, and all the waters on the table sloshed around as if moved by a great storm. They each looked at each other in disbelief.

"Well, that was something," Aunt Jo said matter-of-factly. "But back to my thought, I see something else occurring in Autumn. There's more earth energy in you than usual, and James said he saw you walking out of the woods at Gran's tonight. Something about needing to be grounded." Jo looked at her niece, needing some confirmation.

"I have been feeling really torn between the thoughts in my head and being in the present moment. And when I found Gran tonight, I just couldn't shake all the worry and thoughts in my mind. I had to get to my sanctuary in the woods, where Gran taught me to go when I needed a reprieve. But when I was walking out there... I levitated, Jo." Autumn looked at both of them with wide eyes. "I rose off the ground, and the surrounding winds picked up so much that I created a little tornado around me. And the whispers on the wind spoke to me about being the four-points witch. Somehow, in the middle of it all, I put myself back down on the ground and walked into my clearing, which is where the lights appeared to me."

"Holy cow, this is big. How much off the ground are you talking about here? Like, was it a few inches or several feet? Because I mean, levitation is levitation, but you've never done this before. Ever." Simone's mouth just dropped open at Autumn's words, and she let her dark bob hang around her cheeks.

Autumn laughed and covered her mouth with her hand for a moment as she shyly looked up at them. "It was a good few inches in the air, and I could control it somehow to get back down. So, is this what you were thinking seemed different, Aunt Jo?" Autumn didn't really know what to think at this point.

Jo pushed her chair back from the table and paced around the garden. "This is something. Definitely something," she said as she grabbed a piece of the pumpkin bread from the table and kept pacing.

"I could sense that your strength had grown, but I had no idea. The prophecy says that our family will once again have a four-points witch. That means there is one who can control all four elements of earth, air, fire, and water and bring them together as one coven to protect the land, sea, and sky of our mountain region. For a good century, that honor has been bestowed on our family. Your great-grandmother, Gran's mother, was the last four points witch. When she died, Gran was responsible for holding the bloodline together, and I promised to help her. Autumn, your mother was too strong of a healer, and her gifts were needed elsewhere. So we knew she had to follow her path. That was when I stayed with Gran here to raise you and Simone together and to protect the family until we found the next four-points witch... But now I know that you have been here with us all along. We raised you until the key was ready for you to claim it." Jo sat back down at the table, looking directly into Autumn's eyes now.

"But what does that mean, exactly? How are we supposed to protect our lands and activate a full coven? I mean, I don't even know of any fire witches, and I can barely even protect our little shop from the storm that came through this morning. Not to mention that I couldn't even protect Gran from whatever happened today." Autumn replied with a shrug. "This is just too much. Gran was such a powerful part of our community, and to think that I might have to fill her shoes and then some. It's just too much." Tears formed in her eyes as she spoke.

"It's okay, cuz. We're strong together, and I'll always be right here by your side. You know that." Simone's tough exterior always gave Autumn a boost of confidence, but deep down they were all feeling so much hesitation at this moment.

"Listen, we don't have to figure this out tonight. In fact, I say we take advantage of this full moon while we're out here. Girls, leave the dishes. I'll clean up in a while. Right now, I need you to gather the supplies laid out on the kitchen counter: sage sticks, moon water, scrying bowl, tarot deck, and taper candles. Just grab it all and meet me back here in the garden. We have some divination to do," Aunt Jo instructed as she made her way to the darker end of the garden, lit only by moonlight and where a circle of large logs sat on the ground.

As Autumn began moving toward the kitchen, she saw a tiny figure making its way around the edge of the house. Stopping to squint at it, Autumn tried to determine what it was. Just then, she heard a meow and saw the hints of orange fur rubbing against the corner of the house.

"It's you again!" Autumn exclaimed. "Look, Simone. It's our little friend from the storm today. He's back again. And I saw him hanging out near Gran's house earlier, too. I don't know how he's gotten around town so quickly, but he seems to be following me." She went over to the cat and bent down to pet him.

"Sounds to me like he wants to be adopted. I mean, he is pretty cute, and he did grow on me today. I don't think I've seen him around anyone else's house in town," Simone encouraged.

"Yeah, I think you're right. Let's keep him around a bit and see how it goes. You stay here while I get a few things inside, okay?" Autumn scratched the cat's head and went inside to gather what Aunt Jo requested.

Aunt Jo had already pulled open a tarp at the back of the garden and grabbed several pieces of firewood from underneath to arrange within the center of the log circle. Something Aunt Jo was famous for in the family was bathing or dancing under the light of the moon. She would usually choose to do it near the creek behind the property or in the garden around a bonfire. Tonight it was necessary to stay close to home with the uncertainty of what may come from this moon's energy.

Autumn and Simone came out to meet Jo with arms full of the ritual items. They arranged them neatly by the northernmost log as a position of emphasis intended for Aunt Jo. Simone lit the sage sticks, blew the flames out, and gave one to Autumn. Both girls started from the north end of the circle, working their way around and letting the smoke of the sage billow around the log circle to clear the energy of the space.

"Elements protect our circle and all inside. Let there be no place here for bad energy to hide." The girls chanted as they walked the perimeter, lighting each of the four taper candles as they went, and ended back at the north. As they placed the last of the burning sage down in a wooden bowl, Aunt Jo finished setting the bonfire in the center of the circle.

"Okay, girls. We're ready. Take your place around the fire, and we'll begin." Jo took her place at the north end. They all took a deep breath and stretched out their arms to their sides, looking up at the moon.

"Sacred moon above, I call on your energy to bring forth the water within me and help us see the unseen. Give us the sight of a hundred moons that lie ahead to reveal what lies beneath and what must be brought to the surface." Jo bent down, poured a carafe of water into her scrying bowl, and gently swirled the water with her pointer finger. The silver moon ring on her finger sparkled with light as she made the movements. When she stopped, she gazed deep into the bowl as the girls watched.

"I see a tree with branches split. One of the branches on the ground seems to be on fire while the tree itself is flourishing." Jo kept her gaze on the water as she took in more of the visions coming through. "I see the both of you holding hands amid a raging storm. Howling wind and rain. The necklace glowing around Autumn's neck. And James in the background, trying to anchor himself in the storm." Jo began swirling the water once more with her fingers to encourage more messages to come through.

Simone and Autumn glanced at each other as the orange tabby encircled Autumn's feet with a meow. As they shared a glance, the wind picked up and a few drops of rain fell onto the fire.

"Girls, focus your energy on the elements. Keep them under wraps while I finish," Jo said hurriedly. She grabbed at her tarot deck and shuffled. "Ancestors and guides, what do we need to know right now to understand what happened to Gran?" She fanned out the cards on the ground before her and carefully drew one out.

"The moon card," Simone said as she leaned over to see what card her mother had pulled. "That's a card of hidden shadows and bringing the unknown to the surface. It's about diving into the subconscious and the uncomfortable to bring things to light. The water element at its finest." Simone looked at her mother as she confirmed what Simone was saying.

"Intuition and dreamwork can give us more insight into the shadows so that we may release them," Jo said as she looked up at the sky to find more raindrops falling on them. "I think this is all we're going to get tonight. Let's close the circle before the weather does it for us." Jo gathered her cards, threw the water from the scrying bowl over the last embers of the fire, and raised her hands.

"Elements and ancestors, we thank you for these insights. We ask for the strength to go forward with open hearts and minds as we are led onto the path of our destinies." And with that, Jo blew out her taper candle, then Autumn at the east, walking to the south candle to blow it out. Simone finished at the west with her candle.

With the tabby cat following her feet closely, Autumn started picking up some items the girls brought out to the garden. They hurriedly made their way to the garden table and piled as many dishes as they could into their arms to head into the house with the cat underfoot.

"All right, you can come inside, too," Autumn said as she kept the door open just enough for her new little friend to join them in the kitchen. And just as they all retreated for the night, the clouds opened up and poured the rest of their rain down on the garden.

GROUNDING TEA

1 Tbsp rooibos red bush tea leaves

2 tsp dried apple peels

1 cup water

1 cinnamon stick

Heat the water until boiling. Remove from heat. Place the tea leaves and apple peel in a sachet or tea strainer and steep in the water for four minutes. Wrap your left hand around the tea mug as you stir the cinnamon stick into the liquid using a clockwise motion with your right hand. Chant the incantation,

I anchor to the earth for strength and stability.

Repeat the chant three times and sip the tea slowly until empty.

CHAPTER 7

Autumn woke up the next morning with something warm covering her feet. She lifted her face out of the blankets to find a furry orange tabby lying in a circle on top of the covers.

"Well, good morning," she said as she gave the cat a scratch under the chin. "I guess if you're going to be staying, we should probably give you a proper name. Maybe something to do with your soft orange and white fir. Or perhaps your stubbornness to find me around town?"

The cat only seemed to care for the affection Autumn gave him at the moment and walked up to the head of the bed to snuggle in closer to her.

"Aw, I'm glad to have you, little guy. I need some comfort right now, and you come around right when I need you most, so thank you." With a few more head scratches, Autumn nuzzled her face into the cat and let him have the bed all to himself.

She made her way downstairs to the smell of cinnamon toast and found Aunt Jo and Simone already in the kitchen.

"Ah, there you are, my dear," Aunt Jo said as she came over to hug Autumn. "I know it wasn't the greatest of nights, but how did you sleep?"

Simone raised her eyebrows and rolled her eyes around at that. "Mom, give her some space. She's in a different house and not waking up to Gran as usual. So let her just sit down and breathe for a minute."

"No, it's okay. I actually completely crashed last night. I'm not used to being up that late. There was just so much happening that I must have fallen right into bed, and that was it. Plus, I had a bed warmer with me of the orange kitten variety," Autumn smiled right as the tabby walked into the kitchen.

"Oh yes, I think that little guy stayed with you all night. And from what Simone has told me about his strange appearances around town, it makes me think that he's shown up to be your new familiar. They always seem to find us when we most need their guidance and support." Aunt Jo got a ceramic bowl down from the cabinet and filled it with water to put down for the cat.

"It's so strange, but I felt as though he'd been following me around town. First at the shop with the storm, then at Gran's house, and now here in the garden. And if my gifts are being heightened now, then maybe he has come to me as my little familiar. I mean, he's a really cute one, so who am I to complain, right?" Autumn shrugged. "Anyway, he needs a name. I need tea, and then we all need to discuss how we're going to deal with all of this."

"I don't know how you both feel, but worrying and feeling sad isn't what I think Gran would have wanted. She would want us to be diligent about finding whoever did this and then making things right. She'd probably say something about how the energy isn't right in the air, and it's up to us to shift it," Simone conveyed as she spread butter all over her toast with the same determination with which she spoke.

"You're absolutely right, Simone. We don't want to enable any bad energy to linger around us. So we're going to remember Gran with love and affection, and we're going to sort this out because we are MacKinnon witches. We decide how to shift the tides and the winds and everything in between, and no one is going to do this to our family and town and get away with it." Jo confirmed as she topped up the tea mugs with rooibos for each of them.

"Good, then you're both on board with helping me figure out what happened. And from the looks of this little guy jumping up on my lap, he's interested in helping, too. So first things first. What should we name him?" Autumn asked curiously.

"I love how he's been popping up all over the place. It's so mysterious of him, and I'm really digging it. Maybe something like Shadow? Or how about Calcite because his fur totally looks like an orange calcite crystal?" Simone started getting excited about these suggestions.

"I feel like it should connect with our family somehow. Perhaps something Scottish to connect with our ancestry? He has been like a little twin to you, following you around town as if to mimic you. How about Tavish? That means twin, and I have a feeling he's going to be a bit of a twin for you as your new familiar." Jo clasped her hands together and waited expectantly for an answer.

"Tavish. Hmm, what do you think, little guy? Does that sound like you?" Autumn questioned as she petted him on her lap. The cat started immediately shaking his tail back and forth feverishly and purring under Autumn's hand to give his full approval. "Looks to me he's chosen Tavish."

"Yeah, I think it suits him. He's such a cutie, and that is an adorable Scottish name. Sounds like a keeper to me," Simone agreed.

"All right, now that we settled his name, I wanna head back to Gran's house this morning to gather a few more things and just look around. Since we don't open the shop until later today, I figure I'll go back and pull the spell book out of the cabinet to see if I can find any more clues about what may be going on. This may be my only chance to do it before the police really start their investigation." Autumn sipped on her tea and peered over the lip at the two of them. "Do either of you wanna come with?"

"Definitely. I don't want you going back by yourself. Who knows if the person who did this to Gran is still lurking around? There's no way I'm gonna let you go back on your own right now. I'll just throw some clothes on, and we can head out when you're ready." Simone finished the last swig of her tea, kissed her mother on the cheek, and headed upstairs.

Giving Autumn a soothing smile, Aunt Jo tilted her head and remarked, "You girls will be each other's defenders until your dying days. I'm so thankful that you've had each other all these years, and now I feel as though you're both going to be leaning on the other even more as your paths unfold. After all, the moon foretold it."

"It did? I thought all it said was something about a tree with a branch burning and things being kept under the surface." Autumn was curious about what else Jo was referring to.

"Ah, but it also gave me feelings that prophesied events to come. Like when it showed me you both holding hands in a storm, I felt the bond growing stronger between you two. Stronger than it's ever been before. I don't know exactly what's coming, but I know that you both are the start of a very strong coven. One that has the potential to protect these lands for many years to come." Aunt Jo nodded as she took her teacup and made her way out of the kitchen and into the garden to rearrange the crystals she had previously laid out under the full moon.

Autumn sighed and looked down at Tavish, "Let's just hope we can handle whatever is lurking under the surface."

CHAPTER 8

Autumn and Simone parked the car on the wooded road in front of Gran's house. "Do you think we need to call the police station and let them know we're here?" Autumn suggested.

Simone thought about it for a moment as she got out of the car and slammed the door. "Better to ask for forgiveness later. Let's just go on in and get what you need."

Autumn nodded as they made their way up to the cottage. She approached the front door to open it when a mailing tube fell at her feet from behind one of the porch chairs. The only label on the outside of the tube read "Garrett Developments."

"What's that?" Simone asked.

"I don't know. It just fell from behind the chair, but I don't remember seeing it here before. Maybe it was getting too dark yesterday when I got here after work. It's possible it's been here for a while, but I have no idea what it could be." Autumn opened the front door as she fumbled around to open one end of the tube.

The house seemed so quiet and still now, unlike the lively spirit it had when Gran was alive. She brought the soul of this home to life with her thoughtfulness, playful character, and the kind wisdom she showed to everyone who crossed through those doors.

Perhaps that was the problem. Whoever was here was probably someone Gran trusted or at least felt comfortable enough to invite generously into her family home. This wouldn't have been something she had seen coming. Even with her wisdom, some things about our destinies remain concealed.

After letting the unsettling feeling of the house sink in, Autumn pulled out several large pages from the tube.

"It looks like they're plans for some kind of development. That's the riverfront downtown." Autumn pointed to one of the drawings and read the print aloud. "It says here that this is a riverfront revitalization, and it's got food trucks, a new parking garage, and a plan for a new hotel by the water."

"Whoa, Gran would never have gone for all of that in the historic downtown. She would have had the preservation committee all over that one to make sure it didn't happen." Simone tugged at the plans to move them closer to her.

"So why are the plans here, then? It doesn't make any sense for her to have wanted plans for a project that she had no intention of backing." Autumn let Simone keep glancing over the drawings as she walked around the house.

"And then there's the matter of all the books being thrown on the floor. Do you think someone may have been looking for the family Book of Spells that called to me? Because that would mean that someone knew more about our family than we did." Autumn turned around to look at Simone and see if she thought that was even possible.

"How could that be? Mom just told us about all of this last night, and she and Gran and probably your mother have all been keeping this a secret for as long as we've been alive. If someone else knew, then that means they've known about our bloodline from our great-grandmother or something." Simone started pacing back and forth.

"Yeah, but your mom suggested we could trust Chief Walsh with our family secrets. So maybe he knows about our gifts, and if he knows, then other people could, too." Autumn unzipped the pocket of her backpack as she spoke. "Let's just see if I can pull the spell book back up for some answers."

She pulled the locket out of her bag and closed her eyes, hoping the key would reappear inside it. As she tried to concentrate, she heard footsteps on the front porch. Autumn quickly opened her eyes and closed the locket back up, shoving it into the pocket of her black skinny jeans.

Simone scurried to the front door to see who was outside, only to find Chief Walsh's son, Ben, pushing the door open on her. She stumbled back right into Autumn as Ben gave them both a surprised look.

"Oh hello, ladies. Uh, I know this is your family home, but technically you're not supposed to be here until we have a bit more time with the crime scene closed off," he said, staring directly at Simone.

"Oh okay, officer. We just needed to get a few things for my cousin, Autumn. This is where she lives, but she only grabbed a couple of things last night before heading to my house. So... I guess we'll only take the important things and be on our way."

Autumn had never seen Simone so mesmerized by someone before. He had some kind of hold over her attention. Smiling and nodding, Autumn interjected, "Wait, did you say this was a crime scene?"

Distracted away from Simone's gaze, Ben turned to Autumn. "Yes, my father confirmed it this morning based on what the coroner was coming back with. Turns out your grandmother had traces of a rare herb in her system that caused her heart to stop. But... maybe you should hear this from the Chief. I shouldn't be the one to explain all of this. I just need to get you two out of the house while we process any remaining items."

"Okay, how long do you think it's gonna take before I can come back to the house, then? And when can we talk to the Chief about what happened to our grandmother?" Autumn pressed Ben for more answers.

He threw his hands up at her. "Hold on, let's take one thing at a time, okay? I'll radio to the Chief that you wanna know everything we've got so far, and he can call to meet you later today. But for now, just grab the other items you need and let's close up. Some other officers are coming back soon to finish processing."

Autumn nodded in agreement and gathered her bag, the tube she had found, and Gran's tea recipe book from the kitchen. She didn't want to leave that lying around where anyone could grab it and ask questions. There were too many magical references on those pages for just anyone to see.

"I'm just gonna head out onto the porch for a few other things," she called to Simone and Ben, who seemed to be immersed in a conversation.

She walked out the front door and let the screen door slowly close behind her so as not to disturb them. Throwing all the items piled in her arms onto the Adirondack chair, Autumn made her way across the front porch, moving her eyes from top to bottom in search of something else that may give her a clue.

The wind picked up as she snuggled into her oversized sweater and crossed her arms. The wooden wind chime hanging from the corner of the porch sang, and she faintly heard the whispers of the voices returning.

"The book abides by protective intentions."

The message carried on the wind as it began to shift and blow directly from the west straight at the house, which was unusual. The wind chime thrashed around, and Autumn closed her eyes, telling the air to calm down with her mind.

The air gradually slowed to a smooth breeze as she chanted, "Calm winds surround me, calm winds temper your energy." Her hair stopped flying in her face, and she opened her eyes to focus on Gran's wind chime in front of her. It had been here at the house since Autumn was a child. She and Gran made it together and hung it up in the porch's corner to tap into all directions.

"Hold it up higher." Autumn recalled Gran's voice as she helped her raise her arms and lift the wooden wind chime up to the top of the porch ceiling. Autumn perched on the porch railing, smiling with excitement as her gran helped her hang the new chime made of twigs from the cottage forest and the twine that Gran always kept around for such projects.

"Won't the wind take it down?" Autumn replied as she twisted the screw gently into the ceiling hole meant for the chime.

"No, child. The wind will carry the song on the chimes, and they'll blow through the air to bring the messages the wind needs us to hear. Nothing is more sacred to us than the wind, and it will abide by the tools we use to harness it," Gran continued with a gentle but instructive tone.

"But Gran, how will I know what the wind is trying to say? I don't speak its language," Autumn worried.

"But you will, sweet girl. In time, you will." And with that, Gran gave Autumn a smile and her signature warm hug that made her feel the comfort of the coziest winter day, all snuggled by a hearth fire.

"Gran, I'm so thankful for you," Autumn whispered as she closed her eyes and gave Gran a sweet kunik kiss by gently brushing her nose against Gran's.

"Now let's go inside. I have just the right tea blend to send the aroma of coziness into the air." And with that, the two gathered themselves up and walked side by side into the cottage where Autumn had grown all those years.

"Autumn. Autumn," Simone called to her and suddenly shook Autumn out of her daze.

"Yeah... I'm done. I have everything right here, so I'll scoop it all up and be ready to go," she replied, looking as though she was still considering something. Autumn grabbed everything off the porch chair and brushed past Ben on her way to the car.

"Okay then, I guess we're leaving." Simone gave Ben an apologetic look. "I'm sure I'll see you around town as we figure this out. Or, you know, you could always stop in the shop for a chat about how things are going." Simone walked backward down the front steps, looking at Ben the whole way down, and then returned to the car to find Autumn already inside.

"Geez, why the sudden rush? What's going on?" Simone looked over at Autumn.

"The voices came back and triggered a memory of Gran with the wind chime. It was all just so intense and made me feel like she was right here teaching me to use my gifts again. Almost as if I need a refresh to jumpstart something I've been holding onto from long ago."

CHAPTER 9

Simone pulled the car out onto the road in front of Gran's house when the girls saw a woman waving her hands in the air and running toward them through the fog of the trees. When she got closer to the old wooden ranch fencing that lined the edge of the road, Mrs. Pendleton appeared in her wellie boots and a quilted jacket thrown over her kitchen apron.

"Oh girls," she panted as she approached Simone's car window. "I'm glad I caught you! I'm just so sorry about what happened to your grandmother. With all the jarring and preserving I've been doing to prepare for the harvest market days, I haven't stopped by properly, and I didn't want to interfere while the police were here. But I have heard some strange rumors around town that the police think this is no accident. My nephew works for the department, you know, so I hear things."

The girls looked at each other, wondering if they should be concerned about how much gossip was going around. "Oh, Mrs. Pendleton, we've just been trying to process everything. It happened so suddenly, and we just don't know what exactly happened yet," Autumn responded, trying to downplay the events a bit.

"Well, I didn't want to say anything before talking to you girls and Jo first, but I saw a rather strange man over at the house the other day whom I've never seen before. He looked to be a bit of a businessman, and he was poking around the front porch. I saw him carrying a long brown stick from my kitchen window. I couldn't tell you where he was from, but I knew from the look of him he was rather serious."

She wrapped her quilted jacket more tightly around her waist to cover up from the chill in the air. "Oh girls, I just don't care for strange happenings around here. I like things to be quiet and peaceful, and this just keeps me up at night to think something may have happened to your Gran right next door, and I wasn't aware of it."

"We completely understand, and we wanna continue keeping our town safe and sound just as much as you do." Autumn's words were heartfelt, and she could tell that Mrs. Pendleton felt better for getting this all off her chest. "Thank you for letting us know all of this."

"This could be really important in helping us figure out what happened to Gran, so anything else you can remember at all, please just let us know." Simone reached out to grab Mrs. Pendleton's hand and reassure her they were concerned. "I'll also let my mother know about what you've told us."

"Okay, dears. You stay safe. And Autumn, I imagine you're staying at your aunt's house, but you're always welcome to stop by for a chat and some fresh fruit jam. So please don't be shy about coming around." Mrs. Pendleton waved at them and then turned to head back to her house just beyond the treeline.

Simone turned toward Autumn as she put the car in gear to get moving. "So, do you know who she's talking about? That strange man that came by Gran's house the other day?"

"I honestly don't know who it was, but I'm assuming she was referring to this as the long brown stick." Autumn pulled out the mailing tube that the girls had just opened to find the development plans. "So it must have been someone from the development office or someone related to this project. We're gonna have to ask around at the preservation society or maybe even the mayor to see who may have brought this over. Because, like you said, there's no way Gran would have gone for this redevelopment. But if this is connected somehow to what happened, we need to find out more details and do it soon."

Simone nodded and headed the car back into town toward the shop as they both tried untangling the newest clue Autumn held in her lap.

Just as Autumn flipped the open sign over at the front door of the shop, Aunt Jo came strolling through carrying Tavish in her arms, all snuggled in a flannel blanket. "Hello, my dears. I thought you could use this little guy to keep you company in the shop today. He's been quite the helper in the kitchen this morning, and he kept standing near the door as I was trying to leave. So I decided he needed to come along."

"Well, hello there, cutie," Autumn said as she took Tavish from Aunt Jo and snuggled him into her face. "We can keep him in the back. Simone already helped me put a little bed together for him during the storm the other day, so he should be fine back there, and we'll get him all that he needs."

"Yeah, he'll be our little shop mascot and maybe even get us some more paying customers with that adorable face of his." Even with Simone's tough exterior, she always had a soft spot for cuddly animals. "Plus, he'll make the day go quicker for us, too."

"I hope so! I have so much to do this week with putting together new cards and paper crafts for the season. We need to order some new wrapping papers that Simone designed, too. But now all I can think about is Gran and how we need to unravel what happened."

"Oh yeah, Mom, we talked to Mrs. Pendleton this morning," Simone said as she lit a fire in the hearth at the back of the shop. "She told us about a strange businessman she saw at Gran's cottage the other day, and then Autumn found some redevelopment plans on the front porch. Do you know anything about this?"

"Hmm, redevelopment plans. Well, I know that the city has been open to suggestions for revitalizing the downtown and making it more of a cultural landmark that draws in greater tourism. But I know Gran would always uphold the integrity of our town and the charm that it holds. She would never go for anything that didn't align with that." Aunt Jo adamantly spoke of Gran's attachment to the town.

"You're both right. It makes absolutely no sense for Gran to want to see plans for a complete redesign like what we found. So maybe this was someone who was trying to convince her. Someone probably knew she was head of the preservation society and that she had a lot of sway in town. I mean, Mrs. Pendleton said that the man looked pretty serious at the house. Maybe he was more than just serious. Maybe he was angry or frustrated." Autumn gave them both a curious look.

"Angry enough to kill an old woman just to get their way? That sounds like someone willing to go way beyond business ethics. If that's the case, then that would have to be someone with some serious stakes in the development game." Simone stoked the fire and wiped her hands on her black leggings.

"I know, that's quite disturbing if someone would go to those lengths to get what they wanted. And yet, here we are. Gran is gone, and we know now that it wasn't of natural causes," Autumn looked over at Aunt Jo. "Ben confirmed it for us this morning at the house. We need to speak to Chief Walsh further about it, but it looks like someone may be at fault for Gran's death. They're doing another sweep of the house today, and then the investigation will open."

Aunt Jo put a hand over her mouth in disbelief. "Oh girls, our poor Gran." Tears began rolling down her cheeks. "She loved us all so dearly, and to think that someone treated her this way is just so upsetting." She hugged them both and said decidedly, "I'll speak to Chief Walsh to get any other details I can from him. I expect you girls to keep your eyes and ears open today as customers come in. See if you can find anything else about what may have happened, but please be careful. Apparently, there's someone in town who's not entirely who they appear to be, and we need to heighten our awareness now more than ever if we're going to figure this out."

"Agreed, and I also wanna talk to someone about this redevelopment plan and those strange herbs I found in Gran's teacup the day she died. That's been replaying over in my mind since I found them, and I can't quite shake that there's something to that." Autumn picked up Tavish, and she and Simone walked Aunt Jo to the front door.

"Mom, let us know what you find out from Chief Walsh. He seems to like you, and between that and your natural charms, I don't think you'll have a problem getting some details out of him." Simone clasped her mother's hand briefly before Jo walked out the door.

"All right," Autumn said, heading to the back of the shop. "Shall we put this little guy to work helping us make the new card collection? I have a few messages in my mind now, and I want to inscribe them onto the cards before I lose them. I have a feeling the customers needing them will arrive in the next few days."

Autumn started collecting supplies from the baskets lining the wall shelves behind the counter. She and Simone's gifts paired well to give their customers exactly what they needed. Autumn's clairvoyant messages, sayings, and even intentionally chosen items gave their customers exactly what they needed at that moment in their lives.

Simone's incredible design sense brought it all together with patterns, textures, and layouts that blended warm, cozy feelings and nostalgia. Her wrapping paper designs were the quintessential purchase of the upcoming winter season, and the girls knew from past years that they had to prepare early for the customers needing them.

Tavish jumped up on the counter as they both got to work laying out foil cards, embossing tools, ribbons, and more. Simone opened her design application on the computer and went straight to a wrapping paper pattern featuring hints of sparkle between snow-capped pine trees and winter cottages. Autumn glanced over Simone's shoulder as she unwrapped a spool of brown twine next to her.

Just as they were easing into the new designs, the chime rang at the front door.

"Welcome to Parchment and Pine. Come on in and warm up. Would you like a cup of tea while you wander around?" Autumn smiled warmly and came around the corner of the counter.

The woman's eyebrows rose, and she gave Autumn a quick look. "Uh, no, that's not necessary. Thank you. I was just walking down Main on my way to the preservation society meeting, and I thought I'd pop in to express my condolences about your grandmother."

"Ah, yes. Kennedy, right? I think we met a while back when you first got to town, and Gran brought me to one of the preservation meetings. Thank you, yes, it's good to see you again." Autumn shook the woman's hand and noticed she was wearing a root chakra bracelet with red and black crystal beads.

Simone popped up from the computer and wandered over as well. "Hi, I'm Simone. I think I've seen you around town a bit, but we've never really had a chance to talk. I'm Autumn's cousin."

"Right, I think I remember Lorna mentioning both of you girls at some point and one of her daughters that was still here in town," Kennedy said, referring to Gran and Aunt Jo.

"Mm-hmm, yeah. Her daughter, Jo, is my mother. She runs the bath shop across the street. You've probably run into her around town as well."

Simone eyed Kennedy, not sure what to make of her. She felt a peculiar energy around Kennedy, but she wasn't getting any proper colors around her to decipher what that energy was.

Kennedy walked through the store, heading to a table of handmade beeswax candles the girls batch produced every season to imbue the town with hints of intentional energies. Smelling one of the burnt leaf candles, Kennedy nodded her head. "Oh right, I met your mother at her shop. I've gone there a few times to get some special bath products. She really has a keen sense of what will work for someone."

"That's Aunt Jo," Autumn said smiling. "It's almost as if she has a sixth sense about helping people care for themselves better. Her products are always a huge hit around here."

"Mmm, I can imagine." Kennedy walked over to the register with the candle she chose and placed it on the counter. "What about those paper lanterns you have hanging in the front window? Did you make those yourselves? I think two of them would be just right for my late fall plans."

"Autumn makes these lanterns herself from some of my computer designs. We always work together that way. Family and all, and we include the people of Hollow's Glenn in that family, too," Simone mentioned pointedly.

Something just didn't sit quite right with her about Kennedy, and Simone didn't mind being obvious about how protective she was.

"Let me grab a couple of lanterns down for you, and Autumn can ring you up if you'd like." Simone walked over to the window to pull down the lanterns and noticed a smirk on Kennedy's face as she eyed them.

"Nice, yes, I'll take them. I'll put them to good use this season." She handed her credit card to Autumn while glancing around the shop one last time. "Well, please accept my condolences again for Lorna. We'll miss her at the preservation society." Kennedy grabbed her shopping bag and walked toward the door, giving a quick glance behind her as she left.

"Were you feeling what I was feeling?" Simone hopped up onto one of the counter stools.

"I don't know exactly. She seemed nice, and I know Gran mentioned her a few times as part of the preservation society dealings. But I noticed her bracelet with red jasper and black tourmaline." Autumn fiddled with a set of emerald green foil papers, fitting one into a green, linen envelope to become the liner.

"Protection crystals? From what is the question?" Simone squinted as she paced around the shop. "I couldn't get a sense of her aura either. It was really weird, almost as if it were masked."

"Okay, let's not jump to any conclusions here. She probably just wears that bracelet for a little grounding, or maybe just because she likes the colors. Who knows? And the energy around here is all over the place right now. There's no telling what's happening with our gifts either."

"Yeah, but we were just talking last night about how much our gifts are actually heightening. I feel like they've actually been clearer than usual, especially when I'm with you. So for me to be unable to read her aura is strange. I think we should see what she's about a bit more before we just drop it." Simone poured them both a cup of cinnamon apple tea and went to peek through the front window as if the answers might be right there in plain sight on the sidewalk out front.

CHAPTER 10

"Autumn!" Simone yelled as she flipped the front window curtain forward. "It's..."

Before she could say anything more, a tall woman with dark auburn locks tied up in a bun plowed through the door. "Ah, Simone! I saw you in the front window. Come, give your Aunt Penelope a hug." She opened her arms and walked over to an utterly shocked Simone. Simone glanced back at Autumn, who put down the foil envelopes to come forward and see what was going on.

"Mom?" Autumn said with hesitation.

Penny released Simone from the hug and turned to see her daughter standing in the middle of the shop with a questioning look on her face. "Oh, sweetheart! I've missed you so much. Jo called and told me what happened to Gran, and well, I just couldn't stay away any longer. I had to come home and be with you all."

"You haven't been back in at least two years. The last time I saw you, you were off to the outskirts region to tend to the diseased lands there. You haven't called in months, so I assumed you wouldn't bother coming back for this." Autumn gave her mother a stern tone as she spoke.

"I know, I've been gone a while, and I'm so sorry for that. But I'm here now. I couldn't just disregard my mother's passing, and especially not when

Jo's told me what's at stake now with her curious death and the necklace. I had to make sure you were all right, and that you knew I was still here for you."

"Okay... Why don't I put the teakettle on again, and we can all have a chat in the back, away from any customers coming in?" Simone pulled Autumn back toward the fireplace, and Penny followed.

Autumn took her place in the emerald green wingback chair beside the fire and rubbed her hands back and forth as she thought things through. Her mother silently sat across from her and began removing her olive green barn jacket and flannel scarf. She folded her hands together on her lap and waited for Autumn to say something.

"Meow," Tavish interjected as he pushed his head through the curtains and made his way up onto Autumn's lap.

"Oh, look at this little guy. He's adorable."

"This is Tavish. He just started showing up recently, and he seems to be my familiar." Autumn rubbed Tavish's ears gently as he purred on her lap. Penny lifted her eyebrows and smiled at her daughter. She could see that things were happening in Autumn's life. Perhaps she had come at the right time after all, and so had Tavish.

"I didn't expect you here." Autumn looked into the fire as she spoke, unable to meet her mother's eyes. "Now that you are here, I honestly don't know what to say."

"Well, let me start over by saying how unbelievably sorry I am that I've been gone. Leaving you and the family has always broken my heart, but Gran always understood that my path led me elsewhere. You know that with the gifts I was given, it was never really a choice. We're all given things we must share with the world. It's our duty and honor, no matter how hard that may be on us. Mine was that of a healer, and I was always called to heal further afield. I'm just sorry that's taken such a toll on you."

Simone walked in, placed some cups on the small table between the chairs, closed the curtains that hung around the archway to the hearth room, and proceeded to the front where some new customers were waiting.

Autumn took a deep breath and looked her mother in the eye. "I never understood the need for you to go so far away. All I saw was my mother leaving and the rare occasion when she came back. So how long will you be here this time? Because I don't know if I can handle much more right now. With everything going on, the last thing I need to deal with is the drama that comes with a temporary stay."

"Autumn, I spoke with Aunt Jo. Gran left quite a hole in our family, and it's not something that can be easily patched. It's going to take all of us to understand what's happened and to... teach what may lie ahead on the path for you." She tilted her head and gazed at Autumn with compassion in her eyes. "You are my daughter, after all, and you have my blood running through those veins. I'm here to help support you in whatever you need right now, including making amends for the past. Being gone has hurt me as well."

Autumn nodded as she took a sip of the tea Simone had brought. She could hear her tending to the customers in the front of the store, but it seemed so distant from where she sat with her mother in the back.

"You're right." She took a breath and sat back in the chair. "We need to move forward, and we need you to be part of this family again. In whatever way that we can get you. Gran would have wanted that." Autumn hesitated before saying, "And I do, too. But that doesn't mean we can just pick up like you've been here this whole time. You're going to have to really get to know us all again, and show us you intend to be here, no matter what."

"Absolutely." Penny stood up and walked over to give her daughter the hug she had been waiting to give her for years." I want all those things again as well. And you will be my main priority. After all, if I can't heal my own family, then what good is my gift, right?"

They smiled hesitantly at each other just as Simone busted through the curtains. "What did I miss?" She looked back and forth between them and came over to pour herself a cup of tea.

With a laugh under her breath, Autumn shook her head. "We were just saying how my mom is going to stay awhile to help us heal the family." Autumn took her mom's hand and swirled her tea with a spoon in the other.

"All right, so family again eh? Cool beans. That means one more witch around to help sort things out with Gran and figure out all this business of you being the four-points witch." Simone popped her eyes up at Autumn, as if she had said something she wasn't sure she should have.

"It's okay. I think Jo told Mom already. I suspect that's part of why you're here then?" She questioned her mother.

"Yes, Jo hinted at the fact that the necklace was calling to you, and, to be honest, I've had my suspicions for years now that you possessed more power than your gifts were letting on all this time. And a mother's intuition is never wrong. I imagined it was just a matter of time as you grew older that you would need help to take on the responsibilities you've been given. If there's one thing I know about our gifts, they sometimes come with heavy burdens and sacrifice. So I'm not only here to support our family, but specifically to support you in all of this."

Penny bent down and peeled back her thick boot socks peeking out over the tops of her ankle boots. She unclasped a bracelet that she wore around her ankle and dropped a small metal charm into Autumn's hand. It appeared to have a tree root design embossed on it.

"This symbolizes the roots of our bloodline. They run deep in these lands and connect us to the earth, air, fire, and water here. With these roots, the strength of all those who've come before us protects us. Wear this on the necklace that you got from Gran. It'll be an extra layer of safety, and

I'll put a protection spell around it this evening at Jo's house so that you'll always have the strength of our ancestors."

Autumn pulled Gran's necklace out from under the cowl neck of her sweater and put the charm on the chain along with the locket. "Thank you. I'll keep it safe alongside me."

"Good, now that the fire's dying down, why don't we see about some lunch and your Aunt Jo?" Penny suggested.

"Definitely. She should have some news by now from Chief Walsh, and she'll definitely wanna see you as soon as possible," Simone approved. "I'll go flip the sign at the front door and grab our coats. Meet you at the front?"

They all nodded and left, while Tavish curled up by the fire to monitor the last warm embers before his nap.

CHAPTER 11

Autumn turned the antique doorknob and pushed the door into Jo's bath shop just as Jo approached them at the entrance. "I knew it!" Jo said as she hurried Autumn and Simone inside to pull her sister into a hug.

"Pen, I'm so thankful you're home. I could feel you as I woke up this morning, but I wasn't sure exactly when to expect you." Jo stepped back to have a good look at her sister. "My goodness, you don't look like you've aged at all these last few years."

"Well, it helps that I've been tapping into the earth's energy every day, doesn't it?" Penny said with a grin. "It's so good to see you, sis. I'm sorry it's under these circumstances, but nevertheless, it's so good to be home with you all." Jo took her sister's coat and hung it on a coat rack at the front of the store.

"The girls say you may have some news from Chief Walsh about Gran's death. Shall we get right into it without wasting any time?" Penny followed the girls to a couple of couches on the far wall of the shop.

"Yes, well, I agree. Let's have a chat. I assumed from our phone conversation that you'll be staying awhile, so we can catch up on everything else in due time. For now, we need to discuss what's happening with Gran." Jo sat in an armchair beside the couch and leaned in.

"The Chief confirmed for me that there was foul play. Gran was, in fact, poisoned. Autumn, you were right to suspect those tea leaves in the cup you found. There were bits of a poisonous herb called foxglove in her system and some in the tea strainer they processed. Someone definitely wanted to cause Gran harm." Jo wrung her hands together as she spoke.

"Now, I don't know much about foxglove, but I do know that it's a leaf you shouldn't mess around with. The leaves are dangerous to ingest, and I steer clear of it, although I have seen the flowers growing in the mountains before." Jo had concern in her voice. She always wore her emotions on her sleeve, but Autumn could hear some shakiness in Aunt Jo now. It gave Autumn a lump in her throat to hear.

Penelope spoke up as Jo trailed off. "I've had dealings with foxglove. It's not something that anyone should handle under most circumstances. Only in dire situations can it be used to support healing in those who need their hearts revived. I had a case like that in one of the outer regions, and I barely saved the lass. However, in most cases, the leaves are deadly, creating an irregular heartbeat that ultimately leads to death. There should have been no good reason for it to be anywhere near Gran. Also," Penelope persisted. "The foxglove plant most commonly grows in the woodland on the other side of the mountaintop. That would mean that someone would have had to have known it was there and intentionally have gone looking for it, specifically for this purpose."

"Of killing Gran," Autumn said with disgust.

"Exactly. It doesn't sound like there is anything accidental about this. There must have been intent and some sort of reasoning behind it." Penelope's face looked grave as she stopped talking.

Simone rose off of the couch and began walking across the room. "This is horrible. I can't understand how anyone could do this to another person, let alone Gran, who was such a pillar of the community. We all absolutely love her, and she always stood up for every one of us here in Hollow's Glenn. I mean, that's what she was all about."

"But maybe that's just it." Autumn pointed her index finger in the air as if a strong case had to be made. "Maybe she would stick up for those from Hollow's Glenn and the mountain region, but an outsider may have felt differently about her. It's possible someone felt threatened enough by her stature and position in the community that they wanted her out of the picture. Maybe they felt like she would be in the way of whatever they wanted or needed to gain."

Simone nodded along, "Yeah, like a developer perhaps. Someone who would have gained quite a bit if Gran hadn't stood in the way of his plans for a bigger, more tourist-friendly Hollow's Glenn."

"Precisely!" Autumn felt as if they were onto something with this.

"Wait, girls. What developer? You haven't mentioned any of this to me yet. Was there something else that you found out?" Aunt Jo pressed.

"I found a tube of development plans at Gran's house this morning when we went back to have another look around. That was the one thing I found before Ben Walsh showed up and asked us to clear the area. I grabbed the tube and brought it back to the shop with us, but Simone and I glanced at the plans at the house first and saw an entire redevelopment plan for the downtown area. And there's no way Gran would have gone for it. On top of that, Mrs. Pendleton next door, told us she saw a serious-looking businessman snooping around the house the other day with the plans."

"All right, well, that does sound suspicious, but let's not get ahead of ourselves. That could all just be a legitimate bid for the preservation society to review. We don't know yet. So let's keep that in our back pocket and do some investigating of our own. My guess is the police department will do all they can with this, but it'll be up to us to sort out the more... magical aspects of the situation. And I imagine this foxglove herb is going to lead us more in that direction if I had to guess." Penny looked over at her sister to confirm her thoughts.

"Yes, I agree." Jo nodded. "I have a feeling there's more here that lies beneath the surface, just as in that moon card we pulled the other night. We need to uncover the unseen and not make any assumptions if we can help it. There's something deeply hidden here, and I get the sense that it's going to shift the tides immensely when we discover what it is." Jo fiddled with the moon charm on her bracelet as she spoke.

"Well, now that we're all officially spooked, I say we head over to the Forest Brew for a warm toastie and a cider. That should bring the mood up a bit. Shall we?" Simone rubbed her mother's shoulder and decidedly led the way to the door as they all slowly followed.

Autumn felt much better about things after talking with the family over lunch. As usual, the Forest Brew cafe was always a cozy, inviting spot to grab a bite and let the rest of the world melt away for a bit. That was exactly what Autumn needed. Now, she just wanted to finish the day at the shop and head home for a quiet night to get grounded.

She waved goodbye to Aunt Jo, her mother, and Simone as they headed back to the soap shop to help Jo wrap up the last of her new cranberry swirl bath bars. Autumn needed some alone time to finish lining the envelopes for her winter stationery collection anyway, and this would give her some space to do that.

She wrapped her billowy infinity scarf around her neck as she walked down the chilly Main Street. Feeling a nudge against her shoulder, she popped her head out of her scarf to apologize when she saw Kennedy beside her. "Oh, Kennedy. Hello again. I'm so sorry, I was putting my scarf on and wasn't quite watching where I was going."

"That's all right. I always have a way of wandering into things or people at just the right time." Kennedy twisted her long strawberry blonde ponytail up with a clip she pulled out of her pocket as Autumn attempted to process her odd greeting.

"You know, now that we're meeting again, I would like to get to know you a bit better. I'm on the preservation committee, and I imagine the mayor will invite you to step in for your Gran to fill her spot on the committee. So maybe we could grab a cup of tea or something afterward. I'm dying to know how you make those paper crafts of yours, and I actually could use some advice on running a booth at this year's market days. I've heard your shop has a booth at the event every year."

"Oh okay, I thought you were a researcher for the university, which is why I assumed you were on the preservation committee. What were you intending on selling at the market days?" Autumn remembered her conversation with Simone about how they needed to learn more about Kennedy, and she attempted to gather some quick facts.

Buttoning up the collar of her peacoat, Kennedy gave a muffled reply from behind the layers. "Yes, that's right. My cultural research has brought me here, but I've got some time now that I'm not an assistant professor this semester. So I thought I'd work on some of my other interests, like baking, and I can't eat all of those baked goods myself. That's why I was thinking of having a booth at the market. Although, it's just me making everything, and I have no idea what I'm getting myself into." Kennedy appeared to be asking for help, which Autumn hesitated to give, but she didn't want to make assumptions, as Aunt Jo recommended.

"Well, we want your first market days to be a success here in Hollow's Glenn, so if you need support, I can lend a hand. I don't know about the preservation society, but I'll talk with the mayor and see what that's all about. Then, maybe I'll see you for that cup of tea at the meeting, okay?" Autumn didn't want to commit to anything before getting a better sense of what Kennedy was talking about. She waved and politely headed down Main Street again considering all that she had heard.

No one had mentioned anything about taking Gran's place on the committee. Autumn knew the position rested with their family for decades, but she thought it would immediately go to Aunt Jo, who was also a prominent woman in the community. It was news to Autumn that she might be the one the mayor asked.

Just as she approached the door to the shop, the winds picked up and the dry leaves rustled under her feet. Autumn felt a strangely warm sensation in her coat pocket and reached in to pull out the necklace. Concealing it between herself and the door of the shop, she saw the emerald green light glowing from within it again. The tree root charm from her mother somehow welded itself to the top of the locket and made the light shine from underneath it as well.

"Below the surface, roots run deep." The voices whispered in the wind. Autumn looked around her to see if anyone was watching, but the street seemed calm for the time being.

"Wind of these lands, give me more guidance. Help me understand." Autumn clenched the necklace tightly and closed her eyes to concentrate.

This time, a red cardinal flew into the entryway before her and rested on the doorknob to the shop. The voices repeated the message. "Below the surface, roots run deep."

Autumn opened her eyes to the sight of the bird and shoved the necklace back into her pocket. She stood there, eyeing the bird as it seemed to look back at her calmly. "I'm listening, and I want to understand," she said to the bird before it flew away.

With a sigh, she unlocked the shop door and pulled off her coat before making her way to the back hearth room. She plopped down beside Tavish, who hadn't seemed to have moved from his position by the fire.

"Hey, cutie." She said as she grabbed him off the floor and onto her lap. "If you really are my familiar, I could use some help right now." She scratched under his chin to pay the toll for more guidance. "I don't know what this all means, and I'm scared that something much bigger than I am is taking hold in our little mountain region. I know you're a cat, but if you have any bird friends at all, would you mind putting in a good word for me? I need more than just a fly-by if I'm going to figure all this out."

She lifted Tavish up to look in his green eyes as his legs hung down like limp noodles. "Come on. I've got some messages coming to me for our new cards, and I need to get them printed and packaged up before the customers who need them arrive." She grabbed the cat and headed over to the counter to get back to work before anyone else showed up to rattle her.

Autumn spread out her new set of foil winter landscape cards along the countertop of the shop. She carefully reached a higher shelf on the back wall to pull down a tall glass mason jar full of calligraphy pens. She looked up at the shop to ensure no one was on their way in, and she reached her hand into the jar.

The pens shimmered with golden light as she dangled her fingers above them. Autumn peered inside the jar to find one in particular that rang little chimes into the air. She pulled it out of the jar and held it up to her ear to hear the soft sounds that only a small jingle bell could make. She smiled and knew that was the pen that had the messages to share today.

With a swoop of her hand, Autumn got right to work with one card after the other. She let the pen glide gently over the paper as the words flowed effortlessly onto the cards. One by one, she inscribed the cards with the words specifically intended for those needing them in the coming days. Some would be grandparents wanting to give smiles to their grandchildren feeling down. Some would be words of encouragement to those needing a boost after a low point in their lives. Others would be words of love given from one spouse to another.

As her hand moved over the papers, Autumn wished that maybe one of these messages would be exactly what she needed. After years of bringing wisdom to others, now more than ever, she deeply desired a message to bring her comfort. But, of course, that's not the way her gift worked. It gave others understanding and comfort, which was why she and Simone began the shop a few years back. Although now with Gran being gone, she longed to have that comfort restored for her own family.

As she felt the emotion welling up inside her, the bell rang at the front door. She put her pen down gently on the counter and unexpectedly looked up to find James staring back at her. Her mouth dropped open at the sight of him. Perhaps the wind swooped him into the shop at the exact moment she was looking for some comfort.

"Hi," he breathed as he walked up to the counter with his hands in his pockets.

"Hey, I... I'm glad you're here." Autumn came around the front of the counter and looked up into his brown eyes. "I've been meaning to thank you again for the other day, and I didn't know how to reach you."

"Oh, yeah. Well, it was nothing. I'm just glad I could help a bit, and hopefully I gave you a reasonable warning so you weren't as blindsided by your gran's passing. I know that doesn't take away how hard it is, though, and I want you to know that if you need anything, you can ask me."

He saw Autumn's watery eyes as he spoke. She turned away and headed back around the counter.

"Thank you. But I couldn't ask you to do anything more. You sat with me when I needed someone the most, which was really considerate of you." She had never felt so vulnerable with someone outside the family before, especially in such moments. "Just promise me you'll tell me if you have any more dreams, okay?" She said with a bit of a smile.

"Yeah, about that. Listen, I have had another dream, and I think it may be pretty important. You were..." He paused as the front doorbell chimed.

"Hello, there," Mrs. Newbury interjected as she entered the door. "Oh, I hope I'm not intruding on anything, but I've only got a little time before all the afternoon pickups at the coffee shop. Eve is there holding down the fort right now, and the customers love her recommendations for all the delectable pastries she whips up for me. But you know, I can't leave her all by herself for afternoon teatime."

"Oh, that's all right, Mrs. Newbury. Come on inside, and I'll help you find whatever you're looking for." Turning to James, Autumn whispered, "I'm sorry."

James smiled at her and checked the time on his phone. He couldn't wait for Mrs. Newbury's shopping trip, so he'd have to cut his visit short and get back to work.

"Uh, listen, Autumn, go ahead with Mrs. Newbury. I'm actually gonna be at the preservation society meeting tomorrow since my father's contracting business was just hired to do the downtown refurbishments. I have a feeling I might see you there, so let's talk after that, okay?"

"Well, I have a lot of questions for you, and I wanna make sure we have time to talk. I don't know anything about this preservation meeting." She started walking around with Mrs. Newbury as she spoke to James.

"Oh dear, the meeting is at the Forest Brew tomorrow at noon, as always. Why don't you just come back to the shop with me for some tea and a scone, and I can give you the details." Mrs. Newbury always loved lending a hand wherever she could. Perhaps that was why she was so good at running the Forest Brew coffee shop with her daughter. They both were always so accommodating and inviting.

James started walking out the door just as Autumn replied. "Okay, I guess I'll plan to see you tomorrow then." Smiling with contentment at her answer, James nodded and walked out the door.

"Okay, then. What are you in such a hurry for today?" Autumn put her hands on her hips and looked at Mrs. Newbury.

"This is my only chance to get a few cozy items and some message boards to make our booth look inviting for the market days. You always know just the right thing to call to our customers and make things feel extra special. So I was thinking you might help me gather some things up today because we've only got another couple weeks before the event kicks off the busy season, and I'll be completely swamped before then."

"All right, I think I may have a few things that'll be perfect for you and the Forest Brew booth." Autumn smiled as she remembered creating some new bunting banners, hand-calligraphed chalk signs, and customer thank-you cards just a week ago. It must have been on the air that Mrs. Newbury needed some market decorations, and Autumn picked up on it inherently.

"How do you feel about these bunting flags?" Autumn pulled out her recently made cardstock bunting stamped with pine trees from a tall wooden hutch drawer on the shop's side wall.

Mrs. Newbury took the bunting in her hands, and her jaw dropped as she read the flags. "Warm brew for warm hearts. Oh my goodness, Autumn, how do you always know? I mean, really, did you make this just for me? It's absolutely perfect for the market days, and it even has our signature pine trees on the flags. I'm definitely going to take this. Now, what else do you have?"

Autumn smiled and made her way over to the chalkboard signs and the new kraft paper cards and bags she'd recently lined with a pine tree green paper. "I've got a few more things over here," she replied.

"I just don't know what I'd do without you and all of your inviting preparations. I'm so thankful you're still open through all of this with your grandmother." She patted Autumn on the arm. "Let me look at all the things you have here, and then you have got to follow me back to the coffee shop for that scone and a quick chat. I know Eve would love to see you anyway since she was busy earlier when you were in."

"Okay, let's get you sorted, and then we'll go." Autumn turned to show off all the display items, but she couldn't quite focus on Mrs. Newbury as her mind wandered back to what James mentioned so quickly. He had had another dream, and he had expected to see her at the preservation meeting. She wondered if the two connected somehow and if this dream would be as pressing as the last. But first, she had to figure out why everyone wanted her at this preservation meeting.

CHAPTER 12

Autumn helped Mrs. Newbury down to the coffee shop with all her items for the market booth. Having known her while growing up in Hollow's Glenn, Autumn saw Mrs. Newbury as another staple of the community, just like Gran and Aunt Jo. A genuine sense of belonging existed in a place where you'd known the people since childhood and they'd all be there to support each other no matter what.

As happy as she was walking down Main Street, Autumn sensed something in the wind. Her skin tingled as someone bumped into her elbow. Stopping to pick up a few pine boughs that had fallen out of the bags she carried, Autumn looked up to find an older woman she saw Gran with every so often, but whose name escaped her.

"I am so sorry! Oh goodness," The woman said as she saw Autumn's face peering up at her.

"Oh Vera, it's so good to see you! I think it's been a couple of weeks since I've seen you around town." Mrs. Newbury put her bags down on the wooden bench beside where they stopped and took the bags from Autumn as well. "You know Lorna's granddaughter, Autumn, I presume." Mrs. Newbury put her arm around Autumn and smiled.

"Well, I don't think we've ever properly met, but yes, your grandmother spoke of you many times. I'm so sorry to hear of her passing." Vera fumbled with her purse as she turned away to walk again.

"Wait, Vera," Mrs. Newbury called. "Is everything all right? It's not like you to miss your regular bread pickups. I've been worried that you've been sick."

"Oh yes, well, Bill and I were talking about how I go into town too frequently these days, and he and I both thought I should refrain for a while. We need to keep a tight budget and all, and he's had me so stressed over all of his..." She looked over at Autumn before continuing. "His habits. That was something your grandmother was helping us with. Anyway, here I am now. No sickness, just trying to sort some things out at home."

"Vera, if there's anything I can do, then you just stop by the coffee shop and ask for me. I mean it. I'm always here, and even if you want to give me a ring at home, I'll be glad to listen, okay?" Mrs. Newbury reached out and hugged Vera.

Vera nodded at her while looking down at her purse. "Thank you. Ever since Lorna passed, I've missed having someone to talk to. I may just take you up on that if you don't mind, but please don't say anything to Bill. We haven't been seeing eye to eye, and I don't want to stir him up any more than he already is."

The ladies all looked at each other and nodded. Mrs. Newbury and Autumn picked up the bags off the bench and prepared to walk the last block to the Forest Brew as Vera slung her purse over her wool coat and headed off. "Talk to you soon, and Autumn, it was nice to meet you finally. Again, I'm sorry your Gran is no longer with us."

"Thank you," Autumn waved at her as she walked briskly ahead and turned down the next street.

"Well, that was interesting! I haven't seen her in some time now, and that's just not like Vera. You know, she mentioned your Gran helping her work things out at home. I overheard them in the coffee shop one day. Vera suspected her husband of lying about their finances. I got the feeling he'd been gambling and racking up quite the debt. I bet your Gran was seeing what she could do about that." Mrs. Newbury gave Autumn the eye, hinting that she knew Gran could fix a thing or two by special means.

"I see. Yeah, I guess that would make sense. I saw Gran give her a box of tea blends before, but I don't usually ask about all the people who come to Gran for help." Autumn hesitated before saying, "I mean, I didn't usually ask, when Gran was still here."

"Oh, sweet girl, I know this is hard. Have you found out anything more about what happened to Lorna?" Mrs. Newbury stopped in front of the Forest Brew and waited for Autumn to respond before heading inside.

"Well, not exactly, but we learned from the police that Gran didn't die of natural causes." A lump rose in Autumn's throat as she spoke the words to someone outside the family.

"My word, you're not saying that someone did this to Lorna? That there's someone who caused her harm?" Mrs. Newbury shook her head and let her eyes fall to the sidewalk.

Just as Autumn was about to explain that they were still keeping things quiet while they discovered what happened, the two ladies heard yelling on the next block over. They looked over to the mayor standing with an unfamiliar man in a gray suit, both speaking at each other with their hands in the air.

"This is completely absurd!" The man blurted out. "Your town needs more development, and you know full well that we're the firm that can deliver what's necessary. You're just letting ideals get in the way."

The mayor seemed to calm the man down enough for him to walk away swiftly without causing an even bigger scene. Relieved to be done with him, the mayor put his hands on his hips and took a breath as he walked toward the corner. He caught Autumn's eye as he came closer. "Ah, Autumn!"

Autumn and Mrs. Newbury looked at each other with confusion. They waited for him to come closer before responding.

"Hi, Mr. Mayor. Is everything all right?" Autumn adjusted the bags on her hip as she waited for his reply.

"Oh yes, that was nothing. Just an unhappy developer looking to take over the town. In fact, I'm quite grateful to your Gran for blocking his proposal in the preservation committee. Their firm wants to do some major new developments downtown, and they submitted a proposal to the committee for the new refurbishments that we requested. Thankfully, your Gran had the sense to make sure we passed on their proposal. It just wasn't in keeping with the historic charm that we'd like to remain here in Hollow's Glenn, and well, it would have opened up a great deal of additional issues."

He looked at them both with all the bags they were carrying. "Well, now! Let me help you with those! Autumn, I need to have a chat with you anyway about the preservation committee, and this is as good a time as any, I imagine. Can we step inside?"

Autumn nodded back to him as Mrs. Newbury shooed them all in the door and to a table in the front window of the coffee shop.

"Just sit down here and put the bags along the wall. I'll bring you both a cup of warm cider and some menus."

Giving her a tight-lipped smile, Autumn did as she was told and plopped down at the corner window table with the mayor. "Now then, first things first. Autumn, I'm so sorry about your grandmother. She's been a pillar of this community for decades, and she's leaving quite a hole in all our hearts. She will most definitely be missed."

"Thank you, mayor. I really appreciate it. I know Gran respected you very much. So it means a lot for you to say such kind words."

Mrs. Newbury came over with the cider and menus as expected. "Both of you take your time and just give us a wave if you're ready to order something."

When she walked away, the mayor cleared his throat and leaned in. "I've spoken a bit with Chief Walsh about Lorna's death, and I know that they're treating it delicately. They've opened an investigation, and the Chief will see to it that they uncover whatever occurred. I'm going to keep your family in the loop of anything I find out as well. I know that there are... things... that may be of a sensitive nature surrounding your grandmother. Your family has been in Hollow's Glenn for generations, and it has a close bond with this region. We need you just as much, if not more, than your family needs these mountains."

Autumn shifted in her chair as he revealed this. "So you know about our connection here?" She wasn't sure exactly how much he knew about their gifts and responsibilities to the region, but she wanted to learn more.

"Yes, of course." The mayor widened his eyes, surprised that she didn't know as much as he did. "Our families have been intertwined for decades. When my father was mayor, he swore to uphold the secrets of our family links to the region. He and his father before him both knew your great-grandmother well and her duty to protect these lands. Together, our families have passed down the secret knowledge of our gifts and leaned on each other for support. Your family oversees the founders and handles the sensitive situations that arise with the region's energy, and my family upholds the governing side to keep things under wraps. We are also here should there ever be a dire need for our gifts. Each of the founding families of the town has its role to play in ensuring we thrive long term."

"So our families have used their gifts to protect Hollow's Glenn for generations?" Autumn vaguely remembered hearing Gran and Aunt Jo discussing these things while growing up. Now and then, she'd interrupt a conversation about the shifting energy or the importance of keeping the town's history intact.

"Yes, but I think you better get more specifics from your Aunt Jo because I can't stay too long. She'll know what to tell you, and frankly, it's not my place if you don't already know your family history. While I have you here, though, I want to ask if you'll take your grandmother's position on the preservation committee." He stopped briefly to wave Eve over from the counter.

"Ah, Eve, I'll just take one of your ham and cheese toasties to go, if you don't mind."

"Of course, Mr. Mayor. Coming right up! Hi, Autumn. Anything for you?" Eve smiled at her, pen and paper in hand.

"Oh, I'll have a warm cranberry scone, but I'll stay and eat at the counter while I chat with you and your mom a bit." Autumn handed the menus back to Eve as she walked away.

Autumn shook her head in confusion as she stared back at the mayor. "Mr. Mayor, I don't understand. I don't know much about historic preservation. I mean, I've lived here my whole life, yes, and I absolutely adore this town, but why would you want me instead of someone already on the committee or maybe even my Aunt Jo?"

"Autumn, this is part of your family's legacy. That spot to oversee the committee can't go to just anyone in town. It has to reside with your family, and that's why it's written in the bylaws. Each founding family gets a seat on the committee, and your family holds the primary chair."

He cleared his throat again before he continued. "Now, there are some who balk at that rule and believe it should be overturned, but that's because they're unaware of the necessity of it. Those of us aware of your family's value and that of the other families will keep the bylaws intact. It's just up to you now to claim the position, and I need you to do that tomorrow at the meeting."

"I don't know what to say, other than that I need to speak with Jo before I decide." She stirred the cinnamon stick in her cider mug and thought for a moment.

"All right then, I have every confidence that Jo will guide you in the right direction. So I assume you can get the details of the meeting from Mrs. Newbury here, and I'll expect to see you tomorrow taking up your new position. I know you're the right person for the job, Autumn, and I very much believe that your grandmother did as well." With that, the mayor walked up to the counter to claim his takeaway order and head out for what most likely would be another busy afternoon at city hall.

Autumn gathered her cider and bag and moved over to the back bar stools at the pastry counter.

"Okay," she glanced over at Eve, who was behind the counter warming her scone. "Well, I guess I need some more info from your mom about the preservation committee. But first, I've gotta have some of those famous scones of yours! I could smell them as soon as I walked in. And we need to catch up! Tell me about these amazing pastries you've been baking here."

Eve gave Autumn a shy smile as she put the plate down on the counter with a laugh. "Yeah, I guess you could say I found my strong suit."

Eve brought over some warm cinnamon butter to accompany Autumn's scone and gave her a heartfelt look. "Autumn, I'm really sorry to hear about your Gran. We all loved her so much, and it's gonna be hard thinking about this town without her."

"Thank you, Eve. I know. She was an incredible woman, and she absolutely loved this town. But enough about that right now! I'm curious how you started making these amazing pastries here. I know you've dabbled in baking before, but I guess I didn't realize how good you were."

"Thanks! Yeah, my mom taught me different things about herbs and spices. I guess, I just picked up quite a few things along the way, and recently, she asked me to make things to sell here in the shop. So the rest is history!"

"That's really amazing! You know, I may just have to sell some of those cinnamon sugar popovers you have over at my shop. They would be the perfect cozy treat for shoppers." Autumn gave her a scheming eye and then dug into her scone.

"How's everything, dear?" Mrs. Newbury came around to the back of the counter. "Things are picking up for the afternoon tea rush, but I wanted to check on you and give you all those details about the meeting tomorrow."

"Right! Yeah, I actually don't quite understand the importance of me taking Gran's spot on the committee, but I'm gonna talk it over with Aunt Jo to see if I really should. The mayor seemed to think it was a done deal, though, and that he would definitely see me taking the position tomorrow."

"Well, Autumn," Mrs. Newbury leaned over the counter and whispered. "Lorna's position on that committee wasn't just one to give to anyone, you know. It's your family's rightful place to uphold it."

Autumn put her scone down and gave Mrs. Newbury a squinty look. "The mayor said the same thing to me. Something about being a founding family."

"Exactly. Your aunt will tell you more and be discreet about it, but I believe Lorna intended to prepare you for the position. She just didn't realize..." Her voice trailed off as she thought of Gran's death. "Of course, I know that Marion Bennett has been eyeing that position for years now so that she could have control over both the chamber of commerce and the preservation committee, with her husband practically running the chamber and all. Oh, but that would never happen as long as our founding families have something to do with it."

Mrs. Newbury stopped for a moment to pour some coffee for a few tables, which gave Autumn a chance to think about all she was saying. Autumn took a sip of her cider and realized that the mayor and Chief Walsh weren't the only ones who knew about the MacKinnon family gifts, and that apparently there was much more to their family responsibilities than she ever realized. It was time to have a long chat with her mother and Aunt Jo and get to the bottom of all this.

One step at a time, though. Mrs. Newbury mentioned that Marion Bennett also had it out for Gran. That wasn't something Autumn wanted to overlook, especially now that the circumstances behind Gran's death were getting increasingly suspicious. She couldn't rule anyone out just yet for culpability.

Mrs. Newbury wandered back behind the counter to continue the conversation as if nothing had stopped it. "Anyway, if there's one thing I know for sure, it's that Marion Bennett really resented your grandmother's power in this town. She wanted to be the one with all the sway over the mayor and all the businesses, but that's not the natural order of things here."

She put a hand over Autumn's on the counter. "Go talk to Jo and then come back at noon tomorrow for the meeting. Just be prepared for a few grumblings about you taking the position, especially from Marion Bennett. But know that it's rightfully yours."

Autumn smiled. "Thank you, Mrs. Newbury. I appreciate you talking with me."

As Mrs. Newbury walked away to attend to the afternoon rush, Eve came over to top up Autumn's cider. "Oh, thanks, Eve. Do you think I could take this cider to go? I do really need to get back to the shop, and apparently, I have some things to sort out as well."

"Yeah, absolutely! Let me get it ready for you." Eve walked to the back corner with Autumn's cider and pulled out a to-go cup. She poured the drink carefully into the cup, and just as Autumn was about to turn away, she saw sparkles of light in the air above the drink. Eve's fingers gently swirled over the top of Autumn's cup, and then she stuck a cinnamon stick into the liquid, closed it up, and turned briskly around to deliver it.

"Here you go! One warm cider for the road," Eve said with a smile.

"Oh, okay. Thank you for this." Autumn tried not to come across as so confused, but she was still going over what she had just seen. Could Eve be a witch? There was no doubt Autumn had seen tiny sparks of light, and she definitely appeared to be doing something with her fingers.

"I'll just leave this here. That should take care of lunch, and I don't need any change. Thanks!" Autumn left some money on the counter beside her plate, grabbed her coat, backpack, and cider, and rushed out the door.

She needed to get some fresh air, and she needed answers. Too many questions hung in the air, and nothing seemed to connect. Autumn walked down to the end of the block and pulled her coat on when she reached a bench. She looked down at her cider cup and then at the trash. Autumn threw it in, saying under her breath, "Just in case."

The winds were picking up again, and she could smell a hint of secrecy in the air, almost like lingonberries, yet with an overtone of darkness. As she made her way down Main Street to Parchment and Pine, Autumn knew it was time to call a garden dinner and get some answers. She just couldn't let all of this hang in the air anymore.

GOOD FORTUNE
TEA

1 1/2 cups water

1/2 tsp ground cinnamon (or one small stick)

1/8 tsp nutmeg

1/8 tsp ground cloves

1/8 tsp ground cardamom pods

1/4 tsp vanilla extract

1 Tbsp black tea leaves

drizzle of honey

1 tsp almond milk

Heat the water in a saucepan on the stove. Add each scoop of spices to the water, each time saying the ingredient out loud. When all the spices have been added, repeat the phrase,

Each one for a heaping of good luck and fortune.

Add the splash of vanilla extract and continue heating until the spices have blended and the liquid is boiling. Remove from heat. Please the tea leaves into a sachet or tea strainer and steep in the liquid for three to four minutes. Pour into the tea mug that most draws your attention and add the milk and honey. Envision good fortune coming into your life as you drink the tea down to the last drop.

CHAPTER 13

Evenings in Aunt Jo's garden always felt so enchanting. She made it a point to have the string lights lit for family dinners with hints of water sounds serenely filling the background. No one knew how she did it, but the babbling sounds from the river deep behind the house always soothed each person at the table.

Tonight, Autumn needed to focus on getting as much information from her mom and Aunt Jo as possible. She didn't think Simone knew any more than she did because they practically grew up side-by-side like sisters. Yet, the wise woman in Autumn knew that Jo and Penny would do what they needed to protect the family, even if that meant keeping some things from the girls all these years.

Autumn and Simone set the table outside as Penny brought out three tall taper candle holders to display in the middle of the feast. Aunt Jo pushed her back through the garden door as she walked out with an enormous platter of roasted duck surrounded by brussels sprouts and cranberries.

"Wow," Autumn exclaimed as she fixed her eyes on the duck. "I didn't know we were going all out tonight."

"Yes, well, I wanted to celebrate your mother being home with us again. It just didn't seem right to keep wallowing in all the sadness around Gran, so I'm hoping to turn the energy around with a good meal and some family time. Okay, and maybe a bit of magic while we're at it." Aunt Jo smirked as she put the tray down on the table. "Oh, and Simone, I made a nice stuffed butternut squash just for you, dear."

"Thanks, Mom. Yeah, keep the duck away from my side of the table, please." Simone said with wide eyes.

Jo nodded in understanding as she slid the duck platter to one side. She pulled some crystals out of her apron pocket and arranged them across the table's centerline in a color range from clear and white crystals down to purples and deep blues.

"These will help with any insights we need tonight." Then, she pulled out two small glass tincture jars filled with clear liquid and rose buds. "And these will strengthen our family bond of love and togetherness." Jo placed one on each end of the table and placed her hands on her hips, quite pleased with herself.

"All right, I called this garden dinner because several things have just come up, and I can feel it all hanging in the air." Autumn sat down on one of the rickety wooden chairs and folded her hands on the table. "And to be honest, I know some things are still being kept from me... and Simone. Things about our family and our responsibilities in the mountain region."

Everyone sat down at the table in silence. Simone went first to dish out some food on her plate and reply.

"I agree with Autumn. Things are definitely changing, and you can't leave us in the dark about it. We're old enough to know everything, es-pecially since Autumn is apparently the new four-points witch. And I almost made it rain again today on my way home!" Simone sighed and looked around at them. "I'm pretty sure I activated that storm we had the other day before we heard about Gran. I felt frustrated about staying up late for my design classes only for the submission to not record properly. My frustration may have activated the storm. I just didn't connect the dots until now since I've been seeing myself actually control the weather." Simone appeared to be more apologetic than usual. "I need to learn to control my gifts better now, I guess."

"So that's where that storm came from!" Jo threw her hands up in the air as if everything finally made sense! "I can always feel the water energy, but on that day, I didn't feel it until suddenly the clouds were raging above us! And now that you say something, I felt your frustration when you came down for breakfast that morning."

Autumn took a sip of some iced chamomile tea and shook her head. "That may just be the beginning. You know I've had some things happening with my gifts, too, like the levitation the other day and all the voices. In fact, I heard them again out on the street, and Gran's locket glowed. The root charm that mom gave me fused to the side of the locket, and the voices told me that below the surface, roots run deep."

She scooped out some mashed sweet potatoes from a ceramic bowl and plopped them onto her plate. "So things are happening with the locket that I don't understand. And these messages have got me really confused. Plus, James came into the shop again."

"Oh, he did. Did he?" Simone raised her eyebrows at Autumn and smiled.

Penny looked around at them and questioned, "Who's James? I don't think I remember that name."

Aunt Jo leaned toward her sister sitting beside her. "He's Sorcha Allan's son. You remember Sorcha? Very intuitive friend of mine who always seemed to have predictive dreams."

"Oh right, I remember her," Penny nodded. "She always acted lovely to me, and I actually remember healing her knee once when we were children. She fell and got a nasty scrape while we walked home from school through the woods one day. There was nothing nearby, and I think I pulled out a bit of calendula or something and did a little healing spell. I recall her being such a sweetheart about it all."

"Yeah, Mom, James is the one who actually tried to warn us about Gran. He told us about a dream he had where he found me at Gran's cottage, along with the Book of Spells."

The two older women exchanged serious glances before returning to Autumn. "He came to the shop today and said he'd had another dream. I didn't get any other details from him because Mrs. Newbury showed up. But apparently he's going to be at the preservation meeting tomorrow, and I'm supposed to take Gran's seat there. I guess everyone expected this but me!" Autumn threw her silverware down on her plate and sat back abruptly in her chair with a sigh.

"I see." Jo sat back and pressed her apron down over her skirt with her hands. "I guess it is time for you girls to know about our family. Penny, would you mind walking to the edge of the garden and putting a cloaking spell around us?"

Penny stood up and walked over to the corner of the house where Jo grew a large sage bush. She pulled several leaves from the bush and crumpled them in her hands. Starting in the north corner of the garden, Penny sprinkled the leaves along the ground as she whispered something into the air. Autumn couldn't help but watch as she'd never seen her mother doing magic before, and it looked quite peaceful to see her movements.

When she came back around to the table, Jo proceeded. "Now, I've already told you girls of the Book of Spells and how our family are protectors of sorts for this mountain region. The necklace from your Gran connects us here and strengthens our ties and magic. But ours isn't the only magical family anchored here."

"Mrs. Newbury mentioned that to me today, and the mayor hinted at it, too. So... you're saying more families like ours protect these lands? And they're also magical?" Autumn seemed excited by this discovery.

"Well, yes and no." Jo took a sip of her chamomile iced tea.

"There are other magical families here. They are the founding families, just as we are. Our bloodlines go back for over a century at least. We all connected through an original Scottish-born wise woman. The families worked together here when the lands were in trouble from a plague of drought and wildfires. They stabilized the earth and ensured the waters returned. And because of their bravery and service to these lands, the wise woman gave each family gifts. The gifts we know today as our magic." Penny rolled her hands together in a spinning circle and then lifted her palms to display a bright green sprouted plant in the center. She laughed softly and closed her hands, looking around the table.

Simone's eyes glistened with excitement. "Aunt Penny, I forgot how amazing your gifts were!"

Autumn stared into her mother's hands. "I remember you sprouting the oak tree at Gran's cottage for me when I was young. It was how I remembered you while you were gone healing the lands. But that means... we're one of those founding families meant to protect the land?"

"Actually, we descend from the wise woman. The one who started this all, and that is why our family's bloodline leads the founding families and carries all the elements within it. All four energies resided in your great-grandmother, Gran's mother. She was our four-points witch for decades. Of course, earth and a bit of air came to your gran. Earth resides in my sister, Penny. Water in Simone and I. And while we thought you, Autumn, had earth and air like your gran, it turns out that you take after your great-grandmother. You now carry the four-points, and I'm very interested to see how the water and fire come out of you."

Autumn rubbed her forehead and closed her eyes for a moment. "This is all so much. I don't know what to think about any of this."

Simone rubbed her cousin's back a bit. "It's okay, cuz. We're figuring things out together, remember? I won't let you take all of this on by yourself. I'll always be here."

Penny looked down at her plate and shifted her food around with her fork. "I'm so sorry I had to leave you all for so long. I never wanted to hurt any of you, and I feel like I've missed so much! I wanted to be here to raise you, Autumn, more than anything. But I had an obligation that I fear you're going to have to take up yourself now. But I'm just so thankful that you have Simone by your side to be part of this learning process."

Penny turned her eyes tearfully toward her sister. "And Jo, I'm staying to help you teach these girls to start their own coven and control their expanding powers." She looked over at the girls. "That's the next step before you can resume your new roles as protectors of these lands. Our bloodline is the only one that can hold it all together. The only one that can shift the energies and transform the land, sea, and sky. The other families here guide and support us with their gifts, but we sustain it all."

"That's right," Jo grabbed one of the clear crystals off the table and twirled it between her fingers as she spoke. "James's family has intuitive gifts passed down through his line that came from the founders. I don't know if he's completely familiar with the history, but he grew up with his mother, Sorcha's abilities. Now he's discovering his own dreamwork."

"What about the Newburys?" Autumn inquired. "I went back to Forest Brew this afternoon and could have sworn that Mrs. Newbury's daughter, Eve, did something to my cider. And with everything going on, I didn't know what to think. I've known Eve all my life, but I don't think she would ever do anything to hurt anyone. I definitely saw tiny sparkles of light around my cup, though, and her fingers swirling above it."

Penny and Jo exchanged a laugh as they both nodded. "Oh yes, the Newburys. I just love Catherine Newbury so much! She's always such a delight with all the love and kindness she puts into her food. It has been a gift to enjoy all these years. So yes, she must have passed it onto her daughter, Eve. Of course, they are one of the founding families, and I believe her husband is on the preservation committee. They have such pure hearts, so I'm sure Eve was adding a bit of extra love and comfort to your cider today, nothing more."

"Interesting... She was asking about Gran, and heard me talking with her mother about all that's been happening. Maybe she just wanted to comfort me, but that really surprised me." Autumn rested her chin in her palm and thought for a moment.

"Okay, so we know about James's family and the Newburys. Geez, no wonder those scones over there are so popular. The Newburys sprinkle in some magic! I'll be eating there more often now that I know there's a hint of something extra. But what about others? Chief Walsh's family? They seemed to know about us, and he was definitely keeping this under wraps at Gran's house." Simone wanted to know all the details now that this was out in the open.

"The Walsh family is different. They aren't a founding family, but they know about us. Many of the Walsh men swore to protect these lands in their own way as law enforcement. Our families long ago decided it was best they knew what they were dealing with, and they've kept our secrets for decades."

"Mmm, yes, along with other things," Penny hinted. "I think Chief Walsh always had your heart, Josephine MacKinnon. And something tells me you've always had his as well."

"Don't be silly, Pen. He married a wonderful woman and had a beautiful son. They had a long marriage together before she died, and I never interfered with any of that."

"Whoa, Mom! What's all of this? It sounds like there really was something going on between you and Chief Walsh all these years." Simone perked up and leaned in to hear about this.

"You're all being ridiculous! We may have been keen on each other throughout school, but we went our separate ways. I was always fond of him, but I just wanted him to be happy. I knew his choices were for the best and that I needed to take my own path." Jo looked out into the garden, and everyone's eyes followed hers. "Is that... a bobcat?"

Penelope stood up immediately. "Yes, you're right. I feel it just on the other side of my cloaking spell. I don't think it can see or hear us out there, but it feels as though it wants to find us. Like it's someone's familiar or something."

Just as Penny uttered the words, Tavish pushed through the back door and ran out into the middle of the garden to stare into the darkness beyond the trees. Maybe she was Autumn's familiar after all. But there weren't usually bobcats that came this close to town. Someone had to have sent it here.

"A bobcat familiar in Hollow's Glenn?" Jo slowly moved to the center of the yard near Tavish who kept eyeing the bobcat, and Autumn followed. Jo raised her arms to shoulder height and looked up to the sky, murmuring some words under her breath. In less than a minute, clouds appeared overhead and thick raindrops fell.

The bobcat cowered down and scurried away out of sight. Autumn and Jo turned toward one another with relief. "Aunt Jo, you made it rain. I don't think I've ever seen you do that. And you, our amazing little guard cat!" Autumn bent down to give Tavish a good petting. "You've been so brave. What would we do without you?" Tavish purred and shook his tail with pride.

As the rain gently softened and subsided, Jo made her way back to the table. "Well, we'd better just head inside to finish this conversation away from prying eyes and ears. Who knows what that was all about, but I don't like it one bit."

They all cleared the table following Jo's lead. Autumn piled a few dishes high onto her arms and agreed. "You're right. Something is definitely going on, and I haven't even told you all yet about everything I found out today."

"Come on, girls. Let's get inside, and I'll make a pot of Gran's peppermint awareness tea while we chat." Penny guided them all inside and peered out the back door window one extra time before shutting the shade.

CHAPTER 14

Autumn and Simone sat on the rug in front of the fireplace, warming their hands as Tavish circled between them. Aunt Jo piled a batch of cranberry cardamom scones from the Forest Brew onto a plate and brought it into the living room as Penny followed with a tray of steaming tea cups.

"All right, now that we're tightly inside, let's chat." Aunt Jo and Penny put everything down on the large ottoman in the center of the room. "Chief Walsh told me we can go back to Gran's house if we need to now. They've collected all the evidence, and they're handing the house back to us now."

"That means we can get the Book of Spells back along with anything else that may be handy in that wardrobe of Gran's." Autumn looked at Simone as they nodded at each other.

"Plus, I really wanna go back and grab some of my personal things. I've been missing my journals, and I've just been yearning for all my cozy socks and sweaters now that we're fully into the fall season. I just didn't want to make a fuss about it before because we've had so much else to think about. Which brings me to all the things that I found out today." Autumn grabbed a tea mug and wrapped her hands around it as she spoke.

"Yes, tell us all about what you've been up to! We need to sort out this mess." Penny scooted in closer off the edge of the sofa to grab a scone and some tea while she waited.

"Okay, I mentioned James came into the shop and told me he had another dream just as Mrs. Newbury was coming into the shop. So I let James go and told him I'd see him at the preservation meeting. But several things came up as I walked through Main Street with Mrs. Newbury and went back into the coffee shop again."

She stopped for a moment to take a bite of the cranberry scone and savor how good it was before she continued. "Besides finding out how amazing Eve is now as a baker! Anyway, Mrs. Newbury and I saw the mayor arguing with a man outside city hall. It appeared to be over the development intentions, and I got the feeling that this was probably the developer that Mrs. Pendleton saw with that mailing tube on Gran's porch. I mean, it seemed about right, given that this man in a suit, who I'd never seen around before, was pretty adamant with the mayor about things. He was flailing around saying that the town needed new development and his firm was the one to do it, but the mayor seemed to calm him down without really giving in."

"That would make sense that this developer would still try to finagle his way into town through the mayor. But if I know our mayor, I can be sure he won't back down on what the town needs and wants. He'll stay true to preserving our history and the integrity of the energy here. So, I'm sure he's giving this developer our clear views on what we want, just as Gran probably did. But that makes me nervous about how far this developer would have gone to get what he wants. Did he look like he would be capable of such a thing as killing someone over this?" Aunt Jo had a worried look on her face as she peered over her teacup toward Autumn.

"It's hard to say. If we're being honest, people can be capable of many things when they let anger get the best of them. So I just don't know, but the mayor seemed to shrug him off as if it was just a thorn in his side. That doesn't mean that I want to dismiss the developer, though. We need to find out more about how much he's been around here and what else he may have done at Gran's house."

They all sat for a moment and watched Tavish stretch out his front legs, spread his paws out, and then plop down again into a new cozy position. Autumn scratched at the inside of his furry ear as he closed his eyes to drift back to sleep.

"So there was that, but also I ran into someone else with Mrs. Newbury. A woman I've seen Gran with several times before, named Vera, but I don't quite know her." Autumn glanced up at Jo and Penny to see if they knew who she was talking about.

"Ah, yes, Vera Cunningham! She's an interesting one. Vera and her husband can both be rather uptight and rigid, but she's lived here all her life. What happened with her today, dear?" Jo snacked on her scone and found a flannel blanket to throw over her lap.

"It was strange, to be honest. She mentioned not being in town lately because she had to watch the budget and something about her husband's habits. Apparently, that was something Gran was helping her with. Aunt Jo, I don't know if Gran mentioned anything about that to you, but it sounded to me like Gran was probably making some of her special tea blends for a specific problem that Vera needed to fix. Maybe something with her husband. Does that sound familiar?"

"Now that you mention it, yes. I recall Gran saying that Vera's husband was a bit of a gambler. And if I inferred correctly from the teas that Gran was blending, I would say they were trying to get him to open up about what was really going on with the family finances. I know she had been carrying a lot of geranium leaves and myrrh oil lately, and if I had to guess, they would have been for a communication tea." Jo slipped her ballet flats off her feet and tucked them under the flannel blanket.

"So Gran was still up to her usual tea magic. Nothing had changed, had it? She was still the same old wise woman of the village that I always knew and loved." Penny shook her head and looked down at her lap. "I wish I would have seen her one last time before she passed. I've missed her so much."

"She knew you were doing what you were supposed to do, love. You were right where you needed to be, helping heal those in the region that needed your gifts. We were still all tethered together as we'll always be with our energy." Aunt Jo tried to console her, but she knew Penny's heart would hurt for quite some time from not seeing her mother in the last days. "Let's just focus on what we can do in the present, shall we?"

They all perked up a bit, and Simone stoked the fire to keep the flames going. "So what makes you bring up Vera now, cuz? Was there something that made you suspicious about her?" Simone threw her legs out behind her and grabbed a throw pillow to prop up under her elbows as she laid down.

"Well, she definitely seemed odd," Autumn called from the kitchen as she topped up her tea and brought the kettle out for everyone else. "But it was more about all that she was saying. Like how she had these mysterious things going on at home that Gran was helping with. And now, if Jo is right, maybe something was going on with her husband. If that's the case, then her husband could have had some issue with Gran being around or giving Vera these teas to use on him. Maybe he should be on our suspect list, too."

"So we've now got this angry developer who wants his bid for the town development approved, and we know Mrs. Pendleton saw him at Gran's house the day she died. Plus, we potentially have Vera's husband, who may have been upset about Gran giving his wife these honest communication teas to spill all of his gambling secrets. Wow, this is shaping up to be an interesting town! Who knew we had such diabolical people running around?" Simone enjoyed finding a bit of drama and intrigue wherever she could get it.

"Oh Simone, honestly! The town isn't like that, and you know it! We're good people, all in all, and this hasn't happened here for..." Jo stopped herself and looked over at Penny.

Penny raised her eyebrows at Jo's words, but kept a tight lip.

"Wait, what? This type of thing happened before in Hollow's Glenn?" Autumn wanted to hear what the two women seemed to share in secret.

"It's just that for years, Gran maintained a state of normalcy in the mountain region. It was her duty to keep the energy of the lands, sea, and sky stable, especially until we found another four-points witch. So we haven't had any major disturbances to affect the balance of nature here for a very long time. In the past, people caused imbalances by harming others, or devastating draughts and things damaged the lands. It's our family's responsibility, along with the founding families supporting us, to maintain the energy balance." Penny explained all of this fairly matter-of-factly, as if she was more detached than Jo from the emotional side of it.

Autumn sighed with frustration and paced around the room. "Okay, so now that the torch is passing to me, things are going haywire? Apparently, I'm shirking my responsibilities, which I didn't even realize I had." As she spoke, the flames quickly shot up from the fire and intensified the heat in the room.

"Whoa, Autumn, did you just do that with your power?" Simone raised herself off the floor, and Tavish startled himself up to a sphinx position and turned toward Autumn as well.

"Uh, did I? I mean, I imagined it in my mind just now, and I could feel the heat inside me. But did I really just make that happen?"

"Yes, child. You did. The four points are within you, and they're being activated more fully now that you're engaging with the people of the lands more deeply. Your gifts are calling to you." Penny eyed her daughter with a newfound maternal mentorship that had lay dormant for years.

"I don't know if you can do this. The women who've come before us have been incredible, powerful, wise women. I'm just me, Autumn. I run the cozy paper shop and hand out messages people need to hear through my paper crafts. How am I supposed to protect the energy balance of the mountain region and figure out who killed Gran?" She flopped down on the floor next to Tavish. "My head hurts."

"My dear, you were born for this. Whether or not you realize it, you are a MacKinnon, and MacKinnon women manifest great things. You will be no different." Jo smiled at her gently.

Autumn rubbed her temples and nodded to herself. "I can do this. I can do this." She snatched Tavish up into her lap to help calm her down. "You all know this makes me super anxious, and I don't know what tomorrow is going to bring. But I do know that I want to be the witch you all think I can be. So help me figure out Gran's death first. I feel like that's a good starting point for me, seeing as how wisdom is a strength of mine. So I have one more thing to share that I found out today."

They all grabbed another scone as if that would miraculously bring all kinds of new insights to light. Autumn chewed and gathered her thoughts before starting again.

"Mrs. Newbury mentioned Marion Bennett today while I was at the coffee shop. She said Marion's been very interested in getting Gran's spot as chair of the preservation committee and adamant about controlling the chamber of commerce with her husband at the head there as well. It sounded like she and Gran had quite a few differences of opinion, and Marion wanted the upper hand as the town spokeswoman."

"You're right. She resented Gran's status in town and Gran's ability to sway all the leadership and businesses here for as long as I can remember. I think the picture Catherine Newbury painted of Marion is fairly accurate. She's privileged, arrogant, and entitled enough to think she can get whatever she wants." Jo took a moment to think through what she just said aloud. "To be honest, I never would have thought she could do anything so drastic as to harm someone to get them out of her way. Yet, I believe that's where we stand now. Someone has killed your gran, and we just can't rule anyone out, I'm afraid. We'll have to add her to the list."

"Right, that's what I'm thinking, too." Autumn ran her hand along Tavish's back and down his tail. "I'm going to that preservation meeting tomorrow to get closer to these people. That's the only way we're gonna find out more of what's going on around here. And apparently, that's what I need to do to get things back into balance as well."

"I'll hold down the fort at the shop while you attend the meeting. Maybe this will be good for us to all cover our bases around town then, between both shops and the meeting." Simone turned to her mother and aunt, and they both agreed.

"Yes, I think this is a wise start. But, Autumn, you'll need to figure out how to keep that under wraps before you go." Her mother pointed to Autumn's hands.

She glanced down to her lap to see Tavish snuggled right up next to the warm flame that had sparked right in the palm of Autumn's hand.

CHAPTER 15

Autumn laid out a teal blue linen-bound journal on the counter at Parchment and Pine. She put a gold foil message on the front cover that read, "May The Days Ahead Be Filled With Joy And Inspiration," tied an eggplant and gold plaid ribbon around the journal in a large bow, and inserted a lovely wooden fountain pen through the middle of the it.

"Simone, I need to head out to the preservation meeting, but I'm leaving this journal out on the counter display. There'll be someone coming in who needs it for a last-minute gift before we close, and it might pair well with a bag of Gran's tea blends for inspiration. Would you mind pointing them in the right direction?"

"Of course! You know I always do." Simone said with a smile. "And maybe I'll suggest some of my new wrapping paper designs while I'm at it."

"There you go! That intuition of yours is pretty spot on, so I know you'll make a good choice for whoever it is."

"You just stay focused on the meeting and gather as much information as possible. Oh, and try to stay grounded so you don't start any fires or levitate off the ground while you're there, okay?" Simone shot Autumn a sarcastic look and went back to adjusting some table displays.

"Ha-ha, very funny, Miss I-start-random-thunderstorms." Autumn grabbed the soft white hand-knit scarf Gran had knit for her several years back for a Yule gift. She wrapped it around her neck once and let the ends hang down in front of her shoulders. It comforted her right now to think Gran was with her in small ways, especially as she was about to take up her chair on the preservation committee.

Autumn went to the back room as Tavish circled through her feet. "Tav, I'm just going out for a bit. You stay with Simone, okay?" Autumn grabbed her light gray wool coat and wrapped it around her before flinging her bag over her shoulder. "Okay, I'm off," she called to Simone as she walked toward the shop's entrance.

"Don't get into too much trouble while I'm gone," Autumn smiled.

"I could say the same to you, cuz." Simone joked back at her.

Walking down Main Street, Autumn smelled the aroma of cedarwood in the air but couldn't see where it came from. The scent was strong, and she got an overwhelming wisp of it as she stopped by the bookshop window. There was a large basket in the window full of cedarwood logs and beside it sat Gran's favorite book she read to Autumn occasionally, Little Women.

Autumn laughed to herself, "Subtle, Gran. Cedarwood, huh? I guess you want me to be strong today."

A gust of wind blew through, and the small wooden wind chime at the bookstore's front door made an earthy, mellow chime. "I know. I'll try to make you proud," Autumn whispered under her breath as she turned to keep walking.

She got to the corner of the block and waited for the stoplight to turn. The wind howled and rattled the branches on the maple tree beside her, and Autumn could sense the voices in the distance.

"In the photo, lies what you seek."

Autumn turned to check either side of her before addressing the voices. "What do you mean?" As the light turned, she drifted across the street as the voices spoke again.

"In the photo, lies what you seek."

Why were these voices always so vague? It was as though her ancestors took pleasure in dropping breadcrumbs of no real consequence. She shrugged it off for the time being and would come back to the message later. For now, she stood eyeing the Forest Brew, and it was time to act like she belonged inside at that preservation meeting.

Autumn pulled the door open and lifted her chin as the air carried her swiftly inside. Eve looked busy behind the counter, but she waved at Autumn and pointed to the back room. Autumn took that as her sign to head back and join the group.

"Ah, Autumn, you're here!" The mayor ushered Autumn toward a long banquet table for about twenty people.

"Hi, Mr. Mayor. Thank you for having me here." Autumn smiled, taking her bag and coat off her shoulders. She found a chair toward one end of the table to place them on.

Everyone made small talk around the room as they sipped on hot drinks. From the corner of her eye, Autumn saw Marion Bennett looking her way. She stood with the owner of the landscape nursery around the corner from her husband's restaurant. They made small talk, but Marion appeared uninterested now that Autumn came in.

Kennedy slid into the chair next to Autumn's at the table. "Hello, again." She said in her low voice. "I thought I might see you here at the meeting to take your grandmother's place."

"Hi, Kennedy. How are things with your research and the new baking booth?"

"I'm just taking things one step at a time. I don't wanna rush anything coming together too soon."

"Right," Autumn said, unsure of what they were really talking about. "Well, it's good to take your time with things. I'm sure everything you're doing is very important to you, so it will come together in time."

"Exactly," Kennedy waved her hand to show she had everything covered.

Autumn poured herself a cup of what appeared to be Eve's hot apple cider on the table. She smiled to herself, thinking about how Eve probably sprinkled a little something extra into the carafe just for good measure. Aunt Jo seemed to think the Newbury family always had the best magical intentions, so this time Autumn would let herself enjoy a cup or even two.

"All right, everyone. Let's get started." The mayor interrupted all the conversations with a big clap of his hands.

As he began speaking, Autumn looked up from her cider to see James walking in behind the mayor and an older gentleman beside him. She caught James's eye, and he gave her a smile that made her feel like she was the only one in the room. James took his place on the back wall along with the older man as the mayor started the meeting.

"Now, I'm sure most of you have heard by now that we lost our dear friend and preservation chair, Lorna MacKinnon. She passed away a few days ago now, and the family is making preparations for a celebration of her life."

Everyone turned toward Autumn with sympathetic eyes as the mayor spoke. She felt uneasy but just smiled at them to say thank you.

"So as you well know, our bylaws denote a few key positions on the committee to be handed down to founding family members here in Hollow's Glenn. Autumn here is Lorna's granddaughter, and she runs the paper shop up the street if you're new here. It was Lorna's wish that the position pass straight down to Autumn, and I approved Lorna's request." The mayor said it as if it was already a done deal and there would be no discussion about the matter, or perhaps that's what he had hoped.

"Mr. Mayor, if I may for just a moment," Marion Bennett raised her hand to interject.

"Okay, Mrs. Bennett. Go ahead." The mayor looked at her with hurried eyes, and Autumn felt the fire rising inside her.

"Well, as much as I appreciate Autumn's responsibility in attending to her grandmother's wishes, I would like to ask us all if this bylaw is still in the best interest of our town. After all, it was written almost a century ago, and we've upheld it ever since. Do we still feel that passing down a chair to the next of kin is giving us the most experience on our committee?" Marion looked around the table to gauge the expressions of everyone else.

Autumn tensed a bit, feeling a spark of something warm inside her hand under the table. A slight panic rose inside her as she imagined the flame in her hand that could set the entire coffee shop on fire if she didn't control it. She closed her eyes for a moment and took a breath as she heard the mayor speak up.

"Marion, our founders put this bylaw in place as an important part of preserving our history and protecting our town. The founding families hold this responsibility highly, and changing a founding bylaw is not up for discussion today. Thank you for voicing your opinion, but as the bylaws state, any changes to our rules must be approved by myself, the mayor, and three of the five founding families."

His words gave Autumn a sense of security, but she still felt the flame rising from her palm. She pressed her hands together under the table and remembered a few words her gran had taught her.

Inside her head, she repeated, "By my breath, I extinguish the unwanted."

She carefully lifted her hands to her mouth and blew her warm breath between them. Marion eyed her as she pretended to warm her hands from the chill in the air.

"I see. And while we are the town preservation society, I don't think it's a century's old bylaw that we're preserving. It's the historic nature of our town." She adamantly responded with her hands waving in the air, but quickly calmed herself down and placed her hands gracefully back down.

Autumn persisted and tried to ignore the stares as she slowly felt tingles instead of flames. She moved her hands into her lap and opened them slowly to find tiny specs of light dancing in her palms instead of flames. Autumn breathed a sigh of relief and focused on the conversation at hand.

If only Marion actually knew that preserving the bylaws firmly protected the town. That bylaw ensured the gifted families in the region would pass their responsibilities down and preserve the balance in our mountain area. It wasn't just about preserving the downtown and the charming nature of the town. Autumn could see that now. This was so much more, and what was at stake went far beyond having prime voting rights at this table.

"Excuse me, but I'd like to say something, please." Graham Newbury, Eve's father, sat at the table and held the chair for his family.

"Yes, Graham. Please go ahead." The mayor waved him on.

As Mr. Newbury stood up from his chair, Autumn immediately sensed a shift in the room. Everyone respected Mr. Newbury, and his opinion held weight in this town, just as Gran's had. The fog in the air practically dissipated when he spoke.

"I hold the chair for my founding family here, which is a great honor given to our family and the other four. We don't take our responsibilities lightly. That's why we've passed down a generational knowledge of this town through our children, and each one of us is prepared to protect this town in every way we can. We breed our children to honor Hollow's Glenn and always uphold its history, its culture, and the needs of this region. Not just anyone can come in here and say that, even if you have lived here for years."

Mr. Newbury glanced over at Marion as he continued. "Now, we will always consider what the people here want, but to keep the stability and continuity we have now, we must maintain our founding family positions. Thank you." Mr. Newbury sat down as everyone around the table began nodding and clapping. Marion appeared to take offense at his ideas, but she kept silent for the time being.

"I agree wholeheartedly. So let's not waste any more time in welcoming our newest chair to the committee, Autumn MacKinnon!" The mayor lifted his arms in Autumn's direction as if to welcome her to stand.

Autumn tucked her hands into the pockets of her dark skinny jeans for fear there may still be specs of light, or worse yet another flame, that would show. She rose out of her seat and nodded in agreement with the applause.

"Thank you so much, everyone. I know I'm new to this committee, but I am my grandmother's girl, and she taught me to respect and care for this town. I will do my absolute best to honor it, and those of you who know me know I don't take this responsibility lightly. So, I'm here ready and willing to learn, to understand, and…" She looked around at all the faces staring back at her. Autumn took a deep breath and finished her thought. "And to step up to preserve this town's integrity. Thank you."

She sat back down as the mayor patted her on the back and tried to move on before anyone else could contest.

"While Autumn gets her feet under her at these meetings, I'll run the first few, and then she can take over from there. Some important matters need to be discussed today, the first one being the downtown revitalization."

As the mayor continued with the meeting, Autumn looked over at James standing against the wall. He met her eyes with a smile and mouthed, "Good job" into the air.

She smiled shyly and whispered back, "Thank you."

Next to her, Kennedy leaned over and asked, "Did you say something?"

"Oh no, sorry." Autumn shook her head, and Kennedy returned her attention to the mayor.

"Now, moving on. We approved the final bid for the revitalization project," The mayor continued. He introduced James and his father, Patrick Allan, whose construction company would oversee the project.

As he discussed the different phases of the renovation, Autumn let her eyes wander around the room. She pinpointed a couple of other potential founding families and wondered what each of their gifts might entail. She knew her curiosity would nag at her until she discovered exactly how they all fit together.

The mayor continued on about the construction starting after the upcoming harvest market days, and Autumn tuned back in.

"That reminds me, since the chamber of commerce spearheads the market days, you can talk to Marion about it as her husband runs the chamber." The mayor cleared his throat and took a sip of water as Marion perked up with a larger stature than she had all night.

"We'd love to see as many of you with a booth at the market days as possible. We only have about another week before the event begins! So let's make it the best one yet! All right, everyone. Please enjoy some small talk and pastries, and thank you for coming."

Everyone clapped and returned to their conversations. Autumn poured herself more cider when she felt the warmth intensifying from Gran's locket around her neck. She'd worn it underneath her tunic sweater and the hand-knit scarf Gran gave her. That way, it wouldn't attract attention, but she could still hold onto it at the meeting tonight. The energy within it kept dormant this whole time, even through the flames she ignited in her hands, and yet, now it called to her.

She could hear the voices in the air, "In the photo, lies what you seek."

The same message she heard earlier repeated. The locket grew warmer on her skin, and she knew the glow returned to it underneath her sweater.

"Autumn, are you okay? You seem off. Do you need something?" Kennedy turned and put a hand on her shoulder.

"No... I'm fine. Just heartburn, that's all." Autumn touched where the locket lay on her chest as she spoke. "I just need a croissant, and I'll be fine." She leaned over the table to reach for a croissant as Kennedy monitored her.

"You know, I really appreciate you offering to help me bake for the market days. Do you still have time to meet up next week?" Kennedy leaned in closer, studying Autumn to see what was really going on.

"Oh right, your baking booth. Yes, of course, I'll help. You probably want to get things going a few days before the event, right? So I could probably stop by one evening next week, say Wednesday or Thursday?"

"Let's make it Thursday around seven o'clock at my house, the Winter House on Pine View. How does that sound? I'll be done with my research for the day by then." Kennedy grabbed an almond croissant and looked at Autumn to confirm.

Still distracted, Autumn heard the voices again on the air as she tried to pay attention to Kennedy. "Right, seven on Thursday. I'll be there." As she replied, her eyes drifted away from Kennedy to the wall behind her.

Autumn squinted and noticed the images framed along the back wall. She eased out of her chair and walked to the wall with her croissant in hand. In front of her hung a photograph of the mountain valley, and just on the edge of the image, she could make out a grove of what Autumn thought were foxglove flowers.

She walked along the wall to find two more photographs, each taken in what seemed to be the same area of the mountain valley, on the other side of the mountain. Each photo showed a long line of pine trees bordered by an open space that led into a valley. The foxglove flowers appeared to grow toward one side of the valley and hint at their purple color in an otherwise sea of green.

Autumn turned around quickly and popped the rest of her croissant in her mouth as she scanned the room. She noticed Kennedy looking at her strangely still, probably wondering why she got up so quickly to roam around. Then, she spotted Mrs. Newbury bringing in a new tray of teacakes.

"Mrs. Newbury," Autumn waved at her as casually as she could, given that she just found the photo of the very thing that killed her gran.

"Oh yes, dear. Here I am. How can I help?" She put her hand on Autumn's arm.

"Can you tell me about these photographs? Where did you get them, and how long have they been here?"

"Oh well, these are from Bill Cunningham. You remember Vera, who we ran into on Main Street just yesterday? Yes, well, her husband, Bill, takes photos for the nature conservancy around the lands. He was more than willing to sell us a few of his mountain photos to keep around the coffee shop, so we put these up about a month ago. I'm sure I have the Cunningham's contact information around here somewhere if you'd like to know more about them." Mrs. Newbury patted Autumn on the back and went on with filling teacups and catering to the crowd.

Autumn felt dizzy at the thought of Vera's husband taking these photographs. He knew exactly where to find a grove of poisonous foxglove leaves and had a motive to get Gran out of the way. He knew Gran helped Vera uncover his gambling debts by making those teas for him to drink. It must have been pretty bad for him to go to these lengths to get rid of Gran. But if Vera had already learned of the debt, then why kill Gran? It was already all out in the open, unless he wanted revenge for his secrets being exposed.

Autumn felt a hand on her shoulder, and she turned to find Kennedy behind her. "Autumn, is everything all right? You don't look so good. Would you like me to help you outside?"

Just then, James walked up beside them both, and Autumn eased with relief. She didn't know how she could handle one more minute around all these people without letting everything out into some earth, wind, and fire spectacle. Yet, when she saw James, Autumn let her whole body relax.

"Oh, it's all right, Kennedy. Actually, I know James, and I think I'll have him walk me back down to the shop now that the meeting's over. I appreciate it, though." Autumn smiled at her and took hold of James's arm.

"Is everything okay?" He whispered into her ear.

She picked up her coat and bag, and James followed her toward the front of the coffee shop. "I don't know yet, but just keep walking with me until we get out of here."

Without saying another word, he kept up with her like it was his duty, and they pushed the coffee shop door open with a clattering of the bell.

CHAPTER 16

Autumn threw her coat on quickly and curved around the doorway to the front of the Forest Brew. She turned to find James directly behind her and smelled the aromas of roasted chestnuts and cherry cordial surrounding him. A sense of home enveloped him and gave Autumn the most intensely grounded feeling of safety.

"Thanks for coming out with me," Autumn snuggled into her knit scarf and leaned closer to absorb the scents.

"You were great in there, you know? Strong about your position, but it came across that the town really means a lot to you. Now, I get the feeling something's wrong, though. What is it?" James met her eyes as he took a step in.

She was about to answer, but the bell to the coffee shop chimed. A few people fell out onto the sidewalk. One of them backed into James and shoved him into Autumn. She grabbed onto his arms to steady herself and felt his whole body press up against hers.

"Oh, sorry, loves! We seemed to have stumbled our way out. Didn't mean to disturb you. Have a good night, okay?" A man from the preservation committee yelled as they all walked away.

Autumn focused solely on James while his hands rested on her back, still cradling her from a fall. The wind swirled around them excitedly, but their eyes locked on each other.

"Uh, why don't you walk me down the street to my shop? We can talk privately if you have some time." Autumn got the words out while she straightened herself up and stretched out her coat.

He gave her a quick nod and looked inside the coffee shop window. James saw his father talking with one of the committee members. He waved his hand to get his father's attention and let him know he was leaving.

Together, James and Autumn walked down Main Street toward Parchment and Pine. "So I don't know if Jo mentioned anything to you or your mom, but the police confirmed that Gran's death wasn't an accident. Someone intentionally killed her."

"Oh, Autumn. I'm so sorry. I mean, I kind of suspected from the feeling of my dreams and when you seemed to be uneasy about things at your gran's house. But to hear you say it, I just can't believe it."

"I know. I can't really believe it myself. It turns out there are several people around town that may have had an interest in harming my grandmother. Tonight, I found some interesting photographs in the Forest Brew meeting room, which triggered some potential leads I need to look into. But it all made me feel really uneasy back there." She looked over to him and stopped walking as they reached the corner.

"I guess, you know by now that my family is... different. That I'm different." Autumn swallowed hard, unsure of how much he knew exactly and whether this would scare him off. Somehow, though, she knew deep down that none of it mattered. He would be here no matter what.

"Look, Autumn, my mother told me a few things over the years about our towns and how many of us have interesting gifts attached to us. I knew the moment I stepped into your shop and your aunt introduced us I was connected to you somehow. It doesn't matter what any of that means. I just know I'm meant to be here for you and that I feel like I've known you my whole life. Does that make any sense?" He rubbed his hand over his stubble beard as he spoke.

Autumn looked around them at the warm streetlights that were flickering on now. "Yeah, it really does, actually. I feel the same way, and I can't explain it. All I know is that whenever you show up, it calms me down, just like home."

She wrapped her coat tighter as a strong wind swept through the street. The clouds rumbled, and Gran's necklace grew warmer again. She sensed it glowing underneath her sweater, just as it had done inside the coffee shop. Autumn put her hand on her chest for a moment to confirm it.

"What is it?" James gave Autumn a concerned look.

She spoke, but her answer was overpowered by a yell coming from down the side street.

"You don't know what you've started!" The voice came from a strange girl pointing at Kennedy on the sidewalk. "This will not end well," the girl said, storming away.

Kennedy stood on the sidewalk alone as she glanced up and saw Autumn and James looking at her.

"Is everything okay?" James yelled to her.

"Yeah, fine," she said, dismissing the scene. "Sorry for all that. I'm good. I'll see you soon okay, Autumn?" Kennedy called back as she waved, hopped into her car parked at the curb, and drove away.

Autumn and James looked at each other with surprise. "What do you think that was all about?" he asked her.

"I have no idea. I've never seen that girl around here before. Kennedy is fairly new, though, so I guess it's someone she knows. Strange, though."

The streetlight changed, and Autumn tugged on James's coat sleeve to get him to follow her. They made their way down the street under the lights to talk privately again.

"Are you okay?" James questioned. "Something bothered you a minute ago at the stoplight and also at the meeting earlier. You can tell me, you know. If you want, you can trust me."

They made it to Parchment and Pine, and Autumn smiled at him while she fumbled around her backpack for her keys. "I know I can."

She opened the door with a push and let them both inside. Simone had gone for the night, and it looked like she had taken Tavish home with her.

Autumn slid her coat and bag off and put them on a hook by the front door. Then, she grabbed James's coat while she flicked on the lights.

"There was something of my grandmother's I took with me when we found her at the house the other night. It was a locket she always wore, and it's one of our family heirlooms." Autumn pulled the locket out from under her sweater and held it up by the chain so James could see it.

"I've seen that necklace before." His mouth dropped open at the sight of it. "It's been in my dreams, particularly this latest one. I think it's time I told you what it was about."

She ushered him to the back of the shop and into the hearth room, where she threw a couple of logs into the fireplace and struck a match. "What do you mean, you've seen it in your dreams?"

"The dream I came into your shop yesterday to talk about. Yeah, I've had it twice now." James sat down in one of the wingback chairs and warmed his hands next to the fire.

"Basically, I saw you in the dream walking toward that necklace. It was sitting on a table and had the roots of a tree glowing on the outside of the locket. Underneath the necklace, you found a parchment paper with the image of a family tree imprinted on it. I watched you pick up the paper, and as you did, another branch appeared on the image of the tree. One that wasn't there before."

Autumn curled her legs underneath her on the other wingback chair and folded her hands into her sweater. "What else? Tell me the entire dream."

"After the branch appeared, you turned around and saw me there." He hesitated for a moment and looked into the fire. "I wrapped my arms around you to protect you from something. And as we both turned around, everything went black, and I woke up."

"You protected me in your dream?" Autumn didn't know whether to feel concerned or comforted by this. They'd already confirmed that James had predictive dreams, clearly a sign of something to come. Yet, she couldn't help but focus on the fact that even in his dreams, he tried to protect her. Something extremely gallant existed in all of that, and yet, it was highly likely she would be the one to protect everyone else from whatever lay ahead.

"I don't know what to say to all this. My head is spinning from tonight. First, the fire in my hands, then the photographs, and now this dream about a family tree. It's a lot to handle." She rubbed her temple for a moment as he caught up.

"What fire in your hands? What haven't you told me?"

She raised her eyes to his and opened her mouth, but no words came out. Then, struck by some cord of trust, Autumn replied, "I think we better put the teakettle on. This could take a while."

CHAPTER 17

Autumn clasped Gran's locket around her neck and slid it under her evergreen cowl neck sweater while looking into the mirror by the stairs at Aunt Jo's house. She put an extra set of white fleece gloves into her bag for the day and gathered her things to head out.

"Why are you leaving so early? We don't have to open the shop for another couple hours." Simone rubbed her eyes and slid across the wood floor in her fuzzy gray socks.

"I know, but I wanted to look up a few things at the library before we opened today. James mentioned his new dream to me last night, and I just can't get it out of my head. So I'll pop over to the Forest Brew for a quick brekkie and then head to the library for a bit. Would you mind taking Tavish to the shop with you when you go?"

"Yeah, of course. We're getting to be pretty good pals, and I wouldn't mind someone to keep me warm on my way to work." Simone looked down at the cat as he moseyed in and circled around Autumn's feet.

"He's great at that. He kept my toes warm all night." Autumn bent down and gave Tavish a good head scratch. "Be good for Simone, okay? You can help me assemble a new display at the shop later." Autumn waved goodbye to Simone and headed off on her usual morning walk into town.

The air contained an extra crispness today, and a pink hue swirled through it. Gran taught her to be aware of all things brought through the air, and pink was a color she knew well. It meant a sense of family and connection, and with it, came things that tied people together. As she walked into town, kicking the fallen maple leaves under her feet, Autumn decided it must be another sign. After all, she planned to go to the library to research the family ancestry and some insights into James's dream. The air elevated her curiosity even more about what needed to be revealed.

She made it into town and saw that the Forest Brew had already opened. Autumn grabbed a hot tea and a cardamom roll before heading to the library. As soon as she walked in, Autumn noticed Kennedy standing at the counter looking at the pastries.

"Oh hey," Autumn moved closer to her and thought this would be the perfect time to ask about last night.

"Autumn, hi," Kennedy responded. "Did you get home okay last night? You seemed like something was bothering you. Everything all right?" Kennedy looked Autumn up and down as she spoke.

"Yeah, no I was fine." Autumn dismissed her. "I think something didn't sit right with me last night." Kennedy looked directly into Autumn's eyes for a moment, trying to read through what she was saying.

"Actually, I wanted to check on you and make sure you got home okay. I don't mean to pry, but I saw you arguing with that girl on the street, and it looked a little... heated." Autumn put her bag down on the ground and perused the pastry case, acting as casual as possible.

"Oh, that was just... an out-of-town friend trying to... get some details about my research." Kennedy appeared uneasy and hesitant to talk about it. She brushed her long strawberry hair behind her ear and moved closer to the register to pay for her pastries. "Did you wanna sit for a minute and go over my baking ideas before you head off?"

"Sure, I can stay for a few minutes while I eat. I wanna get to the library, though, before I open the shop. I don't wanna be late for my early customers, you know." Autumn smiled at Kennedy and then pointed out her pastry selections to Eve behind the counter.

"Right. Well, meet me at the window table when you're ready." Kennedy called out.

Autumn moved to the register and brought out her wallet. "Hey, Eve, how are you doing this morning?"

"Oh, Autumn, I've had so many people commenting about my new pastries! They all just loved them last night at the meeting, and I had several large orders come in this morning. It's all a big hit!"

"I can imagine! Everything has been wonderful, and I could not be more thrilled for you. That's really great. Plus, I don't wanna forget an order for the Pine, too, so remind me later." Autumn paid for her breakfast and headed over to the front window.

She wrapped her coat around the back of the chair as Kennedy took a sip of her own tea.

"Hey, how are you liking those paper lanterns you bought at the shop the other day? You said you wanted them for a fall project or something." Autumn loved hearing how people used the products from the shop. Although, she didn't know Kennedy well enough yet to know what she'd use them for.

"The lanterns? I'm just getting started with them, but they'll be the perfect thing to clear out some stale vibes that need to go."

Autumn stirred her tea and considered Kennedy's strange demeanor. She wondered if she'd ever find Kennedy to be more of a friend than a mystery.

"So tell me," Kennedy started. "What's at the library this early in the morning? I mean, I'm a researcher, and I'm not even there yet." Kennedy pulled apart her croissant as she spoke.

Sitting down with a sigh, Autumn pushed up her sweater sleeves and laughed. "Yeah, Simone gave me a hard time about being up and about this early, too, but I had some things on my mind about the family that I'm interested in researching. You know, just some typical family tree stuff. I guess, all this with my gran has me thinking about family."

Kennedy coughed and immediately took a swig of tea to calm her down.

"Are you all right?" Autumn asked, reaching her hand across the table to help.

"Mm-hmm, yeah. I'm fine. The croissant just went down wrong." Kennedy cleared her throat and continued in a raspy voice. "All this business with your gran seems like it's been hard for your family. Have you figured out what happened?"

Autumn paused and grabbed her tea mug. She noticed the air shift inside the shop. Her gran's necklace warmed her chest, and the smell of stinging nettles surrounded her. She quickly crammed a piece of her cardamom roll in her mouth and held her pointer finger up to give herself a moment to process this before responding.

Stinging nettles represented struggle, protecting something under the surface, and the doorway between life and death. She wondered if this had something to do with Kennedy's questions about her gran, but she couldn't quite put the pieces together.

"We're still processing Gran's death as best we can. It's definitely been a lot to process, but we're moving through it." Autumn wasn't sure how much the people in town really knew about Gran's murder. Until she figured out exactly what happened, she didn't want to give out too many details to anyone.

"Anyway, I really have to go if I'm gonna open the shop on time. Why don't you just let me know this coming week about whichever items we'll be baking, and I'll just show up ready to help, okay?" Autumn got up from her chair and threw her coat on quickly. She didn't hesitate to collect her things and move toward the door. "Thanks for the chat! I'll see you soon."

Autumn had to get outside and away from the nettle smell before it overwhelmed her. It was all she could do to cover with a canned response to Kennedy's question and then go. She took some deep breaths as she rifled through her backpack on the sidewalk and pulled out a black tourmaline grounding stone her gran gave her. Making her way to the corner, Autumn crossed Havensbrook Place before getting to the library and feeling like she could breathe again.

When Autumn opened the library doors, she saw Simone sitting on a couch by the circulation desk, flipping through an international Vogue magazine. Autumn approached her, confused but relieved to see a familiar face.

"I thought you were gonna meet me at the shop with Tavish. How come you're here at the library?" Autumn plopped down beside her cousin and took a deep breath as she waited for a reply.

"I brought him to the shop and got him all set up with his cozy bed before coming here. Don't worry, the shop is all set for the day, too. But you don't seem so good right now, and I knew you'd get into something when you left this morning. So I may as well help because that's what cousins and..." Simone leaned in close. "And coven sisters do." She gave Autumn a little wink and a clicking noise with her mouth.

"But seriously, what's going on?" Simone turned her body toward Autumn and hoisted a knee up on the couch between them. "You've got your black tourmaline out, and you're doing some deep breathing. That means something stressed you out. Spill."

Autumn looked around the library for a moment to see who else might be there listening. "Let's just go to the back, and I'll explain where it's quieter." Autumn pulled Simone up by her sleeve, and they made their way to the back of the library, where the more in-depth research materials were stored.

They stopped in between a few book stacks and huddled in close to whisper. "I was at the Forest Brew to grab breakfast and sat down with Kennedy from the preservation committee for a minute. She started asking about why I was up this early and then about everything with Gran. The necklace started warming up on my skin, and I had the distinct smell of nettles in the air. So much that I could barely breathe. The smell was so intense it was almost suffocating me, and I had to get out of there."

"Nettles? Like stinging nettles used for protection teas? You know, Mom also taught me that nettle is good for your cardiovascular system, your heart. She puts it in soothing bath oils for people having heart issues."

"Good for the heart? I thought it was associated with struggle and protecting things under the surface. You know, like the thorny nettles of the plant? But now that you're talking about the heart, maybe that has something to do with Gran's death. Kennedy asked me if we knew what happened. Maybe there's some association because your mom told us Gran actually died from heart complications caused by those foxglove leaves."

"You're right, she did. But why would the coffee shop smell like nettles? I don't get it." Simone waved her arms around at her sides and looked frustrated.

Autumn rubbed her hand over her face and shrugged. "I don't know anymore." She sighed and let her bag fall off of her shoulders. "Let's just stick to why we came here in the first place, and then we'll sort the rest out later. Come on, I need to find the ancestry librarian."

The girls found the librarian's desk and asked for someone to assist them with some ancestry questions. After a couple of minutes, a slender young woman with round glasses and brown hair tied in a bun greeted them from the back.

"Hello, there." The woman appeared to know Autumn and Simone. "Autumn and Simone, right? I'm Becca Winsome. I'm not sure if you remember me from Mountain Ridge High. I moved back home about a year ago to be closer to my parents."

"Right, Becca, hi! Long time, no see. You look like you're doing well." Autumn said with a smile. "Uh, Simone and I are here to look into some of our ancestry, and we need help being pointed in the right direction."

"Okay, I can certainly help you, but depending on what you need, it may take some time." She leaned in a little closer and put her hand to the side of her mouth. "Although, we keep information handy on the founding families of Hollow's Glenn. For protecting our collective history, as you can imagine."

"I didn't know the town preserved those things. Geez, I feel like I'm part of some royal family or something." Simone followed Becca and Autumn to a separate room in the corner.

"Well, we like to keep things confidential here unless a need arises. Although, I have been popular lately! Just the other day, someone came in asking if I'd pull information about the founding bloodlines here. Of course, there are certain things that we only give out to the families and to the town leadership. But it is interesting how you're not the only ones who've come in lately!"

Autumn and Simone looked at each other with suspicion. "Uh, Becca. Could you tell us if the other person who came in recently looked for any material on our family specifically? The MacKinnons?" Autumn politely asked so as not to give Becca any reason for concern.

"Now that you mention it, yes. I believe it started with the history here in general, but there was a great deal of focus on your family in particular that came out of it as well. But you know, I only give out so much to those outside of the families. So I only opened up the public section of our archives."

"But you'll be able to open up more to us?" Simone raised her eyebrows at Becca.

Becca looked at the two girls and smiled. "I know you both, and I know your family. You'll have access to our private archives since the documents are basically yours, and we keep them safe. But you can only access them for an hour at a time. We need to limit how frequently we open the vaults to maintain them properly and ensure safekeeping. I'm sure you understand."

Autumn and Simone looked at each other and nodded. "Of course, we completely understand. Would you mind letting us see anything related to our ancestral line and the lineage itself?"

"Mm-hmm, wait here, and I'll bring out what's openly accessed first. Then, if you want to see the more confidential documents, you'll have to follow me to our private vault. Just give me a minute, and I'll be back."

Becca turned and pushed the door open to the little room. Autumn sat down at the small conference table in the center and pulled out her phone to check the time.

She sighed, "We need to open the shop in a little less than an hour. I hope she comes back quickly so we can get as much information as possible today."

"Yeah, especially if someone else is snooping around our family business. We need to find out all we can about this and do it soon." Simone dragged out the chair beside Autumn and sat down, crossing her arms on the table and lying her head down on top of them.

"It's making me nervous to think someone out there right now killed Gran and got away with it. And either they're still digging around to find information about us, or someone else is. Either way, this is all making me super stressed. I'm gonna need to curl up by the fire with Tavish for a good long while today just to reset from all of this." Autumn played with the rings on her fingers as Becca strolled back in with a few file folders in her hands.

"All right, here's what I'm allowed to show everyone about the founding families." She flipped open one of the folders on top of the table and slid it over to the girls. "Basically, these should be things you're already familiar with here. Family trees, ancestry regarding where your family stemmed from, and so on. Have a look at those for a minute, and then if you'd like, I can take you down to our private collection."

"Great, thank you," Autumn took the file folder labeled "MacKinnon" and started sifting through it with Simone looking over her shoulder. "Here's the family crest and a description of our family coming over from Scotland over a century ago." Autumn ran her finger over the page as she described it out loud. Once done with the first page, she turned it over and proceeded through the rest.

"Here's a family tree. Let's see what this one says." Simone pointed to a loose paper sticking out under the others.

"Okay, this one shows our line with us at the bottom. It seems to go back a few generations here. There's both of our mothers, Gran, and her younger brother and sister. Then, it lists our great-grandmother and grandfather and goes up a couple more generations. I mean, it seems pretty self-explanatory. I don't see anything unusual here."

"Yeah, we're already aware of all these people, so I'm not sure what else this is supposed to be leading us to." Simone sat back in the chair and put her hand over her eyes. Mornings were not her thing, and getting up to do some investigative work before she'd had a few more cups of coffee just wouldn't do.

"You know what, Becca? I think we would like to look at the private collection. We're running short on time, though. Can we just spend about twenty minutes there now and then come back again if we need to?"

Autumn started collecting everything into a pile and handing it back to the librarian.

"Yes, of course. Follow me down there, and you can stay for a bit today. Then, whenever you'd like to come back, just ring me at this number." Becca pulled out a business card with a direct line to the genealogy department.

"Fantastic! Thank you." Autumn took the card from her as she and Simone followed Becca into the library again and then through the double doors leading to the employee-only area.

The three of them proceeded down a spiral staircase to the library's basement. Becca went first through a hallway lit by warm wall sconces. Every few feet on both sides, they came to a set of glass double doors where you could see someone typing away inside at an office desk. Becca continued further down the hall and approached an arched door with an old wrought iron handle underneath a modern keypad.

She punched in the numbers to open the door and then flicked the light on for them to enter. Two chandeliers hung above them in the center of the room. On the far side of the room, a half-round window let in some light from street level and the view of foot traffic from passersby.

Autumn looked at the stacks of books piled high on old wooden tables in the center. Bookshelves ran the length of the room on either side along with long drawing drawers at the back under the window.

"Can you point us in the right direction for our family's ancestry?" Autumn asked Becca.

"I think this would be an excellent place to start. These contain more... accurate documents corresponding to the ones we keep upstairs. You'll probably find something of interest here first, and that can get you going."

Becca led them to a long, skinny drawer near the window and pulled the first drawer down. She clicked a button on a remote control at the top of the cabinet, and a shade rose over the half window above them.

"Just for added privacy," Becca relayed. "Once you pull a document, just come over to the tables to read through it so you can keep it flat, okay? I'll be right across the hall in the office marked Genealogy if you need anything." She smiled at them and walked out the door.

"All right, let's see what we've got." Simone flipped through the documents in the first drawer and pulled as many out as she could gather up. She took them over to one of the large wooden tables and laid them flat, just as Becca had instructed.

Autumn grabbed at the locket on her chest. Its warmth appeared almost instantly this time, and she pulled it out from under her sweater. "It's glowing green again. This must mean we're onto something here. Keep going." She nodded to Simone to turn the documents over one at a time.

"Wait a minute, this is the family tree again." Autumn pulled the topmost document closer to her. "But this doesn't look the same as the one we saw upstairs. Look, do you see this section next to Gran's grandmother? The branch extends off the page, and it's torn at the edge."

Autumn flipped the drawing over, but nothing was on the other side. The girls combed through the remaining pages until they noticed a similar discoloration to the document at the bottom of the stack, almost a pinkish hue. Immediately, Autumn pushed the other pages aside and dragged that one from the bottom.

"The pink color is the same as the top page. Pink... just like the hue in the air this morning. Here it is!" She pulled the two pages side by side on the large table and ran her finger along the top of them.

"Here's where the branch continues," Simone pointed to the second page where their great-grandmother's line extended. "She had another sister."

"It looks that way, yeah." Autumn stared at the pages and tried to follow what it was saying. "This shows our great, great grandmother having another daughter with a different man named Thomas Shaw. That daughter must have split from our side of the family somehow. Maybe she was raised separately because she had another father?" Autumn looked at Simone with curious eyes.

"That's definitely possible, especially since it was with a different man than she married. But that means there's another family line somewhere, and if they're connected to our bloodline..." Simone stopped mid-sentence, but Autumn finished it for her.

"They most likely have their own gifts, just as we do." Autumn felt the warming sensation of the locket as she spoke the words.

Interrupting their thoughts, a gust of wind blew open the latch on the half window, and the shade flew open. The girls jumped and put their hands over the laid-out documents, keeping them from flying around in the wind.

"Go grab the window. I've got these." Simone nailed down the papers firmly with her forearms.

Autumn ran over to the half window and looked for a stool to reach the window latch above. She found one propped between the drawing drawers and lifted it out. As she climbed onto the stool, the wind swirled her hair in the air, and she stopped before reaching for the window.

"Beware of the ancestors you do not yet know," The voices whispered in the wind.

Goosebumps rose on Autumn's skin as she listened to the voices. The wind blew with a chill again, and she shook herself out of the trance and latched the window tightly.

"Did you get it?" Simone pressed the drawings flat to the table and picked herself up, pushing her straight dark bob away from her face. "That was crazy! Where did that wind even come from? I mean, did you cause that?" She widened her eyes at Autumn.

"No! It wasn't me, but I did hear the voices again. Gran's necklace warmed on my skin." She pulled the locket out of her cowl neck, but it was back to its usual state.

"Really? Man, I don't get to hear any of this, and I was standing right here with you! All right, well, let's hear it, then. What did the voices say this time?"

Autumn sighed as she rolled up the drawings and returned them to the drawers. "They said to beware of the ancestors we don't know. Like maybe the ones we just discovered on this family tree here?" She closed the drawings up tightly in the drawer and went back to the table to grab her belongings.

"This is getting deliciously complicated! I know we're still grieving over Gran, and I wanna find out who did this to her just as much as you do. She was, after all, the most amazing, loving mentor we could ever possibly have asked for. And yet, you know my darker Scorpio side is obsessed with all the shadowy drama going on here. And I'm kinda thinking you're obsessed with it, too, am I right?"

Autumn gave Simone the eye and waved her on, "Would you stop already? We've gotta get to the shop, and no, I'm not obsessed. Maybe just really interested in finding out what's going on. That's all."

"Mm-hmm," Simone murmured, disbelieving her.

The girls walked across the hall to let Becca know they'd be leaving for the day and then darted out of the library as fast as they could. The pink hue still hung in the air as they hurried back to the shop, and Autumn couldn't help but think the winds would bring more than just a few voices in the coming days. She expected a larger storm, one she wasn't sure whether she could bend to her will.

CHAPTER 18

Autumn sank into one of the wicker armchairs on Aunt Jo's porch that evening and wrapped herself up in a warm flannel blanket. She tucked her legs underneath her, and Tavish jumped on her lap to snuggle. She looked out into the dark evening and felt discouraged. They were no closer to finding out what happened to Gran, and the police hadn't given them any more information. Autumn scratched Tavish's head to relieve the defeat she felt in her heart.

"Hey, cuz," Simone pushed the front door open and scooted another wicker chair next to Autumn. She sat cross-legged and pulled her black tunic cardigan closed around her.

"You know, moping isn't very becoming. Maybe try just talking things out. You're better at that." Simone cheekily said with a smirk.

"I'm tired of not knowing what happened. I'm tired of feeling like I'm supposed to take Gran's place somehow. And I'm tired of thinking I'm supposed to be this wise woman, yet I can't understand what's going on with our family, Gran's death, or even my magic. I'm just tired." Autumn talked with her hands as she spoke, and Tavish gave her an agitated meow.

"Well, here's the thing. It's only been a couple of weeks, if that. Things take time to heal and to process. You can't expect everything to be tied up in a day. I know you like to live in your head, but life needs to flow the way it's meant to. You can't change that. You can only move with it and let it carry you in the direction you're meant to go."

"Wow, now you sound like your mom with all of that letting-things-flow stuff." Autumn rested her elbow on the arm of the chair and put her head in her hand. "You know it's really hard for me to just go with the flow. I don't do that. I'm a thinker and a planner and a worrier. It makes me nervous for things to be so up in the air."

"I get it. I do. But at some point, you're gonna have to trust that the universe knows what it's doing. And yeah, now you are the next four-points witch. So, you're gonna have to learn to find more balance because you're not gonna be able to protect these lands without it, and you know it. Balance comes from within first, and yes, my mother taught me that. We are water witches, after all." Simone laughed a little as she got up and walked to the porch railing.

"What is it?" Autumn snatched Tavish up by his belly and followed Simone to the railing.

"It's just barely a waxing crescent moon. That means we're meant to still be learning and discovering things. Nothing has tied up for this cycle yet because it's not meant to be. It's okay to feel like things are still messy and challenging right now. We're in the thick of it, but I'd wager that come the full moon again, things will feel a lot more resolved." Simone pressed her back against the railing and gave Tavish a head scratch.

"You're right. As usual, I'm letting my worry get the best of me. I need to calm down and focus my energy on what I can do now." Autumn took a breath and sat down again with Tavish. "I can go through the clues that we know again and start actually investigating for real now."

"Okay, what does that mean?" Simone took a seat and brought her knees up to her chest, wrapping her arms around them.

"For one thing, that image of the foxglove flowers at the Forest Brew has been really weighing on me. I think we should have your mom mention it to Chief Walsh so they can check out Vera's husband a bit. But I actually wanna go up and look around the mountain myself. I need to find exactly where those flowers grow and see if I can find any other clues to help us."

"So you're gonna go trekking through the woods by yourself up on the snowy mountain. Uh-uh, I'm coming with you. I'm not letting you go out who knows where and get lost out there, or worse. We've already established that someone intentionally foraged for those foxglove leaves, so who's to say they're not out there all the time? No, I'm definitely going with you." Simone adamantly moved her hand up and down over the arm of the chair as if pounding a judge's gavel.

"Fine, suit yourself. You can trudge up the mountain with me. It'll be fine. There are marked trails up there, and I've been up there once or twice before. We'll just let my mom and Jo know that we're going, and we'll take just enough time to find the foxglove grove and look around for clues. That's it." Autumn said the words as if trying to convince herself at the same time as Simone.

"Okay, now that we've settled that. What else is on your mind?" Simone grabbed one of the flannel blankets out of a basket on the porch floor and draped it over her knees.

"Marion Bennett. She kept eyeing me at the preservation meeting the other night. And I mean, it could just be that she's jealous of Gran's position that was handed over to me. She acted very insulted when they gave me the position, so maybe that's as far as it really goes. But I still don't know for sure because from what I've heard, she really wanted all that new development to happen in town. It would have been great for her husband's business to increase their wealth and connections." Autumn pulled a plate of raspberry thumbprint cookies out from under her chair.

"Where have you been hiding those?" Simone exclaimed, and Autumn gave her a slight shoulder tilt and a smirk.

"They're from the coffee shop. Eve made up a batch as a test run for the Pine, and I picked them up on my lunch break today." The girls both bit into a cookie simultaneously and gave each other a big nod in agreement. "Oh yeah, these are keepers. I'll definitely order a batch of these for the shop."

Getting back on the topic at hand, Simone swallowed and made a rolling motion to signal Autumn to keep going.

"Right, so I'm still definitely looking into Marion because she's very much the jealous type, and you never know how far someone would take that. But then, there's still the developer, who Mrs. Pendleton saw at Gran's house the day she died. I haven't verified when he arrived and whether he went in. So, I think I'll talk to the mayor and find out more about that guy, too."

The girls sat for a moment, chewing on another cookie and looking out into the dark with just a few lantern lights lit around the edges of the porch and some candles in the windows.

"Oh, you know what we really need to know then? We need to figure out from the police when Gran actually died because I didn't find her until later in the evening after work. But it looked like she had been lying on the couch for a while. I could feel her energy still there when I found her, but it was like she was only holding on until she could reveal the wardrobe key to me and show me the clues around the house, you know?" Autumn closed her eyes and snuggled her nose into Tavish's fur for comfort.

"I know you miss her like crazy, Autumn. We all do. And you've been holding it together pretty well, but it's okay to feel all the feelings. Heck, cause a scene if you'd like and start really balling. I'm in for a good show." Simone pulled another cookie off the tray and laughed.

Autumn couldn't help but let out a belly laugh at Simone. "Thanks for always sticking by me, Sim. I don't know what I'd do without your passion. You really make me smile. But I'm serious when I say I'm gonna get focused and get to the bottom of all of this. First, we'll hike up the mountain and check on the foxgloves. Plus, I'll do some sleuthing about this developer in town, too, and maybe Marion Bennett if I can chat with some business owners discreetly."

"You know what would really help with all of this? If we had a proper coven like our moms were suggesting the other night. We need to round out our gifts to be stronger, and that includes doing things like solving crimes. Right now, we've only got water, air, and a bit of earth behind us. I mean, your fire energy is starting to come through, but it seems like you'll always be an air energy. We need to solidify our earth and fire connections before we can really assume our destinies, know what I mean?" Simone had her usual tone of directness.

"I agree. We can't waste any more time imagining that things are fine with just me and you anymore. Jo and Mom were right. We need a coven, and we need to learn to harness the strength of these elements. Although..." Autumn stopped for a moment and tilted her head to one shoulder. "I have been feeling really burnt out the last couple days. I don't know if it's just all that's been happening, but I feel like I'm in some sort of energy burnout."

"You feel like that, too? That's weird because I started feeling that way the other day, too, and now I can't shake it. It's like I'm completely exhausted, and I can't seem to keep up with anything. In fact, before I came out here, I almost went straight up to bed because I could hardly keep my eyes open anymore. And that's totally not like me. You know I always stay up sketching and watching movies late at night."

"Yeah, that's really weird. Are we both just burning the candle at both ends with the shop and all this with Gran? Or is it something with our magic? I don't think I've ever felt this tired and had to push through it even during the day, but the last couple days have been a slog." Autumn put the plate of cookies back under her chair just as Jo and Penny came out onto the porch.

"Girls, we felt the mention of us out here a moment ago and something about a coven." Aunt Jo chimed in.

"Yes, and we know you're out here plotting to stick your noses into things that will probably get you into more trouble than good. And while we know we can't stop you in whatever it is you're working on or be part of this coven that you'll need to form, we know that we can protect you both." Penny gave Autumn a serious look to show that she needed to do this for her.

"That's right. We can't have you both wandering about town looking for a killer while also trying to figure out your magic. It's time we did a protection spell around you both, and a sturdy one at that." Jo and Penny nodded at one another.

"We'll need the Book of Spells in Gran's wardrobe for the proper spell, so we best do it tonight before you both go chasing after things tomorrow." Penny knew her daughter's stubborn side well, even if she had been gone for a few years.

"Right, no sense in delaying what we can do tonight. Up you come, girls. Let's pop into the car and head to Gran's for that book." Aunt Jo shooed them all to the car, and even Tavish decided he was up for the ride.

CHAPTER 19

Penny closed her elbows tight to her chest and rubbed her hands together. "Autumn, sweetheart, please hurry. At this rate, we'll all be icicles before we get the door open."

Autumn twisted the key into the lock as Tavish rubbed his head on the bottom of Gran's front door. When they heard the knob turn, everyone pushed inside quickly.

"Okay, okay. Geez, you'd think none of us knew how to control the weather or anything." Autumn rolled her eyes and found the light switches inside.

They all stood in the center of the entryway and stared into the living room. Other than to grab a few of Autumn's things and find the mailing tube on the porch, none of them had come back to their familiar family home. This was where they all grew up and made memories with Gran right by their side.

"Mom was always such a kind soul. I still can't believe she's gone." Aunt Jo moved into the living room and sat down on the couch. She rubbed her hands over the cushions as she glanced around.

Simone grabbed her cousin's arm and hugged it close. "Autumn, are you okay being back here? This is your home, after all. You lived here with Gran for years. What does it feel like coming back?"

Autumn slowly put one foot in front of the other and walked the perimeter of the living room, with Tavish following close behind her. "I don't know exactly. I miss being here, but the energy isn't quite right anymore. It's like there's still a weight in the air that hasn't lifted, and until it does, I don't know how long I can stay. Does anyone else feel it?" They all shook their heads at her with expressions of sympathy on their faces.

"Let's focus on what we came for now, and we can worry about shifting the energy here later, all right? Autumn, how did the key to the wardrobe appear to you before?" Penny asked her daughter.

"Well, I think it knew I needed it, and it appeared in Gran's locket. There's something about protective intentions linked to the book. Some of the ancestral voices relayed that to me before. I don't know what that means exactly, but I'm guessing it's tied to our intent."

"That's right, dear." Aunt Jo rose off the couch and walked over to the wardrobe behind the entry wall. "The family heirlooms only manifest when we need them the most. They're there to help us fulfill our responsibilities to this place. So, we need to summon the elemental energies and the ancestors and make our intentions known. If we connect with them properly, they should reveal the key to you."

Jo closed her eyes and ran her hand down the front of the wardrobe cabinet, feeling the energy inside it. She whispered something none of the others could hear and turned around.

"Come with me. The energies of the woods will give us the sanctuary we need." Jo opened the front door and ushered them all out.

Autumn hesitated at the door for a moment, seeing her hooded cape on the hook. She grabbed it with a swipe of her hand and walked out with Tavish by her feet as Jo followed them. One by one, they moved down the dirt path into the woods on the side of Gran's house.

Autumn heard a distant owl in the forest, and with each step, she felt more of herself returning. It wasn't just Gran and the cottage she missed these past couple of weeks. It was the forest as well. The owl within it called to her the deeper they went.

She flung the cape around her shoulders and clasped it at the neck like she did on the night of Gran's death. She paid attention to every step she took through the forest, remembering the grief of that night as it billowed up inside her again.

When they got to the clearing, Autumn stood in the center of the dark circle of trees and knelt to the earth. She put her palms down and recalled the night she rose above the it and caused a tornado of air to surround her. This place gave her power. Her gifts stayed fairly dormant throughout childhood, but something activated them the night she found Gran. The land and the sky merged with her here in this space, and she felt it in her bones.

"Autumn, dear, we must begin before it gets too much darker. Why don't you take the north end of the circle? You'll be the one to call the ancestors and guide our intentions. Can you do that?" Aunt Jo helped Autumn up off the ground and over to the northmost position in the clearing.

"Yes, I'm all right to do it, but if you wouldn't mind giving me some direction, that would be good." Autumn had been taught how to cast a circle growing up, but they were getting into unfamiliar territory with calling on strange ancestral artifacts that disappeared and reemerged when the time was right.

"Of course, dear. We're all here to support you. Just remember, the key leads us to the book, and we're looking for the family protection spell within the book. It'll be much more powerful with the exact words our ancestors chose for our bloodline, all right?" Jo patted Autumn's forearm and took her position at the south end of the circle.

"Simone, Penny," Jo raised her arms up to signal them to join the circle at the east and the west. They all held hands and lifted their heads to the sky above. "Autumn, go ahead whenever you're ready, dear."

Autumn took a deep breath and blew a wisp of warmth into the crisp air. Tavish sat up on his hind legs to watch her intently. She sensed the energy of the elements rising within her as she spoke.

"Guardians of earth to the north, air to the east, fire to the south, and water to the west, we summon you to encircle us with protective energy now. Activate the elements within us and bring forth the ancestral artifacts to protect our bloodline."

As the words came out of her mouth, the winds swirled around them. The three other women moved in closer, and Aunt Jo pulled some bay leaves out of her pocket and threw them into the center of the circle. Autumn closed her eyes, and the winds turned into a howling tornado.

Jo looked at Penny, and they chanted. "Ancestors of the land, sea, and sky, hear our call. Ancestors of the land, sea, and sky, hear our call. Ancestors of the land, sea, and sky, hear our call." Simone joined them to repeat the chant as they all drew in and locked hands.

Autumn's feet lifted off the ground, hovering in the air again. She looked around and noticed that she brought the other women up with her this time. Each of them hung a few inches above the swirling winds sweeping below their feet.

Jo gasped and eyed Penny, who smiled with delight at her daughter's abilities. Simone peered below her with curiosity and pointed her toes up and down to confirm being suspended in the air.

"Magnificent," Penny whispered under her breath, in awe of the energy Autumn harnessed through the circle of the four women.

The warmth radiated from Autumn's necklace now, and she immediately knew the wardrobe key sat inside the locket. Autumn took another deep breath and calmed the energy coursing through her body. They all slowly dropped to the ground as the winds died down, and Tavish pranced through the middle of the circle, purring with contentment.

Autumn lifted her arms to either side of her, as she had seen Aunt Jo and Gran do many times. She looked over to her aunt, and Jo gave her a nod of approval.

"Thank you, ancestors, for hearing our call. We are grateful for your help, and thank you to the elements of the north, east, south, and west for the strength and awareness you've given us."

With that, Autumn put her arms down at her sides and slowly walked counterclockwise around the circle, starting with Simone at the west. She moved behind Simone, gently tapping her shoulder, relieving her from her post. Then, Autumn continued around to Aunt Jo and finally her mother. When she completed the circle, she pulled the locket out of her flannel tunic and opened it up.

Inside, she found the tiny wardrobe key that had appeared to her once before. Autumn raised it enough for all of them to see and smiled with pride. She just led her first circle to manifest something into reality. If she could do this, then maybe she was ready to become the four-points witch after all.

Penny walked over to her and put her arm around her. "That was incredible! I'm so proud of you, sweetheart. This is your path, and I know it's the start of many great things."

"Yeah, how wicked was that? I'm loving how your gifts are playing out these days. I mean, I'm kind of jealous I didn't get the levitation energy, but getting in on it with you is the next best thing." Simone gave her cousin a wink and a smile.

"Okay, while that was a wonderful display of your gifts, Autumn, it's time to get that book and do the protection spell to keep you girls safe."

Jo reached out to grab Autumn and Simone's hands, and Penny followed on the other side of Simone. They walked hand in hand along the trail back to the cottage with a line of tiny sparkling lights kicking up behind them and a little cat trotting happily through it all.

Aunt Jo led through the door of the cottage. She piled up all their things on the front entry table and quickly scurried into the kitchen to look for more protection herbs and salts.

Autumn pulled out the key and went straight for the wardrobe. Penny and Simone gathered around her as Autumn knelt and turned the key in the lock.

The doors swung open, and a golden light shone around the edges of a familiar wooden box on the bottom shelf. Autumn had to move aside a large besom broom that also appeared in the wardrobe. She carefully picked up the box and carried it to the coffee table.

"Simone, grab that curtain over there, and I'll close this one," Penny directed. She grew up in this house alongside Jo, and not much had changed in it since. So Penny still knew where everything was. She went to the tea cabinet and pulled out a small handbell Gran kept there for clearing the air.

"Ah yes, here you are." Penny ran her hand over the antiqued bell fondly.

Jo, Simone, and Penny gathered back at the coffee table as Autumn pulled the book out from the box. Simone knelt beside Autumn and peeked inside the box to see what other interesting things may be tucked inside besides the book.

"I'm sure we'll have other opportunities to look through the box, but let's get going with the book for tonight. I don't want to waste any more time." Aunt Jo placed a long black tray in the middle of the coffee table and sprinkled a line of sea salt down the entire tray. She then placed sprigs of bay leaves, basil, and rosemary on top of the salt and added star anise to each corner of the tray.

"Girls, I want you both to stand next to the coffee table here. Autumn, has the book found the right spell for us yet?" Jo glanced over as the Book of Spells flew open in Autumn's hands. Autumn appeared mesmerized by the book guiding itself to the pages it deemed necessary and then stopping at the exact page for a protection spell.

"Uh, it seems to have found it," she said with disbelief. "It stopped on the Protection From Harm And Ill Will Incantation. Looks like it needs a black or red candle, sea salt, and the people you're protecting." Autumn looked up from the book to find her mother had already found a black candle, and Aunt Jo had covered the tray on the coffee table with sea salt.

"Right, I guess we've got those things covered." Autumn raised her eyebrows as she turned toward Simone and shrugged her shoulders.

Simone gave her a smirk to say she was completely loving this. Simone always loved a good spell, especially when it included some shadowy elements. It brought out the water element in her with that deeper, darker side of life.

"All right, my dears. Penny and I will say the incantation as we put the protection circle around you both. Autumn, read us the words so we have them correct. Using them verbatim will be more powerful since they were bound to our bloodline and this land." Jo waved her hand in a circle to give Autumn the go ahead.

"Okay, you're supposed to call on the elements as you envision the circle around us and walk it while speaking the words. You'll say: Unbounded strength and power protect these two. By these mountain lands, may no harm befall you." Autumn ran her finger down the page. "And it seems like we need to put some kind of time limit on the spell."

Jo walked around the coffee table to look over Autumn's shoulder at the page in the book. "I didn't expect to limit the spell, but that makes sense. Protection spells require more energy, which usually comes from the earth. So we mustn't draw from it for too long."

Jo returned to her position next to Penny on the couch side of the coffee table. "We'll just have to set it for three days. That should give us enough time to do some digging around and figure things out. What do you all say?"

Penny grabbed for Jo's hand and squeezed it tightly as she nodded. "We'll make it work. After that, we'll do what we can to keep you both safe, and you both have your gifts to call on whenever necessary." Penny gave the girls a serious look that revealed her concern underneath.

Simone crossed her arms and closed in next to Autumn. "We can work with that, can't we, cuz?" She bumped Autumn's hips with her own as she spoke and laughed.

Autumn felt better knowing Simone was in this right alongside her. "Yeah, okay. Let's do three days, and we'll be ready for whatever comes afterward." Autumn turned the book around so Jo and Penny could read the words as she held it up for them.

"All right, then. Let's begin." Jo moved her hands back and forth in the air to signify the girls squeezing in tightly.

Tavish jumped up on the coffee table while Penny lit the black candle and placed it in front of the salt tray. She rang the antique bell of Gran's three times to clear the air in the room and smiled at Jo to begin.

Jo flattened her right hand, fingers firmly pressed together and lifted it above her head as she spoke.

"Elements of earth, air, fire, and water, we call upon you now. Along with our ancestors, feel our intentions. Draw any harmful energy away from these two girls through the power of my words." Jo nodded to Penny, and they began walking around Autumn and Simone in a circle.

"Unbounded strength and power protect these two. By these mountain lands, may no harm befall you. Unbounded strength and power protect these two. By these mountain lands, may no harm befall you." The two women continued making a circle as their hands drew a faint shimmer in the air around Autumn and Simone.

Jo and Penny created a spiraling motion from top to bottom as they walked, and the girls watched them in awe as they worked beautifully in harmony with each other. "Unbounded strength and power protect these two. By these mountain lands, may no harm befall you." They completed the circle and came back to where they began.

Jo picked up a handful of salt off the tray and did one more lap around the girls as she sprinkled a pinch here and there around them. "For three days and three nights shall this spell hold. And for no other than us four shall the spell fold."

The shimmer of light Jo and Penny drew in the air turned into a larger bubble of tiny sparkling lights surrounding the girls. Tavish chased the lights with his eyes and spun his head from side to side.

Jo smiled seeing her handiwork and finished the spell. "Ancestors and elements of the mountain lands, we thank you for your energy. We close this spell with light and appreciation for protecting these girls. As I say it, so shall it be." Jo placed her hand on Penny's shoulder, and Penny waved her hand over the black candle flame to extinguish it.

"Well, I'd say we can breathe easier for the next few days. And if I may say, Jo, I really have missed these rituals with you. I'm glad to have my sister back, and I can see that you've all come quite a long way with your magic since I've been gone." Penny stared at the two girls admiring Jo's spell work.

Autumn and Simone locked arms and stood staring back at Jo and Penny while the sparks of magic glinted off them both like tiny drops of steam from a heated bath. Whatever they encountered in the coming days, it felt good knowing this magic coursed through them as an added layer of security.

CHAPTER 20

Autumn and Simone carried a bag of warm cinnamon popovers and hot teas from the Forest Brew into Aunt Jo's bath shop. As they moved closer to the counter, they saw Jo and Penny talking with Chief Walsh and his son, Ben. It had been several days since they received any updates from the police department on the investigation, so Autumn was eager to hear what they may have uncovered.

"Chief Walsh, Ben," Autumn nodded at them as she set the bag on the counter. "It's good to see you. Do you have updates for us?"

"Yes, Autumn, the Chief was just telling us they learned the time of Gran's death from the coroner. It was just after four o'clock that afternoon." Penny stood wringing her hands as she spoke.

"That would make sense why she was having tea. It was the usual tea time for her, but the question remains whether she invited someone to have tea with her or if they just showed up." Autumn looked to the Chief as if he had more answers.

"It's hard to say, but we're piecing it all together." Chief Walsh wanted to offer them as much as he could, but the facts weren't clear yet.

"They're also looking into the developer seen at Gran's house by Mrs. Pendleton. That's their best lead right now, but at least it's something to go on." Aunt Jo's voice rose as she flailed her arms in the air with frustration.

Simone set the drinks down on the counter and hugged her mother. "We'll figure it out, Mom. I feel it all coming together." She kept her arm around her mother for a moment longer to comfort her.

"That's right. This developer, uh, Charles Garrett, is the one we're looking into now. He owns Garrett Developments, who've been trying to bid for the redevelopment downtown." The Chief turned and lifted his arm to wave Ben forward. "Ben and my other deputies will lead the investigation from this point forward. They'll be interviewing a few people around town."

Ben stepped forward and gave everyone a smile and a nod. "I'll keep you all informed about what we find out, but it's best to keep everything to yourselves. Otherwise, we may compromise the investigation."

"We understand, officers. Thank you so much for being so open with us." Penny shook the Chief's hand and continued. "We'd like to hold a memorial service for my mother soon, so we'll be planning where to carry out her last wishes."

"Understood. We've collected all the evidence we need now, and her body is ready to be released to you. So please make your arrangements." Chief Walsh moved closer to Ben and waved him toward the door. "I hope you all can start finding some peace with this soon. We'll be in touch." They headed out the door, and Ben gave Simone a particularly warm smile before he left.

"I think we should do a nice memorial service by the downtown water fountain for the townspeople to attend, and of course, we'll do our own memorial in the woods. That's what your gran would have wanted." Jo opened the bag of popovers and placed them on the table to keep herself from shedding tears.

"That sounds like a fine idea. She always said preserving this town was deeply important, so the fountain is a beautiful place to gather and celebrate her values. And you're absolutely right about the woods. It was her home for her whole life, after all. It's only proper that we as a family remember her there." Penny grabbed one of the tall to-go cups and warmed her hands around it.

"I can make the arrangements with the parks office today. In fact, I actually wanna head over there anyway and see some mountain trail maps. Simone and I have an idea of where those foxglove bushes grow, and I wanna check it out sooner than later." Autumn broke off a piece of a popover and stuffed it into her mouth.

"I'll head over to the parks office with you then. We can do it at lunchtime and then just grab a bite from the Forest Brew on our way back to the shop." Simone saw Autumn getting ready to tell her not to bother. "I'm not gonna take no for an answer, so don't even bother. We're in this together, and besides, we need to get the details sorted out for Gran's memorial. So it's best if at least two of us go to nail things down."

"All right, fine. We'll go at lunch," Autumn blew her hair away from her face, too exhausted to argue.

"Let's just try not to have the whole place turn into a tornado this time, okay?" Simone laughed under her breath and took a sip of the tea. Penny and Jo glanced at each other, wondering what they missed, but kept their comments to themselves.

"Yeah, about that. I think we're gonna need some regular... practice sessions if we're gonna control these stronger gifts." Autumn gave Jo and her mother a hopeful look, and they both nodded in agreement.

"That's true. It sounds like if we don't help you girls out soon, we'll all be experiencing the next apocalyptic flood! We'd better order some supplies and make preparations. You girls focus on finding out more around town for now. Let Penny and I handle the magic lessons, and we'll all come back together when we've made progress, shall we?" Jo met eyes with each of them to gain agreement.

"Okay, Mom. We need to open up the shop, but we'll see you tonight at the house, okay?" Simone kissed her mother's cheek and waved goodbye to Penny.

Autumn hugged them both and grabbed her things to head to the door with Simone. When they shut the front door of the shop behind them, Autumn stopped and stared at Simone.

"What if I can't get the elements under control? I'll let everyone down, or worse, it could hurt someone." Autumn had the worried look on her face that usually came up when something was out of her control.

Simone put her hands on Autumn's shoulders. "Relax, cuz. There's gonna be a learning curve, okay? Stop worrying because you've got this. And us elemental witches aren't to be messed with. So, we'll uncover whatever's going on here with Gran's death, and our gifts will help us do it, all right? Just write some affirmations in your journal when we get back to the shop, and you'll feel better."

Usually, Simone made Autumn feel better with her straight talk, but as they walked down the street, Autumn had more of a knot in her stomach than before. The last thing she wanted to do was let her family down. To let Gran down. Somehow, she knew these activating powers were the key to what happened to Gran and stepping onto this new path of the four-points witch. She just didn't know how it all fit together yet, and the fear of everything piling down on her started creeping in.

Autumn unraveled her infinity scarf and looked up to see a group of workers creating a fall display of pumpkins and tall lanterns in the lobby of city hall. She and Simone walked over to get a closer look when Autumn heard the mayor's voice in the distance.

"That Charles Garrett is awfully bold, I'll give him that! To invite us down for a drink and think he can just ease into our town and get the bid. I'll give him points for boldness, though, and I know this won't be the last we'll hear from him. He's not the sort to give up so easily." The mayor spoke to a few other people surrounding him. Autumn recognized a couple of them from the preservation committee and from around city hall.

"Ah, Autumn!" The mayor looked over and waved his hand at her. He turned to the group and nodded. "Give me a moment, will you? I'll catch up."

Autumn and Simone strolled over to him and shook his hand.

"Mr. Mayor, how are you?" Autumn wanted to jump right in and ask about the developer he had ranted about, but she aimed for a polite greeting instead.

"Yes, I'm well, thank you. But I wanted to check in with you and your family. Simone, hello." Mayor Halpin put his hand on Simone's shoulder. "Listen, Autumn, you did a fine job at the preservation meeting the other day, and I personally wanted to thank you for taking over this position. I know it must be difficult with everything going on right now, but, well, we need you and your family more than ever. I think you gathered that yourselves." The mayor presented a more serious look on his face now.

"We appreciate that, Mr. Mayor. It's hard coming to terms with everything, and we're still working with the police about Gran's death." Autumn hesitated for a moment before continuing. "But we need to figure out what happened to our grandmother first and foremost." She spoke sincerely but did her best to nudge him into opening up. "We couldn't help but overhear you mentioning the developer, Charles Garrett, a moment ago. You said he invited you out to drinks to get the bid. Do you remember when that was?"

"Oh, I'd say it was last Wednesday because it was a couple of days after the previous preservation meeting where your gran was adamant about their firm not having a place here."

Autumn and Simone glanced at one another as if telepathically confirming that was the same day as Gran's death. The question was whether he was around the cottage at the exact time of her death.

"I recall him calling the office several times and trying to get through the back door, you could say." The mayor turned to see the group of people waiting for him at the front doors, and he held up his pointer finger to signal he'd be another minute.

"Did you ever end up meeting with him?" Autumn needed to know where Charles Garrett went in town and when he might have been at Gran's house to deliver those drawings.

"As a matter of fact, yes, I went down to the Ridgeline Inn and met him along with a few others that afternoon. Of course, he was there schmoozing everyone and laid out some big ideas. Although, most of us were just there to hear his motives, you know. They're just too grand of ideas to turn this place into a tourist trap, though, and we can't have it. You both know we must protect our town at all costs."

"You're absolutely right, mayor. Uh, do you know when you might have been over at the Inn to hear what he had to say?" Autumn pressed for more answers.

"Well, it would have to have been around, oh, three thirty or so. They have their happy hour specials, you know, and they're gearing up for the harvest days and their Oktoberfest to follow. So I have to say, it was more of an excuse for me to go over and have some of that seasonal pumpkin ale they're bringing out." He gave them a wink and patted them both on the arm. "Ladies, I do have to get going, but please give my regards to your mothers. And Autumn, I will be in touch about the more... energetic concerns about the region as time allows. See you both soon." Mayor Halpin walked away and joined the group just heading out of city hall.

"All right, so we know Garrett showed up here the day Gran died, but he met with several people at the pub." Simone walked and talked with Autumn as they made their way to the parks department.

"Yeah, the mayor said they were over there around three thirty. And Chief Walsh told us Gran died around four o'clock. There's no way Garrett could have left the Inn all the way across town in the foothills and made it back to have tea with Gran and slip something into her cup all before four o'clock. That just wouldn't work. It's too far away." Autumn felt sick saying it because now the developer was off the table as a suspect.

"I guess that means it wasn't him. The mayor basically just gave Charles Garrett an alibi." Simone opened the glass doors to the parks department and let Autumn go inside first.

Autumn turned and whispered to her cousin, "Maybe so, but at least this means we're getting closer to finding the actual killer."

Just as she headed for the counter, someone nudged Autumn's shoulder and knocked her back a step.

"Pardon me," A deep voice began as he stepped closer to the girls. A tall, sturdy man with a bushy brown beard towered over them. "Oh," he eyed both of them and thought for a moment. "The MacKinnon girls. Right, excuse me." He walked away abruptly before saying anything more.

Simone helped Autumn put her backpack onto her shoulder after it slid to the floor. "What was that?" Simone said, looking toward the stranger.

"I have no idea." Autumn went up to the lady at the parks office desk. "Hello, uh, do you happen to know who that man was?"

"Oh yes, that's Mr. Cunningham. He does the photos for our parks department. He can be rough around the edges and mostly keeps to himself, but underneath it all, he's a decent man." The lady replied as she continued typing something into her computer. "What can I do for you both?"

"Sorry, yes, we're here for a couple of things. First, we need to reserve the downtown fountain square for a memorial service. If you have some availability in the next week or so, that would be good." Autumn put her forearms on the counter and waited for a reply.

The lady looked up from her computer and gaped at the girls. "Oh my goodness, of course. You're Lorna MacKinnon's girls. Anything for Lorna's family. She was always such a dear and will be remembered so fondly around here." The lady continued typing and pulled up some dates for them. "How about at the end of next week on Thursday afternoon? You can have the square for two hours. Will that do?"

The girls nodded to each other. "That's perfect. We'll schedule that now then, thanks." Simone took the paperwork from the lady and started filling it out.

"Just fill in your contact information here, and we'll confirm with you before that day, all right?" She smiled at them and pulled a few more pages out of a printer behind the counter. "Now, what was the other thing that you needed today?"

"We'd like to see your hiking trail maps near the mountain ridge. The ones that go around to the other side of the mountain. Do you have those available?" Autumn kept her tone light.

"Ah, you mean the Timberline Trails. Yes, in fact, Mr. Cunningham was just here discussing that very area. He takes the images we use for the mountain region in our tourist marketing. If you're interested in the Timberline Trails, you'll have to be quick because it's getting late in the season. They'll only be open for a few more days, and then the gates close until late Spring. At that point, no one gets through because of the amount of snow and severe weather on the mountain."

She pulled out a brochure from a basket on the wall behind her and gave it to the girls. "Here you are. You'll find a few trails marked on this map, but the blue one is my favorite. That one has some lovely views." She gave them a smile and went back to typing on her computer.

Autumn opened the brochure and smiled back. "Thanks a lot!" The girls walked away toward the glass doors and pushed them open as they buried themselves in the map.

"We may be onto something here, but we can't delay." Autumn found a wooden bench next to a wall in the lobby of city hall, and Simone followed her to sit down.

"So this guy knows the trails up there that potentially lead to the fox-glove grove, and he obviously goes up there regularly. Plus, he had a motive since Gran gave his wife those teas to make him talk. We need to get up there and look around asap." Simone ran her finger around the trails on the map. "But which trail do we choose?"

"Look, this one loops around the back side of the peak where the green treeline seems to stop. From what I saw in the Forest Brew photos, the foxgloves sat on the other side of the evergreen trees. The photos had a definitive edge to where the forest stopped and the foxgloves began, almost like they were in a clearing." Autumn pointed to the trail marked in green on the map. "That trail may be our best bet."

Simone read the legend and widened her eyes. "That one is four miles long, and it says the elevation is over nine thousand feet. Have you been hiking recently, and I didn't know about it?"

"I know, but we're in pretty good shape." Autumn hesitated as the nervousness rose in her stomach. "We can do it, and it doesn't look like that one has any real grades to it, so it should be fairly even and smooth." Autumn nudged Simone with her shoulder. "We have to do this for Gran."

"Look at you, stepping up and being a leader." Simone had a smirk on her face as she leaned in. "I believe this four-points witch thing may be your calling after all."

"Yeah, yeah." Autumn rolled her eyes. She'd put on the brave face for now, but deep down, she worried more than ever about how this would all play out. "Let's just figure out when we can get up there because we only have a few more days, and let's not forget, our protection spell only has a couple more days as well."

CHAPTER 21

Aunt Jo popped into the front hall from the kitchen just as Simone and Autumn put together their day packs for the hike up the mountain.

"Autumn, be sure you've got the locket on. It'll watch over you both and ensure the ancestors are with you. Remember, this is the third day of the protection spell. You should be all right until sundown, but you'll be cutting it close. Don't get too far off track up there."

Jo lifted her hand, and inside it, she held a single stem of lavender knotted inside a piece of twine. She grabbed Simone's wrist to tie the twine around it. "Hour by hour and stem by stem. May these lands diligently protect them."

Jo cupped Simone's hand within her own two hands. "There. Now you have the energy of the land as an extra layer of security. There should also be park rangers up on the mountain, and Penny and I will be here if you need anything at all. If you can get a signal on your phone, send us a message saying you're all right."

"Mom, we'll be fine. It's just a quick hike, and we'll be down in no time. Go to the shop, and we'll see you when we get back." Simone hugged her mother and threw an extra sweater into her olive green canvas backpack just in case.

"You know we need to do this, Aunt Jo. We'll be back before sunset, promise." Autumn hugged her aunt. "Oh, and could you thank Mom for watching Parchment and Pine for us today while we're gone? I didn't get to say thank you properly before she left this morning."

"Of course, sweetie. I'll close my shop early and head over there to help her. We'll make sure everything is in proper order for you both." Jo raised a finger, remembering another important point. "You know what?" She stood in the center of the hallway, paused to receive a download from the universe. "Why don't you both stop at the Forest Brew before you head up the mountain? I have a feeling Eve has something to... boost your luck today."

"Are you getting one of your intuitive hits again? All right, we can stop if it means a little extra energy nudge. I am curious now that we know they're a founding family." Simone picked up her backpack and slung it over her quilted black coat.

"Yeah, that sounds like a good idea. We'll grab some drinks before we go." Autumn laced up her duck boots and slouched down her thick wool socks over the top before grabbing her knit hat and gloves out of a basket on the hallway bench. "I'm all set. Let's head out."

"Right, we'll message you as soon as we find the foxglove and get back to the ranger station. See you soon, Mom." Simone waved to Jo, and the girls headed out the door to Simone's black Jeep SUV parked in the driveway.

Simone pulled the car up along the sidewalk outside of the Forest Brew. Autumn pushed the passenger door open and stepped out.

"I'll just be a second," Autumn slammed the door behind her and walked into the coffee shop. She immediately saw Eve behind the counter filling cups of coffee for the customers sitting on stools. Autumn motioned to her to head to the back end of the counter, and Eve nodded with understanding.

"Hey Eve, I wondered if you may have some tea or something that could... give Simone and me a boost of luck? I mean, if there's a... special blend that could help us track something down we're looking for. Would you have something like that?" Autumn gave her a sheepish look and waited for a response.

Eve put the coffeepot down on a towel and thought for a moment. She wiped off her hands on the towel strung through the apron around her waist and smiled. "I may have something for you. Just some natural ingredients to put into a tea blend, much like what your grandmother may have produced." She broadened her sly smile, as if she was just permitted to let herself loose.

Eve walked behind the kitchen's swinging doors and didn't come out for several minutes. Autumn saw Eve through the tiny window at the top of the doors. She was busy doing something back there, but Autumn couldn't tell what.

After a couple more minutes, Eve returned with two to-go cups in her hands. "A special cinnamon chai blend with a hint of, well, let's just call it fortune." She slid the cups across the counter to Autumn, who could see little sparks of light glinting through the small openings of the lid.

"Thank you! I think we're already fortunate to have you here. Thanks for this! I'll keep you posted on how it goes." Autumn raised a cup in the air in appreciation and slid some money onto the counter with her free hand. She grabbed the other cup and headed out the door to find Simone still at the curb in the car.

"Your mom was right," Autumn said as she got in. "Eve had just the thing for us, and I saw the light of her magic making its way through the cups." Autumn carefully opened one of the lids and a line of lights sparkled into the air.

"She enchanted the tea. Just like Gran used to do." Simone sat wide-mouthed as she stared into the to-go cup.

"Yep. And she didn't seem fazed by it one bit. In fact, I think she got really excited by the idea of me knowing she could do it." Autumn closed the lid and slid the teas into the cup holders between the seats.

"Well, well, well. Looks like we have ourselves another earth witch in Hollow's Glenn, and she's been here all along." Simone laughed as she pulled the car away and started driving up into the mountains.

Simone bent down to tie the laces on her hiking boots tighter, wishing she bought better inserts to make them sturdier and more comfortable. The girls hiked for a few miles through tall evergreens and saw the edge of the trees.

"Come on, slowpoke. I can see the treeline from here." Autumn zipped her burgundy waterproof jacket up higher and took a sip of water as she waited for Simone to walk again.

The winds picked up, and the trees swayed around them. Autumn felt a chill creep up her arms as they moved down the path.

"What is it?" Simone asked with a serious look on her face. "Did you hear something?"

Autumn shook her head. "No, but I know we're close. There's something up ahead."

She took a deep breath to sense if there was anything in the air she should know. There was a slight scent of saffron. Autumn rarely smelled it before unless Gran made saffron buns in early December.

"Gran is here. I can feel her energy." Simone looked from side to side, searching for her grandmother's energy.

"There's saffron in the air. Gran always said saffron reveals the mysteries of the universe. Maybe that's a good sign that we're on the right track here." Autumn kept walking as she whispered softly into the air. "Elements of earth, air, fire, and water, lead us to what we must uncover."

"It's not just Gran here. The ancestors came to surround us with an extra bit of support." Simone furrowed her brow for a moment and looked up at Autumn. "How much time is left before the protection spell wears off?"

"Not much, maybe another hour or two if we're lucky. We got a late start, and driving up the mountain took us a while, so now we're pressed for time." Autumn had a concerned look on her face, but she tried to keep it together.

She took a breath and paid attention to her footsteps to stay grounded. The wind sped up even more now and howled around them.

"Look to the valley for what you seek." A voice trailed off into the wind.

Autumn brushed the hair out of her face and let out a sigh. "We're getting close. The voices started again." She adjusted her bag and raised her hand to feel the locket around her neck. It kept getting warmer the further up the mountain they went. "Let's look for a valley somewhere up here. The foxgloves have to be there."

Simone agreed, and they proceeded as the winds grew even stronger. Branches cracked off of a few trees nearby and fell to the ground, and Autumn had the distinct idea that they were not alone on the trail.

As the path faded into the mountain, more rocky outcroppings surrounded them. The girls veered off from the path and made their way through the last of the trees to a small clearing on the other side. Autumn pulled her phone out of her bag and checked for reception, but she had none.

"I don't have any signal either," Simone replied, pulling out her own phone. "We're gonna have to take some pictures and message Mom and Penny when we get back to the ranger station."

"Yeah, looks like it." Autumn moved around in a circle, eyeing the forest of trees behind them and the small clearing in front of them. No one else was visible out there, but something told her to keep an eye out.

"Hey, the tree line curves around down there before it dips. I feel like that's where we should go." Simone pointed to their right as she walked down a rocky slope.

"Okay, just be careful and stay close to me." Autumn's stomach tensed. She didn't like uncertainty, and there was too much of it in the air right now.

Autumn watched as Simone trotted down the hill and suddenly stopped. "Why are you stopping? Did you find something?"

As the words came out, Autumn noticed the silhouette of a big, burly man hunched over with what looked like a camera in his hand. He slowly rose and turned to see who came up behind him.

Autumn and Simone's jaws dropped as they stood staring at Bill Cunningham directly in front of them, alongside the remainders of what looked like a line of withered foxglove bushes.

He looked stunned to see them there as he gradually let his camera hang around his neck by the strap. "MacKinnon's girls." He stood there for a moment just looking at them and then appeared to get upset. "Did you follow me up here?" Mr. Cunningham pointed his finger down to the ground as if scolding someone. "Who told you I'd be here?"

Simone lifted her hands in the air in surrender. "We were just hiking. The path is only open for a few more days, and we thought we'd come to see the views before the weather got bad." Simone slowly moved to the side and tried reaching for her phone again.

"Mr. Cunningham, is it?" Autumn spoke as gently as she could. She knew he didn't buy them just being up there to hike, so she was going to have to try a different route with him. "We don't want any trouble. We're only looking for something and came up here to find it. That's all. You know what it's like to want to find something special, right? You're a photographer."

Autumn tried to buy some time as Simone slowly crept around the side of Mr. Cunningham, but he quickly jerked around and picked up a long rifle sitting beside his pack on the ground. He pointed it straight at Simone, and she raised her hands and froze.

"I'm not buying it. Your family always causes trouble. You're just like your grandmother, and look where that got her. She poked her nose into everyone's business and stirred up trouble between me and my wife." He stuttered as he spoke and pointed the rifle directly at Autumn now.

She sensed the wind forcefully sweep around her and the foxglove bushes swayed back and forth. Gray clouds moved in above them, and suddenly Autumn felt her feet leave the ground.

Awareness Tea

1 1/2 cups of water
1 tsp mugwort leaves
1 Tbsp peppermint leaves
drizzle of honey

Heat the water until boiling. Remove from heat. Place the herbs in a sachet or tea strainer and steep for four minutes. After the tea cools, sit with your mug in a quiet place, eyes closed, and focus on the point between your eyebrows, considered your third eye. Take a sip of the tea and repeat in your mind,

My eye is open. My awareness is honed.

Say the incantation in your mind three times as you drink the tea and focus on your third eye point.

CHAPTER 22

Jo burst into Parchment and Pine carrying a couple of jars of moon water, a medium-sized copper bowl, and several bundles of sage. Penny and Tavish both popped their heads up from the counter and widened their eyes at her. Tavish stretched his back into an arch and jumped down to see what all the commotion was about.

"Something is wrong. I feel it." Jo moved quickly over to the hearth room in the back and placed everything down carefully on the round table between the wingback chairs.

"Jo, you're being dramatic. The girls will call as soon as they find something. Just try to relax." Penny tried to reassure her, but it didn't work.

"No, my intuition is telling me we need to do something. I'm going to see if I can channel Simone and get a reading on what's happening." Jo poured the moon water into the copper bowl and then went over to the fireplace to light a bundle of sage.

"All right, let me draw the curtains before anyone walks in." Penny unwrapped the tie around the curtains to the hearth room and let them fall into place. "Why don't I keep watch for customers out front while you try to figure something out, okay?" Penny left Jo and made her way to the front of the store to peer out the window. She craned her neck around the window display of new paper lanterns to check if anyone might be coming.

Jo cleared the energy in the hearth room by swirling smoke from the sage bundles around herself and the room. She gently put it on the edge of the fireplace to keep the smoke going. Then, she took her place in one of the wingback chairs and hovered her face over the bowl of moon water. Tavish sat up on the other wingback chair and watched Jo intently as she began.

"Water within me, water within her, call to Simone now and allow me to see what she perceives." Jo dipped her middle finger into the water, creating ripples in the bowl. She searched the water for an image of something and waited for a moment.

Jo gasped to herself as something appeared. She faintly saw Autumn talking in the distance and standing as if she didn't want to move at all. Jo felt an aura of fear around her. Then, the image shifted and showed the large barrel of a rifle in front of what appeared to be a wide open space.

"Oh, my word. They are in danger." Jo dipped her finger gently into the bowl of water again and allowed the image to dissipate. She immediately grabbed her bag and rummaged through it for her phone to dial Chief Walsh.

"Hello, yes, I'm looking for Chief Walsh. I believe two girls are in danger, and I'd like to have a patrol sent at once." Jo rushed over to open the curtain and waved Penny over to her.

Penny had just greeted a customer that walked into the shop and started looking for a new garland to hang over their mantle at home. She pointed them to a section on the opposite wall and then scurried over to Jo.

"Just take a breath, Jo, and tell me what you saw," Penny whispered in a calming tone.

"It's the girls. They are in danger. I saw Autumn standing still, talking to someone, and there was someone opposite her with a rifle!" Jo frantically tried to keep her voice down, although quite rattled.

"All right, let's take it one step at a time. Are you calling the police?" Penny glanced down at Jo's phone in her hand.

"Yes, I'm on hold right now, and they're getting Chief Walsh. Actually, here he is." She returned the phone to her ear once she heard his voice. "Oh, Chief. Thank you for getting to the phone so quickly! It's the girls, Autumn and Simone. They've gone up mountain trails, and I'm afraid they're in danger. Something... tells me someone up there may cause them harm. I think the person has a rifle."

"All right, Jo. I'm going to have you give all the information to my desk clerk, and we are going to send a few officers up there now, okay? Don't worry, we're going to check on them. I trust your sense about these things, so we won't delay. Please, just stay on the line and give the information to Mavis at the desk, all right?" The Chief stepped away from the phone, and Jo presumed he was gathering the officers to head straight out there.

Jo put her hand over the phone and mouthed to Penny, "They're sending some people up there."

Penny seemed relieved but kept her composure to go help the people buying some garland. "Thank you so much! Come back and see us again before the holidays!" She moved with the couple toward the front, flipped the sign to closed, and locked the door.

"Jo, I think we better go down to the woods and connect with the energies of the land. That's probably our best chance of helping the girls right now." Penny went back to the hearth room and hugged her sister. "Everything will be all right. Just focus on that intention and put your energy toward the protection spell we have around them. That's the best thing we can do right now."

Jo threw the bowl of moon water over the remaining flames on the fire, and they both grabbed their coats and took a quick look around the shop. "Oh, Tavish, you stay here. We'll be back for you when we know something more. Be good, cat."

Tavish jumped off the wingback chair and made an infinity circle around both ladies' legs. He let out a big meow to show he wasn't willing to just sit there and do nothing, and then pawed at Jo's leg.

Jo sighed and grabbed a basket full of flannel blankets sitting beside the fireplace. She picked Tavish up and placed him into the basket. "All right, I suppose you can come with us. But no wandering off." She gave him a rub and wound her forearm under the basket handle.

Penny guided her sister toward the back door, keeping it together as best she could. "Come on, then. We're MacKinnons, and we've got our girls to protect."

CHAPTER 23

Autumn hovered about a foot in the air now. She felt the energy coursing through her and pulsing around her. Simone sensed almost a telepathic calling from her cousin telling her to bring about the storm.

"What the?" Bill Cunningham stared wide-mouthed at Autumn in disbelief. "What's going on? Is this another one of your family's witchy tricks?" He raised the gun barrel higher and looked down the sight at them.

The clouds above them grew grayer and closed in as thunder struck. The girls moved in closer to the man as he showed hints of fear on his face. He looked up to the sky and saw barrels of rain fall directly at them.

"We told you we didn't want any trouble, but you pulled out a gun. So now you're going to put that down and tell us what really happened with our grandmother. No one needs to get hurt." As she spoke through the pounding rain, a strength grew within Autumn that she never imagined she had before.

Simone came up beside her with gray eyes the color of the storm. The winds howled around them, and Bill's arms shook as he tried to control the barrel of the gun.

"Why did you follow me here? Why is your family getting between me and my wife?" He stuttered as he spoke and rattled the rifle up and down with aggravation.

"We told you we weren't here for you. But now that we've found you here, lower the gun and tell us what happened." Autumn spoke calmly and resolutely, although the intensity of the power she possessed swirled around them.

The wind raged so strongly that the rain now blew in sideways and pummeled the man so much he had to lower the rifle. He struggled to stand in one place and could barely keep his eyes open through the rain.

"I didn't care for your grandmother snooping around in our business, but I didn't kill her if that's what you're getting at. She had no right to intervene in our affairs, but I'm not cold-blooded. I wouldn't harm anyone unless they hurt Vera. She's the love of my life, you know. But I'm afraid I'm the one who's gone and hurt her with my gambling." He dropped to the ground, still holding the rifle in his hands.

"Police! Put the gun down and move back!" A shout came from up the hill at the tree line.

Autumn quickly dropped her feet to the ground as a sudden rush of officers made their way into the clearing and over to Mr. Cunningham to retrieve his weapon. Chief Walsh rushed over to the girls with his gun drawn but lowered.

"Girls, are you both all right?" He had concern in his voice as he focused on them.

They nodded with relief, and slowly the wind and rain died down. Simone grabbed Autumn's hand, and they both took a deep breath. The light peeked through overhead and shone down on them as the clouds moved on.

"Your mother gave us a bit of a scare when she called the station." The Chief gave Simone a serious look. "Somehow, she sensed you two needed help, and I'm glad she didn't hesitate to call."

He looked both of them over and squinted his eyes at them. "Although, from the looks of things when I came out of those trees, you seemed to be... holding your own. But I think Ben and I were the only ones who really noticed that, so we'll just keep things to ourselves, okay?" Chief Walsh started heading over to his officers restraining Mr. Cunningham and then paused, momentarily turning back at them. "You may wanna come over and say a word to Mr. Cunningham here about what he may or may not have seen before we take him away."

Simone nodded and took Autumn's elbow as they moved closer. Autumn stood directly in front of Mr. Cunningham as the officers put handcuffs on him. She knew he was hurting and that he really didn't know what happened to their grandmother.

Simone leaned into Autumn's ear and whispered, "His aura is a dark grayish blue. Sadness and depression. He was telling us the truth."

Autumn took a step forward toward him. "Mr. Cunningham, if what you told us is true, then we have no issues with you or your wife. In fact, we'll do what we can to help you both. I swear to it." She gave him a sympathetic expression as she continued. "Today just created a terrible storm and a bad misunderstanding, right? A terrible storm and a bad misunderstanding."

She called to the winds in her mind and sent them swirling around him for a moment. They whispered to him, "Just a storm, forget all else. Just a misunderstanding, forget all else."

Mr. Cunningham looked at the officers on either side of him and then back to Autumn. "I'm so sorry. This was all just a misunderstanding."

Autumn and Simone nodded in agreement. "It's all right," Autumn confirmed with compassion. "It was a misunderstanding."

The officers walked Mr. Cunningham back up the hill toward their SUVs and placed him in the back of one.

Ben walked over to the girls and gave Simone a relieved smile. "You had us worried, but I'm really glad you're okay."

"What's going to happen now?" Simone replied without taking her eyes off him.

"Well, we'll take him down to the station and ask him some questions about what happened and also about your grandmother most likely. We just looked at him as a potential suspect when this all happened. So there may be something to it, but we'll see."

"We thought so when we saw him near that foxglove grove over there, but now I'm not so sure. He genuinely seemed worried that we were trying to mess with him and his wife somehow, not the other way around."

"Yeah, I don't think he's who we need to focus on. He probably just had the rifle up here for wildlife and then we startled him." Simone tucked her chin into her coat and tried to bury her face into the warmth.

"Here, let me give you this." Ben slipped his arms out of his uniform jacket and wrapped it around Simone's shoulders.

"Thank you." She smiled at him and got lost in thought for a moment.

Autumn cleared her throat. "Anyway, you should have a look at the foxglove bushes over here. We think this may have been where someone got the tea leaves that killed our grandmother. The question is who else would have known they were up here?"

An idea popped into Autumn's head. She walked over to the shriveled bushes and bent down beside them just as the locket under her coat warmed up next to her skin. It pulsated with energy and encouraged her to pursue her search.

She glanced over the leaves on the bushes as she thought. Anyone who had seen Mr. Cunningham's photos in the Forest Brew could have known about these bushes, just as Autumn had. And there was at least one other person who attended the preservation meetings there who also sat on their suspect list, Marion Bennett.

"We'll get a sample of those and take it back to our lab. They'll be able to tell if it was the same substance or not," Ben affirmed. He was good at his job and suited nicely to take over for his father as police chief soon.

Autumn nodded at him without taking her eyes off the foxglove. "Okay, good."

"Listen, you can write your statements, and then I can follow you back into town if you'd like?" Ben took a few steps toward Simone as he spoke.

"Oh no, you don't have to do that. We'll just stay out here until you're done and then head back ourselves. Thank you, though." Simone gave him back his coat and brushed her hand along his as he took it.

"If you're sure?" He looked at them both with a questioning look, but they both nodded. "Right, then here's my notebook. Jot down what happened, and I'll come back to collect it." Ben eased his way back from Simone and turned to meet up with the other officers.

"Simone," Autumn moved around the line of foxglove bushes trying to find something of interest. She stopped at the third bush and ran her eyes over the leaves. "I can smell the saffron again over here. Look at the leaves. I see faded hints of sparkling lights, and they're in some kind of pattern." She pulled her phone out of her back pocket and turned on the camera as she leaned in closer to take a picture.

"Is that... a tree branch?" Simone questioned as she leaned over Autumn's shoulder to see.

"Yeah, I think so. Just like the one we saw in the library archive on our ancestral documents." Autumn quickly put the phone back into her pocket and tried to look like she was wandering as an officer came over to collect a sample of the leaves.

She leaned and wrapped her hands around Simone's arm as they walked back up the hill together. "Anyone who had seen those photos of the foxglove in the Forest Brew could have known to come here for it. That could be anyone on the preservation committee, including Marion Bennett, who already had it out for Gran and her position on the committee. The only real question is our family tree and why there's magical light residue on these leaves."

"Well, if she's not part of a founding magic family, then a partner could have helped her get the leaves and put a spell on them or something." Simone thought out loud.

"Yes, but why would our family tree be involved then? We're still missing something, and it has to do with that extra branch of the tree. Maybe we need to have another look at those archives to put the pieces together."

"Yeah, I guess. But we better start some of those magic lessons our moms were talking about before we go too much deeper with this. We're completely soaked, and it would've been nice to have kept ourselves dry and only created the storm over the person we needed to stop. I'm just saying." Simone laughed with relief as the girls made their way back through the trees and up to the police cars ahead.

CHAPTER 24

Autumn sipped on a cup of warm chamomile tea as she sat on the sofa in Aunt Jo's shop. Simone perused the shelves and opened jars of new bath salt mixtures her mother had put out for the upcoming season.

"Oh, here he comes!" Autumn put her cup down on the coffee table just as Chief Walsh came through the door.

He took his hat off once inside and gave them all a nod. "Ladies, good morning."

Jo, Penny, and Simone converged to where Autumn sat as Chief Walsh approached them. They expected some news about Bill Cunningham and what they may charge him with after the incident on the mountain.

"As you know, we brought Bill Cunningham back to the station the other day after the incident on the Timberline Trail. We charged him with carrying a weapon on state park land, but we released him since you dropped the charges for anything further." He sighed as they all took seats on the sofa and chairs.

"So you haven't found anything connecting him to my mother's death?" Jo gave him a confused look.

"I'm afraid not. We questioned him and searched his home but didn't find anything. He also has an alibi for the day of Lorna's death. Turns out, he went fishing with his brothers in the next town over at the lake. They all vouched for him, and the fishing shop on the lake also confirmed he was there. Looks like he's not the one we're looking for. I'm sorry." The Chief turned his hat in his hands as he met eyes with Jo.

"We appreciate your efforts, Chief. We had a feeling he didn't do it. Seems like he's caught up in some troubles at home that have him on edge." Penny spoke up, hoping to let the Chief know they understood.

"Well, we're not going to drop it. I've still got my son, Ben, and a couple of other officers looking into the facts of your mother's case. We'll find whoever did this, eventually. It's just a matter of time before the pieces come together." He stood up from his chair and started heading back to the door. "If you have any other insights or need anything in the meantime, just continue to call the station and ask for me or Ben, okay?"

Jo walked to the door to thank him and see him out as the others sat silently waiting.

"What now?" Jo asked as she made her way back to the sitting area.

"I don't think this surprised any of us, so it just means we're narrowing things down. After work today, I'll go over to the library archives for a little while to look at the family tree more. Maybe there's something there we didn't see the first time." Autumn stood up and walked to the large counter in the back to wash her tea mug out at the sink. "Don't wait for me for dinner tonight because after that there's a preservation meeting, and I plan to talk with Marion Bennett to get some more out of her."

"Autumn, you need to be careful. The protection spell wore off, and doing another one so soon could push the limits of the ancestral support we have. Find out what you can, but don't push it. We don't want another incident like this one on the mountain." Penny cared for her daughter deeply. Even though she had been gone for several years, a connection between them still existed, one she wanted to make even stronger now.

"Mom, I've taken care of myself just fine all these years. I'll be fine for today, too, but I won't push it. I know there's still someone out there who has it inside them to do harm, and that scares me. But if these last couple weeks taught me anything, it's that I am strong and capable of more than I think I can handle."

Penny looked at her daughter with pride and smiled. "You've grown into such an incredible woman. You should be very proud of yourself for the person you are."

"Okay, enough of this. I'll come by the house tonight after I've gone to the library and the meeting." Autumn motioned to Simone that they needed to get going.

"Oh yes, and we'll be getting things ready for when you arrive." Jo gave Simone a hug and headed to the door with them.

"Ready for what? I didn't have anything in my calendar for tonight." Autumn threw her hand-knit scarf around her neck and pulled her coat on as she asked.

"Oh, did we forget to tell you both? We've got all the materials we need for your magic lessons. The first one begins tonight as the full moon is in three days. It's the perfect energy to tap into your gifts and get connected to them, so make sure you're back at the house by eight o'clock. Don't be late!" Jo shooed them out the door just as a few customers trailed into the shop.

"Do you feel that they're ready?" Penny went over to the front window to watch the girls walk down to Parchment and Pine.

Jo welcomed the new customers and made her way to the window next to her sister. She leaned in and replied, "They're already being led down this path, and it's not for any of us to stop it now."

Autumn called Becca at the library's Genealogy department before leaving the shop that evening. By the time Autumn got to the library, Becca had the private archives open and ready for her. Autumn went straight for the drawings under the half-circle window, just as she and Simone did previously.

This time, she wanted to find evidence of what happened to the lost bloodline. It was becoming apparent that a connection existed between Gran's death and this branch, but nothing had come to light yet. She dug through the drawer to find the same torn family tree they saw before.

Autumn pulled the paper over to the large table in the center of the room and moved her hand over the names. Thomas Shaw's name sat on the topmost branch. Below him, the tree listed a few generations of children. At the very bottom, where the branches tapered off, two blank spaces sat without names. The only labels for that row of branches read, "Twin daughters, names unknown."

Autumn grabbed a tall stool beside the table and hoisted herself onto it just as she smelled a waft of saffron in the air. The same scent of mystery she sensed earlier. The smell overpowered her, and she leaned over to dig through her backpack for her water bottle. Autumn pulled it out of her bag and took a few big gulps to offset the intensity of the scent.

As she put the bottle back down on the table, it caught the strap of her bag and fell over onto the document. "Oh, no!" Autumn looked around furiously, trying to find a towel or something to wipe up the mess before it ruined the drawings. She scrambled over to the arched doorway where a few dustrags sat on a shelf.

Running back to the table, she mopped up the water as quickly as possible. "Good job, Autumn," she murmured to herself with frustration.

She flopped back down on the stool and squinted her eyes at the document. Something in the paper looked like it was coming to the surface now that it was wet. Autumn leaned in closely and ran her hand over it.

She whispered into the air, "Reveal the truth that lies beneath the surface."

Gasping with surprise, she saw a watermark appear that resembled the image of a bobcat. Autumn eyed the paper in disbelief as a rapping sound startled her at the window. Scraping its claws on the glass, a white owl appeared with wide eyes in the street's darkness. It brushed its wings against the window for a few seconds and then disappeared again into the evening.

Autumn stood in the middle of the room for a moment with confusion before rushing to grab everything on the table and stack it back into the drawer. She grabbed her things, flew across the hallway to wave goodbye to Becca, and swiftly left the library.

Checking her phone, she realized the preservation meeting started soon, giving her the perfect opportunity to find hints of a long-lost twin or a bobcat.

CHAPTER 25

Autumn rushed down Main Street from the library archives. She wanted to be on time for the preservation meeting, but her mind still reeled from her findings. Knowing now that a set of twins existed, she at least had a direction of something to look for, even if just a small clue.

Autumn crossed at the streetlight, thinking about the possibility that the twins also carried some magical genes. The more she discovered, the more questions came.

The light changed, allowing her to cross over to the block with the Forest Brew. She quickened her step toward the entrance and slid through the door as a gust of wind blew right behind her.

"Hold the door!" A shout came from behind her.

Autumn turned to see Marion Bennett following close behind her with a stack of boxes. She propped the door open with one arm and let Marion trail in.

"What's all this?" Autumn asked, eyeing the boxes.

"Well, we all have to do our part to run the events in this town." Marion walked to the back meeting room of the coffee shop as she replied. "I have many responsibilities that I take on diligently, and this one was for all the flyers and signage for the harvest market days. I'll be handing everything out to the business owners at the preservation meeting this evening."

"I see. Well, I can appreciate that. Here, let me help lighten the load." Autumn tried to take one box off the top of the pile, but Marion just turned her away.

"I have it, thank you. Just make sure nothing falls, would you?" Marion stood up taller and gave the impression she could do it all.

Autumn took this opportunity to question Marion. "I imagine you're busy with all you do at the chamber of commerce and at the preservation committee. How do you manage it all?"

Marion set the boxes down on a large table in the back room and let out a sigh. "Oh, managing isn't the proper word for it all. It's a duty that very few can properly handle."

"And you've had some differences of opinion with my grandmother about how to fulfill those duties. Possibly even wanting to handle them all yourself?"

Marion cleared her throat and stood up straight, walking around the table to find her seat near the head. "It's true. There's no secret about our differences of opinion, and I firmly believe this town needs to expand and grow to reach its full potential. No need to sugarcoat things. Development supports the town, and I, for one, am all about lifting this town higher."

"Well, that's an interesting perspective, especially from someone on the preservation committee." Autumn sat down beside her and kept prodding. "I find the town's roots to be strong as they are. We've weathered such significant challenges here in the mountain region, yet through it all, our community's tightness maintains our integrity. Expansion in the wrong direction could disrupt that balance, so it's important to preserve what we have going for us."

The mayor stood over the table and listened quietly to their conversation. He smiled at Autumn as she defended the town, just as Lorna did. "Autumn has some excellent points about the tightness of our community.

It's vital that we not get ahead of ourselves with this redevelopment. We have to preserve the strength and heritage of this town."

Autumn leaned in closer to Marion and lowered her voice. "Was it this latest development project not going to Charles Garrett that upset you?" She wanted to see Marion's reaction toward the developer and identify any resentment that could have led to Gran's death.

Marion jerked her head toward Autumn and pressed her lips together firmly. Autumn knew in an instant that Marion's thoughts were resentful, and a slight piercing scent of rotten eggs suddenly wafted into the room. She watched Marion trying to keep her composure at the table.

"It was." Marion placed her napkin in her lap and thought for a moment before speaking. "I'll have you know that it's not just me who thinks his development plan is a good idea. But your grandmother always got her way with any development in this town, and I, of course, got outvoted." She poured a glass of water and gulped it down.

"Is that why you wanted to take over our family's seat on the committee? You thought you could do a better job of running things than my grandmother? She was always... in the way." Autumn knew she was pushing hard, but she figured Marion wouldn't step too far out of line in a room full of people and risk a scene.

"Yes!" Marion blurted out. She looked around the table and cleared her throat. "Excuse me," she said to everyone and then resumed looking directly at Autumn. "What I meant was, yes, I felt I could do a better job for this committee. However, rules are rules, and the bylaws state the seat passes down through the founding families." She tilted her head with regret, "As I am not part of a founding family, I can only do my best to support this town in the duties I'm appointed for, which currently is not the ideal."

Autumn sat silently, almost feeling sorry for Marion somehow. She genuinely seemed to want to help this town, whereas earlier, Autumn assumed it was solely for her own personal gain. Yet, when Marion spoke, it appeared she really believed the town needed her to run things better. But she wasn't a founding family member, and she didn't understand the need for protection of the town's energy. Marion wasn't connected to it like the others who passed down their gifts through generations and kept the secrets of the land to ensure its preservation.

"I can see you're passionate about our town, Marion. But was that at the expense of my grandmother? Now that she is out of the way, things may be more convenient for you." Autumn had no idea where this brazenness came from, but she certainly didn't want to stop now. Somehow she felt her grandmother's boldness creeping up inside her, and she wanted to find out as much as she could. Her palms grew sweaty and at that moment, a flame ignited in her hand again.

Autumn pressed her palms together firmly under the table, just as she did at the first preservation meeting. Something about this place activated the fire energy she never knew she had. Autumn took a deep breath and tried to analyze Marion's expression and body language as best she could while still controlling the flames within her hands.

"I don't know what you're trying to imply, but I am most appalled. I may be a lot of things, but I would never stoop so low as to capitalize from someone's demise. We better just drop this and focus on the meeting starting in just a moment." Marion grabbed her purse from beside her chair and rummaged through it to pull out a paper and pen. She sighed and looked toward the mayor who was making the rounds and coming back to the head of the table.

Autumn stared at Marion for a moment and waited for some insight. Something told her Marion was telling the truth. No heaviness existed around her. The air felt clear and almost as though it contained a sense of relief. So, Autumn tried one more thing to verify her belief.

She brought her hands to her mouth and coughed into them several times. She sensed the flames dissipating slowly. With a calming breath, Autumn asked the ancestors to bring her wisdom with one remaining test.

Autumn smiled at the others now sitting at the table and addressed everyone. "I just love these images on the walls. They really represent our beautiful landscape here in the mountain region, don't you think? I wonder where exactly they were taken. You know, I would like to explore more of our area."

"Ah, yes!" The mayor said. "Our own Bill Cunningham took those, I believe. No idea where he got such great shots, but he works for the parks department, you know. Taking photographs for their tourist marketing. If you want to know more, I'm sure they could help you find him."

"Bill Cunningham, you say?" Marion interjected. "Well, that's a name I haven't heard in quite a while. I had no idea he did commercial photography now. My word, we could get him to do something for the chamber. Never mind all those plant photos! We need pictures of our businesses and events!" Marion's excitement level rose with the idea. The uneasiness melted away, and she grew intrigued with the possibilities. There was no reason to believe she hid any knowledge of those photos.

"All right then, everyone. Let's get this meeting started." The mayor raised his voice over all the other conversations.

Just as he began speaking, Autumn felt a shortness of breath. She gasped and put her hand over the locket at her chest. Its warmth got stronger with each breath, and with each faint hint of air she could take in, the scent of stinging nettle emerged. She felt someone lean in beside her.

"Those are foxglove flowers, you know. In the photos." Kennedy whispered in Autumn's ear.

Autumn felt a lump rising in her throat as she heard the words. She turned to face Kennedy and took the biggest breath she could. "Oh, really? You recognize them?"

Kennedy's long strawberry locks hung down on the side of her face to hide it from the others at the table. "Yes, actually. I've dabbled a bit with herbs and such in my baking, and well, I've come across it. You know I like to research." She shrugged at Autumn as if it was no big deal, but her eyes said differently.

Autumn tensed as a wind blew through the room from the front of the coffee shop and blew out all the candles lit along the center of the table.

"Oh, my!" Marion shrieked and jumped in her seat. "That was quite a wind."

"Below the surface, roots run deep." Voices whispered across the room as the locket burned against Autumn's skin now and the scent of nettles deepened.

She took a large drink of water and then met Kennedy's eyes. "Where did you say you originally came from again?"

"I didn't." Kennedy managed a small smirk. "But I'm here now, and that's what counts." Kennedy tossed her hair over her shoulder, picking at the food on her plate. "You know, Autumn," she whispered so as not to talk over the mayor at the front of the room. "I meant to double-check that you'd still help me bake this week for the market booth. You still have time to come by tomorrow night, don't you? I won't take up too much of your time, but I could really use your... extra set of hands."

The energy around Kennedy grew cloudy and dense. Why hadn't Autumn noticed this earlier? The air almost weighed her down now like a ton of bricks as she learned Kennedy knew about the foxgloves. Autumn spoke to her ancestors in her mind asking them to give her the strength to breathe through this and be strong for her family.

She rose from the table and caught her breath as she stood. "I'll be there at seven. The Winter House on Pine View, correct?"

Kennedy nodded as Autumn walked to the back wall and found James standing there. She stood beside him for the rest of the meeting, comforted by his calming and gentle energy. Autumn leaned in and put her hand on his arm. "Drive me home after the meeting?"

He saw the worry in her face and didn't hesitate. "Of course. Whatever you need."

Autumn wanted to hug him and bury her head into his shoulder, but she knew Kennedy was watching for her reaction and didn't want to offer any sign of fear.

CHAPTER 26

James opened the door to the Forest Brew and let Autumn out. The crisp air hitting her face gave her just what she needed after the meeting. It invigorated her energy and revived her from the tightness she experienced in the meeting room. Autumn wrapped her knit scarf loosely around her neck to let in more air when she heard a familiar sound.

"Meow." Around Autumn's ankles, she found Tavish circling and looking up at her.

"Tavish? How did you get over here? You're a sneaky one, aren't you?" She bent down and picked him up, holding him close into her jacket as she walked down the street with James. "I'm really glad to see you, though. You must have known I would need a few snuggles after what I discovered, huh?"

James kept walking with her in silence until they reached his charcoal gray pickup truck that seemed to blend in with the night. He opened the door for Autumn and Tavish and moved around to the driver's side.

"So, do you wanna talk about what happened?" He sat for a moment waiting for a reply before starting the truck.

"Just drive me to my grandmother's house, and we can talk, okay?" She snuggled Tavish into her lap, and they headed out.

"Autumn, I'm worried about you. I had that dream again. The one where I stood over a glowing necklace with you, and I tried to protect you from something. And now you're acting strange. What's going on?"

Autumn rubbed Tavish's ears to calm her down enough to talk to James. "I know who killed my grandmother. I'm sure of it now." She swallowed hard and closed her eyes, telling herself she could trust him. Then, she pulled out her grandmother's locket from inside her coat. "And the locket you've dreamt glows around my neck whenever I get closer to an important clue."

He turned to face her for a moment and noticed her holding the antique locket. "So, it really glows? How is that possible?"

The car turned down the long tree-lined road that approached Gran's house. It was dark, and all the street lights faded behind them. James continued down the road and pulled up in front of the cottage to park the truck.

"Let's take a walk," Autumn said gently, as she opened the door and put Tavish down on the ground.

She headed for the path into the woods as Tavish, and James followed. They watched her intently as she moved easily through the leaves and fallen branches in the dark like she knew every inch of this land in her mind.

"I know these woods," James called as he caught up to her. "My mother lives just on the other side of them in the next town over. I used to walk through here all the time when I needed a few moments to myself. It helped me clear my head, and I would usually leave little piles of huckleberries from my mother's bushes at points along the path as a thank you to the forest."

Autumn slowed her pace and glanced at him. "That was you leaving the berries? I always wondered where those came from." She smiled as she watched her boots hitting the ground with each step. "If you hadn't noticed already, this is my sanctuary, too. I connect with the elements here, and it grounds me to be in this space. There's just something about it that's always captivated me."

Tavish ran ahead to the clearing in the trees and found himself a pile of leaves to lie down in. Autumn and James met Tavish and found a large log to sit on as they spoke.

"You asked what happened. At the meeting tonight, I wanted to get more information to find out who killed my grandmother. I asked questions, but it turns out it wasn't who I thought it was at all. The actual killer revealed herself to me by just rubbing it in my face. She wanted me to know she did it without really saying it."

"She? Who was it?" James's voice sounded patient and calm as he asked.

"Kennedy. She just sat there next to me talking about the photos on the wall, which clearly depict the poisonous plant that killed my grandmother. Then she asked me over to help her bake tomorrow. It must be some kind of game to her!"

Tavish stood up from the leaf pile and arched his back before heading out to the middle of the clearing. He looked back at Autumn to ask if she was coming with, so she went to him in the center of the tree circle.

"Kennedy..."James looked shocked while saying her name. "What do you mean she invited you over tomorrow? And how do you know it was her?" He gradually made his way to the center of the clearing as well.

"Because she knew all about the plant, and she spoke like she had other secrets she didn't want to say but was amused by them. She did it. I just have to figure out why and how to prove it."

"All right, let's take this one step at a time. Assuming she killed your grandmother, why would you go over there? We need to notify the police and let them deal with her. I don't want you getting hurt."

"James," Autumn said as she knelt down to grab a handful of dirt from the ground. She stood up and blew the dirt particles into the air in front of her. They separated and immediately suspended in the air frozen in time.

"I'm a witch. If anyone can figure out what's happened and reset the balance disturbed here, it'll be me." She walked in a circle around him and Tavish, tracing a line on the ground with her foot. "I got scared tonight after finding out some things about my family and then talking with Kennedy. And I'm still scared of what may be coming. But I know this is part of my path, and I'm supposed to walk it."

He looked at her in awe, not because she was a witch but because she was stepping into her power.

"I knew you were a witch, Autumn. My mother taught me about our heritage here in the mountain region and the storm that raged through the landscape causing the floods, landslides, and even fires. I learned of the people who remained here to care for the lands. From what I've been told, it was your ancestor who transferred the power of the land, sea, and sky to the founding families."

"It was. You knew that?" He nodded as she stopped to close the circle she traced on the ground and reached out a hand for him to grab.

"My family belongs to the line of founders, although my immediate family is somewhat removed. As you already know, my mother handed down her gifts for predictive dreaming to me, but we've guarded those gifts closely over the years. Still, she taught me about the heritage here, and I knew one day I would find out more about it. Seems that may be now."

They held each other's hands in the center of the circle Autumn drew, and Tavish sat between their feet. The winds howled around them, and the trees danced just for them.

"I can feel the air and the earth within me." She closed her eyes and whispered something under her breath. A fire sparked on the ground beside Tavish, and the cat eased his paws back to give it space to grow larger.

"The elements asked me to reset the balance, to uncover the shadows that lie beneath the surface, and to reestablish the bloodline that has broken." Autumn opened her eyes to see James in front of her. He clasped her hands and never wanted to let go.

The fire flared, and the winds blew sparks around them. The sparks turned into tiny magical lights jetting through the air. Autumn sensed that James added to her magic, but she didn't understand how. Maybe he added a deeper flavor to it. Regardless, she liked how she felt when he was around.

Autumn took a deep breath and released it slowly. With her exhale, the wind blew through and snuffed out the fire in an instant. Tavish shook his tail and stomped his feet to say this was his witch, and she made him proud.

James dropped his hands from Autumn and looked around the woods for a moment as everything died down. "Okay, that was intense." He nodded his head up and down and squinted to see through the darkness now. "Maybe you are ready to handle whatever Kennedy's doing." His eyes met hers as he continued, "Not that I want you to, but it seems you could probably hold your own if you had to."

Autumn smiled sheepishly and glanced at the ground. "I'm getting there. My grandmother left me some big shoes to fill, but I'm slowly building up my confidence. I don't completely know what I'm getting into, but I can feel her with me. So, now I need to confront Kennedy and see what information I can get out of her." Autumn picked up Tavish, and she swept the circle on the ground clear with the bottom of her boot.

"I wish you wouldn't put yourself in harm's way, especially with the dream that I'm worried will come true. But if you still wanna meet her tomorrow, then at least let me be close by in case you need help."

Autumn rubbed her palms together and closed her eyes for a moment. A small flame appeared in her hand and illuminated the woods for them. She grabbed James's hand with her free one and led the way back up the path to the cottage.

As they reached James's truck parked out front, she brought her hands up to her mouth and blew out the flame. Now that she had done it a couple times, she had gotten the hang of it.

"I forgot I'm supposed to be meeting my family tonight. I'm so exhausted, but I know they'll want to hear all that's happened today." Autumn rubbed her forehead. "I better head over there."

"Let me drop you off then. You shouldn't drive yourself now, and it'll make me feel better to know you're safe."

Autumn thought for a moment. She didn't want to put James out anymore, even though she wanted as much of his company as she could get. "All right, but only because I'm tired and could use more company."

"Right, absolutely. Hop in."

She and Tavish wandered over to his car and hopped into the passenger side. James drove them over to Jo's house as Autumn tried to keep her eyelids from closing on the way. Once they arrived, he walked her to the door just as Aunt Jo opened it.

"Finally!" She exclaimed. "We expected you an hour ago. Where have you been?" She turned to see James next to Autumn. "Oh, James! My goodness, I didn't see you there! Please, come in. Did you bring Autumn home from the preservation meeting?" Jo wondered if they had gotten closer than Autumn shared.

"Yes, sorry if she's late. Some unexpected things came up, which I'm sure Autumn will share with you. I better get going for now, though. Autumn, remember what I said. If you need anything, I'll be right here." James put his hand on Autumn's arm and gave Tavish a head scratch before turning back to his car. "Goodnight, Ms. MacKinnon."

"Goodnight, dear. Tell your mother I'll talk to her soon." Jo turned to look at Autumn, who was slowly making her way inside the house. "Good grief! You look exhausted. I'm not sure you're in any condition to practice your magic this evening. What's happened?"

Penny and Simone joined them in the front entry, and Autumn put Tavish down and dropped her things. She sighed as she sat on the bench beside the stairs.

"I know who did it." Autumn looked up at them all staring at her. "And I'm expected at her house tomorrow afternoon." They all looked at each other in surprise.

"The question is," she went on while taking off her boots. "Will I be able to find proof of what my mind tells me is true?"

CHAPTER 27

"**C**ome on, girls! Try to keep up!" Jo yelled back to them as she and Penny went down the winding dirt path to the river behind Jo's house.

The sun had just risen over the trees. Since Autumn felt too exhausted the night before to work through their magic lesson, Jo and Penny led the girls to the river first thing in the morning to get the lesson underway. Now that Autumn sensed Kennedy was the killer, there was no time to waste, as she'd be putting herself in harm's way to find out more.

"Mom, slow down. We've got a couple of hours before we need to open the shops. There's no reason to go so fast." Simone did her best to keep up, but she barely had a cup of her favorite cinnamon latte in her that morning.

They made it to the river, and Jo and Penny set up a small ritual space alongside the river's edge. The water flowed smoothly and crisply that morning, just like the air. It provided the perfect foundation for Autumn and Simone to work on their gifts.

"All right, then. Let's all stand in a line here at the water's edge. Hold hands and take a few cleansing breaths." Jo lived for this. The water spoke to her in ways that gave her soul expression, and everything she did was tied to the water.

They all did as Jo instructed and then released hands. Tavish meowed behind them as he made his way down the path. He never could resist being part of the magic.

"Come here, Tav. You can be part of the fun, too." Autumn scooped him up and placed him on a nearby boulder with a flattened top. "There, that's a good spot for you."

"Autumn, why don't you go first, seeing as how you've got a more pressing afternoon ahead of you." Penny gave her daughter a long white feather with gray stripes on it. "Our ancestors foraged this feather from the mountains. It's said to have the spirit of the boreal mountain owl within it."

Autumn stroked the feather through her fingertips. "It's beautiful. I've never seen it before."

Penny smiled at her. "That's because I kept it for you. I know I've been absent, but I knew I would give you a few things someday. Your gran and I discussed I would be the one to hand them down to you when the time was right. This is one of those things. I kept it in the mountains with me as I've done my healing work so it would more strongly preserve the energy within it. Now, it's time for you to have it."

"Thank you," Autumn replied, trying to hold back a tear forming in the corner of her eye. She knew her mother never intended to leave for so long and that she was called to use her gifts. Autumn realized how much of a burden and a sacrifice that must have been for her.

"Now, first we need to practice your connection to the air element. We don't need to cast a circle this morning since we'll be working individually. But I want you each to keep the intention of positive, supportive energy surrounding you as you perform your magic. That will ward off any negative energies."

Autumn and Simone both nodded that they understood and moved closer to one another as the lesson began.

"Autumn, you've shown since childhood that air holds your greatest strength, so let's use that to our advantage. Try to call on the birds of the air. Get one to come to you and whisper a message to it to carry on the air to one of us." Jo took a step back to give Autumn some space.

She closed her eyes and placed a thought in her mind. The breeze blew around them and kicked up Aunt Jo's dress. She held it down with her arms as she watched Autumn intently.

Then, sailing on the wind itself, a mountain blue jay swooped down in front of them and landed directly on Penny's shoulder. Tavish jumped up abruptly from the boulder he had been lying on to follow the bird. Penny stood as still as possible, eyeing the bird in amazement. The air brushed across pieces of Penny's hair that stood out from her bun, and the bird bobbed up and down for a moment.

Penny heard a faint whisper in the wind saying, "I'm thankful you're here." Then, the bird fluttered back up into the air and out of sight into the evergreens that lined the other side of the river.

Penny smiled at her daughter with pride in her eyes. "I'm thankful, too." She walked over and held Autumn's hands for a moment. "Well done. The jay bird connected with your intention, and you willed it to listen. That was a fine start."

"Perfect. Let's move on then to something that takes more control, shall we?" Jo waved everyone back from Autumn. "You've levitated a couple of times now, presumably when you've felt some powerful emotions and intentions. It happened because your mind tried to take over for your heart. You mustn't be afraid of your heart, my dear. Allow the two to work in harmony with each other. Embrace your feelings and use them to your advantage with your mind."

Autumn gave her a quizzical look. "How am I supposed to do that?"

Jo cleared her throat and sighed slightly. "Let go. Let the feelings flow naturally like water, and the thoughts will arise in parallel to them. This is how you trust your intuition more, just as I remember Gran teaching you with the messages you write on your cards and paper products. Trust what comes to mind, but let it follow the heart."

"Okay, so how do I start?" Autumn shrugged her shoulders and gave them all a blank stare.

"Think of something that's bothering you. This whole thing with Gran works. Let the emotion arise without fear, and then allow your thoughts to guide you. Don't control whatever happens at first, just embrace it and then set intentions in your mind for what you want to achieve." Penny's voice gave Autumn a sense of confirmation that this was all possible.

"Okay, here I go." Autumn closed her eyes and remembered her encounter with Kennedy at the preservation meeting the other day. The tension built inside her. Autumn's muscles tightened, and her body grew stiff. The surrounding air turned dense, and clouds formed overhead. The trees shook with rage, and Autumn slowly hovered off the ground.

"She's doing it," Simone whispered.

Autumn's long auburn locks swirled around her, and she rose another foot into the air. The locket around her neck glowed with the bright emerald green color she grew familiar with these past few weeks. Jo, Penny, and Simone locked arms as they stood looking up at Autumn in the air. The winds circled furiously around them all, and Tavish ran to sit underneath Autumn on the ground.

She opened her eyes and spoke out loud. "Let this raging wind inside me channel into justice. Bring the mysteries to light and the hurtful intentions to be revealed. Winds of the mountains, hear my call. Flow through me with insight and reason." A whistling noise passed through the intense air. "Sail through the town and pick up what you may and send it back to me on this same day."

Autumn clutched the locket in her hand as the wind furiously howled and rushed through the trees, making its way toward the center of town.

She took a deep breath in, and with an exhale, she lowered back to the ground.

Aunt Jo stood frozen, tightly clasping a clear quartz crystal she brought with her. "Oh, my dear. I wish I had seen the power in you sooner, but no matter now. You're finally claiming your birthright." She turned to Simone and took hold of both their hands. "And now, Simone, it's time for you as well."

Simone pressed her lips together tightly and turned to Autumn. "If you're ready, I'm ready." She stepped back from all of them and took a deep breath. "Where should I start?"

"We know you take after me with water, and you've shown quite a gift with controlling the weather as of late. Let's see if you can work with a body of water like the river here." Jo and Penny moved to the side so Simone could see the water clearly. "The water is smooth now, but what if you drove it forward with great strength? Allow it to crash into that boulder over there in the middle. Use your passion to activate it, and then control your emotion to let it subside."

"Right. I've got this." Simone shook out her arms and stretched her neck from side to side. She spread her fingers apart and pressed them into the air slightly at her sides. Then, she swayed them back and forth, almost in a serpent-like motion through the air.

"Strength of the waters carry my intention. Flow with the passion of many moons. Let your rapids move swiftly through and pummel the stone with my motion and cue."

Simone continued to move her entire body back and forth now, snaking it around as her hands pushed through the air. They could each hear the water rising in the distance. In the river's flow, white peaks rose on the edges of the waves. Simone threw her hands to the side, and a rapid crashed against the large boulder in the middle of the water.

Instantly, a slight crack took shape on the face of the rock. Jo squinted to look at it while the waves continued to roll around it. Simone slowed her arm movements down and gave a quiet shushing sound under her breath. The waters eased up and subsided as Simone stood still. Now, the waters only babbled and gently hit the river's edge.

Autumn covered her mouth with her hand and widened her eyes at her cousin. "You did that! That was incredible! Did you see the boulder cracked? Amazing."

Simone shrugged. "I guess I got into it, what can I say?"

"Girls, you must also know your powers grow stronger when you're together. That is the four-points energy at work. Autumn serves as the linchpin to all the elements, so she will elevate whatever you activate within yourself and vice versa. If you are near her while she activates the energy you possess, she will also have a greater amount of force behind her magical workings." Jo smiled at the girls as she placed the clear quartz crystal on the ground between them.

"I think it's prudent if Simone accompanied you to Kennedy's house later today. That way you have the strength of both of you in case something arises." Jo looked over at Penny for confirmation.

"Yes, I agree." Penny gave them all a serious look. "Go together and act like you're just bringing Simone along as an extra set of helping hands. Kennedy won't be able to turn that down. We'll notify Chief Walsh today that we suspect Kennedy so they can start looking into her. But I know Jo and I both will feel a lot better about you heading over there if you go together."

"Keep your phones with you at all times. You should have a signal at her home in town, so that shouldn't be an issue. Look for any clues she may have left lying around. Find anything about where she came from, her motive, or something tying her to your gran." Jo shoved her chilled hands into the side pockets of her evergreen-colored wool cape.

"It's getting chilly out here, and it's almost time to open the shops. Quick, huddle in close and we'll give thanks." they all moved tighter toward each other in a circle. Tavish snuggled up next to Autumn's leg and sat beside her feet.

"Elements of the land, sea, and sky, thank you for the gifts you channel through us with intention. We ask that you remain a powerful presence with these girls as they reset the balance of life. As I say it, so shall it be." Jo watched as the locket around Autumn's neck flickered with light at her words.

"That was a good session today, girls. Now, let's get some good customers in today, and we'll take the afternoon one step at a time." Penny gathered the items they brought and started moving up the path toward Jo's house again.

Simone nudged Autumn with her elbow. "Let's just hope those winds you send through town reveal some key information today."

Autumn shared a worried look with Simone before they followed closely behind Penny and Jo. Learning to control her emerging gifts felt like the straightforward part. Her confidence level was another story, though, and Autumn wondered how much confidence she'd actually have when she needed it most.

CHAPTER 28

Simone pulled her SUV along the front curb outside Kennedy's house and let the engine run for another minute.

"Ready for this?" Simone looked Autumn over to see how she was feeling.

"Yeah, I think I'm good. I just need to remember to breathe." Autumn inhaled through her nose and blew it out with a whistle through her mouth.

"Our moms have Chief Walsh on speed dial if they sense anything going wrong, and it sounded like James is on standby, too. But you know what?" Simone gave Autumn a confident smile. "We were made for this. We're elemental witches, and if the last couple of weeks have taught me anything, it's that we're pretty powerful together. So let's go in there and show this chick who she's messing with."

Autumn laughed nervously and nodded. "Okay, let me do a little mantra to add some power to our words before we head in." Simone sat back as Autumn closed her eyes and concentrated.

"We, powerful witches, protect these lands and channel the elements as a force for good." Autumn spoke the mantra once, and then Simone chimed in with the same words.

"We, powerful witches, protect these lands and channel the elements as a force for good."

They joined hands in saying the mantra one last time to make the power of three.

Autumn opened her eyes and smiled. "I'm ready."

The girls opened the car doors and gathered a few materials they had brought since they were supposed to help bake. Autumn led the way up the sidewalk to the front door just as her necklace grew hotter against her skin. As she stopped in her tracks, she heard an owl nearby in a tree.

"An owl," she noted. "The symbol of insight and bringing knowledge out of the shadows. We had better be on our toes." Autumn walked toward the front porch as the wind picked up, blowing the bags around that they carried.

"The truth lies in the details." A whisper came through the wind.

"What is it? Something in the air?" Simone leaned closer to Autumn and placed a hand on her shoulder.

"The ancestors spoke again. Pay attention to details now. Search for any clues you can find once we go inside."

Simone nodded and looked out into the dark trees behind them before Autumn rang the doorbell.

"You made it." Kennedy opened the door with a sly smile. "And I see you brought... your cousin, right? Simone, is it?" She pulled the door open wider to let them both in.

"Yes, this is my cousin, Simone. She runs the shop with me, remember?" Autumn stepped to the side to let Simone come forward.

"Autumn thought you could use some extra baking hands, so I came along, too. You never know if you'll need some extra support." Simone looked straight-faced at Kennedy and passed over her coat.

"Well, you'll be saving me the trouble... with baking on my own, I mean." Kennedy laid their coats on the arm of the couch and waved them in. "Why don't you both follow me into the kitchen?"

They worked their way around the living room and into the open-plan kitchen directly behind it. A large square island sat in the middle of the room where Kennedy laid out a few baking tools and ingredients.

"We'll be making mince pies and shortbread cookies with jam filling for my market booth. Of course, I don't make the traditional meat filling, so it'll just be apples and currants." Kennedy pointed out a few items on the counter.

"Are you of Scottish ancestry? We're always so fascinated around here by people's heritage." Autumn tried to bring this up as nonchalantly as possible.

Kennedy smirked, "Actually, that was a reason for my research here. I'm a cultural anthropologist by education, and I guess I've veered into Celtic mythological beliefs and practices more, mostly because of my heritage." She opened a recipe book and passed it across the island to them as she spoke. "I'm fascinated by the history here. How there have been several Scottish families rooted here for some time, not to mention the incredible stories handed down. It's quite intriguing, but I'm sure you've both heard many stories having grown up here."

"I don't think you could stay for any amount of time without hearing some kind of story. Every community has their stories, though." Simone measured the filling ingredients for some of the mince pies and placed them into a large glass bowl as she monitored Kennedy.

"Exactly, people here love the history and the stories. It's just part of the charm here." Autumn pushed it off like nothing more than entertainment, while deep down, she knew now more than ever the stories were true.

"So you have Celtic heritage then? What kind?" Autumn made her way around to the other side of the island and grabbed a couple of apples to peel.

Kennedy rolled out a large circle of pie dough on a marble slab while continuing. "My family is Scottish, you're right. I was only raised with some traditions. I pieced others together over the years, but it wasn't the same as being immersed in it."

Autumn began sweating as Kennedy described her childhood. The broken branch of the family tree came to her mind, and she couldn't shake the idea that this was the missing piece. She pushed the arms of her sweater up to cool down, but the heat just got more intense by the minute.

She made herself look busy and found a nearby garbage can to throw some of the apple peels into. Pressing her foot firmly down on the petal to raise the lid, Autumn noticed something familiar inside the can before sliding the peels into it.

A burnt pile of paper lanterns Autumn recognized from her shop sat right on top. Only about a quarter of the lanterns remained with charred edges. Kennedy had purchased them at the shop just days ago, but they were now destroyed, perhaps intentionally.

Autumn quickly brushed the pile of apple peels over the top of them and returned to the kitchen island. She grabbed the glass bowl that Simone was using to combine filling ingredients and threw the apples in, giving Simone a look of concern as she did so.

"So, do you have any other close family, or is it just you?" Autumn looked over at Kennedy cutting the pie dough into small circles.

Kennedy continued placing the dough circles into a muffin tin to line each cup. "We've mostly lost touch over the years. I keep to myself since work is my life, but I see my sister now and again."

"It's a shame you've lost touch, but I've found family to always be there for one another." Simone's voice had an undertone of seriousness to it.

Kennedy came over to Simone to inspect the filling ingredients and stir the bowl. "Yes, well, that may be. I haven't found that to always be true in my case, but who knows? Maybe there'll be something to be said for being blood after all."

Simone's hands grew clammy with Kennedy's words, and she took a step back to create some separation for a moment. She wiped her hands on a kitchen towel nearby, but an overheated feeling crept over Simone just as it had Autumn.

On the other side of the island, Autumn glanced through the ingredient list and made her way to a rack of spices on the wall. She picked through the jars with her finger and let her eyes drift over the labels to find what she needed. One unlabeled jar caught her eye in the back. She nudged another out of the way and squinted her eyes at the familiar leaves inside it. She recognized the oval shape with a small, toothed edge—foxgloves.

Autumn swallowed hard as her ears rang. She glanced at the other jars on the shelf and noticed a larger one labeled stinging nettle, as in the scent she picked up the other day. Her heartbeat got faster by the second.

"Autumn, why don't you bring the cloves and nutmeg off the shelf? We could use those next." Kennedy eyed Autumn as she stood in front of the spices.

She found the requests as fast as she could and returned to the island, thinking of how she might send a message from her phone.

"See anything else interesting over there?" Kennedy questioned as she took the spice jars from Autumn.

Autumn's body tensed, and she sensed sparks in her hands. "Oh no, I was just looking for these," she raised her eyebrows and pointed at the cloves and nutmeg.

Kennedy brought a small mortar bowl from a lower cabinet and opened the clove jar. She grabbed a few cloves from the jar and rubbed them between her fingers, dropping them slowly into the mortar. She whispered under her breath as she grasped the bowl on either side.

Autumn saw the bowl glow in Kennedy's hands, and she looked up to meet Autumn's eyes.

"Runs in the family, doesn't it?" Kennedy said with a slight upturn to her lips.

Autumn's stomach tightened as she glanced at Simone and realized they weren't the only two witches in the room.

CHAPTER 29

Kennedy eyed the girls as something made its way alongside the kitchen cabinets toward her. Autumn looked down at the shadowy figure emerging from behind the kitchen island to find a bobcat sauntering up beside Kennedy's leg.

The house shook around them, and there was an unevenness under their feet.

"I really have to hand it to you for all that sleuthing you were doing, Autumn. Although I knew you were an air witch, you're much more clever than I imagined." Kennedy directed the bobcat to move closer to Autumn. It growled at her slightly while shifting forward.

"So you are related to us? The part of our family that was lost over the years." Autumn needed to get more information out of Kennedy now that this was coming out in the open.

"Well, lost isn't quite true. We were... abandoned. Your great-great-grandmother had an affair with the man who raised their daughter, who was my great-grandmother. After they split, she no longer existed to your side of the family. Even though we separated, we still had the Celtic witch's blood in us. Your great-great-grandmother's blood. That meant the elements passed through our side of the family as well. It just happened that they developed differently in my branch, and we never had the rightful place of being the guardians of these lands. In fact, we had no status, no purpose, and no direction."

"That's what you wanted? Status here in the mountain region?" Simone interjected with frustration, as she steadied herself next to an island bar stool while the bobcat continued to growl.

The ground began bursting at the seams below them now, and Simone felt the deep red energy surrounding them. Her own emotions boiled up, and a crash of thunder sounded outside the house and sounds of rain followed.

Kennedy looked up to the ceiling and smiled. "Not exactly, but I intend to reclaim our rightful place as witches that command the four elements in this region. It's the place we should have had all along, and that's why I needed that necklace of your grandmother's, and the spell book, although I couldn't find it. Of course, I knew she wouldn't just hand them over, with them being ancestral heirlooms and all. She needed some... convincing, and still she refused. Even after she died, I couldn't remove the necklace from her cold, lifeless skin. And then, I found you clutching your neck at the preservation meeting, covering it up under your scarves. I knew if I could appeal to your eagerness to help, then I could get you here to hand it over, which is what you're going to do right now."

Kennedy stepped forward with a smile. "Feeling a little hot, are we? When I saw those paper lanterns in your shop, I knew I could use those to do a little of my own magic. See, I'm an earth witch, but I also have a small amount of fire in me. So the wood from the paper and a nudge from some fire did the trick to get you both feeling a little off while you were here."

Light-headed but intent on overpowering Kennedy, Autumn took a deep breath and focused on her connection with the fire element. The heat rose in Autumn's hands and a spark ignited in one palm. She threw the flame down onto a kitchen towel on the island. It flashed up into a massive fire right in front of Kennedy, who stumbled back to get out of the way.

The flames astonished and confused her, as she only expected Autumn to carry the power of air energy with her.

Autumn and Simone rushed into the living room away from the fire, and Simone grabbed her phone to text her mother.

"Not so fast. Get over there underneath the chandelier." Kennedy made a noise and signaled the bobcat to corner them in the living room. "There's going to be a big earthquake this evening. And you both are going to be pinned under all the rubble that comes down on top of you. Sadly, you'll lose your necklace in all of this, and your lives as well."

Autumn slowly inched over to the center of the room. She took a deep breath in and called to the ancestors for their strength and guidance. Then, she whispered to herself, "I feel my fear, and I own my power." She blew out her breath. "Owl of the night, let help appear in my sight."

The wind howled ferociously outside, and something flapped against the large front window beside the girls. All three of them turned to see the wings of a white owl outstretched as it fluttered against the windowpane in the wind. The trees scratched the glass, and rain pummeled the window.

Simone swayed her hands around at her sides and called upon the water. "Rain, flow swifter than a hundred rivers. Flow with force, flow with strength." She mouthed the words to herself.

"Looks like you're just adding to the intensity of this storm. It'll be perfectly believable that you both didn't make it through, sadly, but I will."

Autumn's mind told her to look at the French doors rattling in the wind behind Kennedy in the dining room. Through the battering rain, Autumn glimpsed James standing there peering inside. Break the glass, she said to herself. Autumn imagined the whistling winds of a tornado barreling through, and she turned to give Simone a look suggesting she was ready to use her full power.

Autumn's hair raised up and swirled around her. Her feet left the floor as the energy swiftly coursed through her body. Kennedy stared at her in disbelief and then pushed the bobcat at the girls. A jolting burst of hundred-mile an hour wind shattered the windows of the house, and the sound of thunder clapped directly above them. The chandelier swayed and pulled away from the ceiling.

Simone ducked down on the ground and covered her head. Glass flew at Kennedy from the windows and the chandelier breaking on the ground, and she waved her arms around furiously. James burst through the broken French doors at the back and tackled Kennedy to the ground. He held her down firmly with his arms and legs wrapped around her tightly. Autumn sent a raging wind through the living room that pulled the couch over on its side and pinned the bobcat down underneath it.

"You found the four energies after all," Autumn said calmly as she pulled the glowing locket out from beneath her sweater. "Turns out, they just respond to anger and resentment with protection and strength. As long as you have this anger in your heart, you'll never command them."

One more powerful gust of rain blew through the broken windows as Simone pulled herself up off the ground. Sirens blared in the distance, coming closer with each sound. Autumn closed her eyes and slowly lowered to the ground with an exhaled breath.

Simone ran to the front door as several officers came through, guns raised. They saw James holding Kennedy on the ground and hurried toward them, relieving James of his restraining duty. He pushed himself back on the floor when Autumn came to his side.

"Are you all right?" She looked at him with worry in her eyes.

"Yeah, are you?" He put his hands on her shoulders and looked her up and down.

"I think so." She said, trying to catch her breath after the adrenaline rush. "I just... can't believe you were there."

The officers rustled Kennedy to her feet as she argued with them and then took one more lunge toward Autumn.

"You don't deserve that necklace!" Kennedy screamed. She tried pulling her hands free from the officers to make one last attempt to snatch the locket off Autumn's neck.

James threw his arms up in front of Autumn to block her from Kennedy just as the white owl flew into the room over Autumn's head. It clawed at Kennedy's face and hair as she backed away and screamed. The officers got their bearings, and the owl flew away. They pulled Kennedy up, cuffing her wrists behind her back and dragging her out to the squad car.

"Be careful, there's a bobcat under the couch over there! You better call animal control to come get it." Simone pointed some officers in the cat's direction, but when they crossed the living room to look, there was no sign of it. Somehow, the cat found a way out at the end of the storm and disappeared.

Chief Walsh entered the door and found Autumn, James, and Simone gathered beside one another. "Well, this has been an eventful evening. Is everyone all right?"

They nodded, and Autumn picked herself up off the floor. "How did you know to come here?"

The Chief smiled at her. "I always listen when your Aunt Jo suggests I do something. She has some kind of effect on me, I suppose." Simone and Autumn both smiled and glanced at each other with knowing.

"Chief, I found a jar of the foxglove leaves in the kitchen on the shelves. Kennedy admitted to killing my grandmother. Turns out, she's actually related to us, and she resented her side of the family being abandoned. She wanted revenge along with... some special heirlooms that she tried to steal, but my grandmother wouldn't let her."

The Chief cleared his throat. "I see. We've already verified her relation to you. Kennedy's sister came into the station a few days ago and notified us that she may cause trouble. She tipped us off with some library archives, so we've actually been following Kennedy, too. Looks like we were just a few steps behind you."

"Sister, huh? She didn't mention a sister to us." Simone stepped into the kitchen along with James to follow the conversation.

"Yes, uh, fraternal twins. I believe she said her name was Lainy. She may still be around town if I had to guess, and it seemed to me like she was a better seed than her sister turned out to be." The Chief roamed the kitchen, eyeing the scene and looking for the evidence Autumn had suggested. "Why don't you all step outside and get checked out by the ambulance? We had quite a storm, but I imagine it's all done now." The Chief looked at the girls with a hint of questioning in his gaze.

James stretched his arms out around both Autumn and Simone. "Thank you, Chief. I'll go outside with them."

The three of them stepped out onto the front porch and heard a meow below them. Autumn looked down to find Tavish licking his paws next to the porch railing.

"Tavish! What in the world? Cat, you must be the most courageous little guy ever! How did you get all the way over here in that storm?" Autumn picked him up and snuggled him into her neck. "Thank you for finding us," she whispered into his ear.

James shook his head in relief. "Let's head over to that ambulance and get you both checked out."

As they walked across the wet grass to the ambulance sitting at the curb, Autumn grabbed James's hand. "You were right about all of it." She stopped and turned toward him. "About your dream, and you being here to protect me. I can't believe you came. I was so scared."

He brushed a strand of hair away from her face. "I told you, Autumn. I'm here for you, and I'm not gonna shy away no matter how serious things get, okay? This is where I belong."

She nodded and gave him a gentle smile. "Okay, I get it. You're not going away, and you're not spooked by your dreams. Just promise me one thing?"

"What's that?" His grayish-blue eyes sparkled in the moonlight.

"You'll let me look out for you, too."

CHAPTER 30

Simone pulled out another basket full of calendars for the new year and placed them out front on the Parchment and Pine market table. The market was supposed to begin in about ten minutes, and the girls had most things in place around their cozy tent wrapped with hanging flannels, inviting bunting flags, and gorgeous paper lanterns hanging from above. They also displayed their latest collection of calendars, paper products, and journals inspired by the mountains to set the perfect tone for the upcoming cold season.

"These look so good, Simone! Thank you for doing the amazing evergreen designs on all the pages. All the customers are going to love them!" Autumn gave her cousin a big hug, and Simone rolled her eyes while fighting a smile.

"You're the one that makes these so special with the monthly fortunes that fit the recipient perfectly. Remember the last one where the mayor came in and personally thanked you for the one he gave his wife? Somehow it said exactly what she needed to hear from him. You're incredible." Simone pulled a folding chair up to the table display and sat down with a sigh.

"I just can't believe how these last couple of weeks have gone. Now that we've wrapped up this investigation and Gran's memorial is tomorrow, I feel like everything is going to be completely different." Autumn sat beside Simone on another folding chair.

"Of course it is!" Simone insisted. Autumn looked at her wide-eyed as Simone put a throw pillow behind her in the chair. "We have shoes to fill now, and that means we're not meant to just sit idly by and look after the shop anymore. The town needs us, and we need to be prepared for whatever comes. Not to mention, we've gotta start recruiting for the spots to be filled in our little coven." Simone laughed to herself excitedly. "I don't know about you, but I'm all about diving deep into this coven thing. I mean, I usually like to hang solo if not with you, but the idea of a full coven sounds pretty amazing."

Autumn started cracking up at Simone and covering her mouth with her hand. "You're hilarious, you know. But you're right, we need to complete the circle, and I'd actually like to work on that today if possible."

Simone agreed and then turned to face the people arriving at the market. Her eyes caught a man in the crowd, and as he noticed Simone, the man nudged his wife to follow him.

"Oh no," she sighed. "This should be interesting." Simone grabbed Autumn's elbow as if to get her to do something.

"What are you doing?" Autumn asked as she tried pulling her elbow away.

A man suddenly stood before them at the market table clearing his throat. Autumn and Simone rose from their chairs and found Vera and Bill Cunningham standing before them.

"Mr. and Mrs. Cunningham," Autumn greeted them with uncertainty.

"Girls, I'm glad to see you made it to the market this year, and I see that you have a display of your gran's teas on the table. It's just lovely." Vera pursed her lips into a smile and then looked over at her husband. "Bill has something he'd like to say to you both."

Her husband's gaze moved back and forth between the girls for a moment. "Yes, I wanted to apologize to you both."

They all stood there for a moment in silence, trying to process his words. Autumn sensed his intentions were heartfelt, and she immediately smelled a hint of lilies in the air, a scent of innocence and rebirth.

"I thought your grandmother was trying to drive my wife and I apart, and the last thing I'd ever want is anyone to hurt my Vera. But it turns out I was the one who hurt her, and I blamed your family for meddling in our affairs instead. I know now that Lorna cared for Vera enough to help us come to terms with our issues, and I'm grateful for that. So I truly didn't mean you any harm, and I just wanted to say... I'm sorry." He wrung his dry hands together as he got the words out.

"Thank you for saying that, Mr. Cunningham. We both really appreciate that and realize it was all just a big misunderstanding." Autumn repeated the words she used with him on the mountain as she tried to remove any memory of their magic. "I hope you know I meant what I said about helping you both in any way we can. In fact, why don't you take one of our calendars for the new year? It'll be our reconciliation gift for a fresh start. I think you'll find it to be a nice reminder of the new beginning you both have together as well."

Autumn sorted through the basket with her fingers and pulled out just the right one for the Cunninghams. "How about this one? The holly depicts a Celtic symbol of goodwill and continuous prosperity." She smiled as she held it up for them.

"Oh, that's so lovely of you, Autumn! You know, I've had my eye on some new holly bushes to line the backyard, and now you've gone and chosen a calendar with them right on the cover. Honestly, I don't know how your family does it, but thank you!" Vera broadened her smile as she took the calendar that Simone had just tied with a dark green bow.

"You're very welcome. Thanks for stopping by and talking with us." Autumn sat back in her chair as the two of them walked away to the next booth.

"Well, that went much better than I would have expected! Maybe the energy around here is shifting after all." Simone rummaged through her black messenger bag under the table to pull out a water bottle. She chugged the water and then plopped down next to Autumn.

"Things are just getting started right now. Why don't you head over to the Forest Brew booth and have a chat with Eve while I hold down the fort?"

"Are you sure? I can wait a while and go over in a bit," Autumn suggested.

"No, do it now while things are still slow. I'm good here. Besides, I think I see your mom heading over from my mother's booth, so she'll be able to lend a hand if I need it."

"Yeah, okay. I'll be back in a few." Autumn got up and slung her backpack over her shoulder. She passed her mother on the way across the market and gave her a hug.

"Hi, Mom. I'm headed over to the Forest Brew, but if you wouldn't mind helping Simone for a few minutes, that would be great."

"Of course, I'll head there now, sweetie." They began walking away from each other as Penny had a thought. "Autumn," she called. Autumn turned back to look at her mother. "I'm proud of you."

Autumn had never heard those words from her mother before, yet they felt right on time. "Thanks, Mom. I'm proud of you, too." For the first time, Autumn could see her mother choosing to honor her gifts in a way that didn't push her farther from the things she cared most about but toward them. And she was still bringing healing to those who needed it most.

She walked toward the Forest Brew booth knowing her family would be different after this. The town would be different, too, and she felt a little more confident in letting it all play out exactly as it needed to, without a plan.

"Oh hey, Autumn!" She looked over to see Eve busy at work behind a tall pastry case sitting on their large market table.

"Hi, Eve. You're just the person I came to see." Autumn glanced at the growing line of customers to her right. "Wow, the customers lined up quickly, I see."

"Oh yeah, they all want the latest coffee blend! Plus, now that Kennedy's mince pie booth is no longer here," Eve's voice stopped. "Oh, I'm so sorry for mentioning her! I didn't mean to..."

"No, it's okay. I'm just glad everything got resolved."

"Yeah, well, they had a shortage of pastries since her booth dropped out, and the chamber called my mom to see if we could make up the difference. Turns out my pastries are a huge hit, and they were actually super excited that I'd be willing to bake and have a larger booth."

"That's amazing, Eve! But, it's no wonder. Your pastries really are incredible. That's what I wanted to talk to you about. I know you're getting busier as people trickle in, but can I steal you away for just a moment?" Autumn scrunched up her face and pressed her teeth together in anticipation of an answer.

"Sure, let me just check in on my mom first." Eve stepped to the side and verified with Mrs. Newbury that she'd be okay.

Eve pulled her apron off and threw a long, crocheted scarf around her neck. She motioned to Autumn to follow her around to the back side of the booth. They walked together until they were out of the way of the crowds forming.

"First, I'm going to put our order in for the Pine today. I wanna have your best pastries in our store before the holiday shopping begins. I think a few things will really... speak to our customers." Autumn hinted at Eve's abilities and gave her a sideways glance.

"Thank you, Autumn. Just order whatever you need, and we can deliver it straight to the shop each week if you'd like."

"That would be perfect, Eve. Thanks! And there's something else, too."

"Okay, name it."

"Well, the boost of luck you gave Simone and me the other day actually worked things out in our favor. So, thank you. Honestly, though, I think you can do a lot more than just manifesting a bit of luck. That's why I wondered if you'd be interested in doing more things like that on a larger scale. Maybe in more of a group setting, like with Simone and me?"

Eve played with the ends of her scarf as she thought. "So we would be... dabbling together?"

"I'd call it a lot more than dabbling, but from what I've seen and heard about your gifts, they'll be a very welcome addition to our new coven, shall we call it?" Her eyes shot up to meet Eve's as she waited for a response.

Eve pulled the ends of her scarf up to cover her face as she jumped up and down, giddy as a schoolgirl. Autumn looked at her with curiosity. She knew Eve was eccentric, but this truly made Autumn love Eve's lighthearted nature.

"Yes, yes, of course! Oh my goodness, this is going to be amazing! Can I tell my mom about this, or should we keep it between us?" Eve couldn't seem to contain her excitement. "It's just that I've never had anyone besides my mom to practice with, so this is huge."

Autumn put her hand on Eve's shoulder to get her to slow down. "You can tell your mom. I have a feeling she and my Aunt Jo have probably already discussed this a bit. But let's not get ahead of ourselves, okay? We'll start slow and see how things end up."

"Oh, that's a good plan. Starting slow works for me. But when do we start?" Eve jittered around a bit.

Autumn pulled out her phone and thought for a moment. "Next Thursday evening around eight o'clock. I'm getting the sense that'll be just the right time."

CHAPTER 31

Autumn loaded her arms down with flowers and baskets of Gran's tea. She pushed her back against the door of Simone's SUV to close it and sighed. Making her way toward the downtown fountain, she could see Aunt Jo, Penny, and Simone getting everything in place for Gran's memorial service.

"Right here, Autumn!" Aunt Jo called, pointing at a spot along the edge of the water fountain for the flowers.

"Got it." Autumn placed two large pots filled with purple iris flowers where Jo had requested. The irises were Gran's favorite, a symbol of courage and wisdom, just like Gran herself.

"Everyone will arrive in just a few minutes. Do we have Gran's tea blends to give out as well?" Penny asked.

"Yep, I've got them here. I'll just put them over where Aunt Jo will be speaking." Autumn walked to a little wooden bench in front of the river. It was the one they requested to be marked with Gran's name. Autumn placed the basket of tea tins on the bench and noticed the nameplate on the backrest. "In remembrance of Lorna MacKinnon, our wisest and dearest champion of the town."

Autumn ran her fingers over the inscription. A powerful scent of the iris flowers wafted through the surrounding air.

"Gran is here. I can feel her energy." Simone walked up next to Autumn and put her hand on her shoulder.

Autumn nodded as a tear came to her eye. "You're right. The scent of iris flowers is strong in the air, and I know she is, too."

The girls looked out at the river in front of them, lined with a long row of flower boxes all the way down the river path. The sun's rays peeked through on the flower boxes as the clouds appeared to break above them. All the flowers opened wide at once, the beautiful colors displayed in only a way Gran herself could have achieved with a bit of magic.

"That's our gran," Simone leaned her head against her cousin's, and they stood for a moment admiring the landscape.

"They're all arriving. Girls, we're starting in just a moment. Please help me greet everyone." Jo straightened her black velvet skirt and buttoned the large collar flap of her dark green vintage coat as she walked into the crowd forming.

Autumn nodded to Jo as she caught the comforting scent of roasted chestnuts and cherry cordial. She turned to find James behind her.

"Hello, stranger," he said with a soft grin.

"Why, hello. I'm glad you came." Autumn took a step closer to him.

"I hadn't heard from you in several days, and I've been thinking about how you're doing. Plus, I wanted to be here to give my condolences along with my mother." He raised his chin toward his mom. She talked with Jo and Penny across the square.

"Right, your mom is fairly close with Jo. Well, I appreciate you being here, too." She brought her eyes back to his.

"So, are you all right? Are things somehow getting back to normal for you?"

Autumn sighed and nodded. "Yeah, I've been fine. I just needed a few days to process everything and take some space for myself, you know?"

"Yeah, I completely understand. That was a lot to go through, and I'm really glad you're all right."

They both turned to look at all the people showing up. Gran touched so many lives not only here in Hollow's Glenn but in the mountain region as well. Autumn recognized people from the next town over and even some she hadn't seen in years.

"Man, this is some turnout. Your grandmother must have been an incredible woman."

Autumn could feel a gentle breeze blowing around them, sweeping through her hair and giving a lightness to the air.

"She really was."

"Well, I can see that she passed quite a few things down to you, too." James turned toward Autumn and put his arm around her shoulders to pull her closer.

"I think you should come around more often. Maybe take me for a coffee sometime." She looked up at him as he held her.

"I'd like that. I hear the peppermint hot chocolate at the Forest Brew is something not to be missed when the weather turns."

Autumn laughed to herself. "You're right. My friend, Eve, knows how to add a special something to a cozy cup."

They both turned toward the fountain as Aunt Jo rang a bell to silence the crowd.

"Hello, everyone. Thank you for coming to this special occasion. We're honoring our dear mother, grandmother, neighbor, and friend, Lorna MacKinnon. She was a pillar of this community for decades, and her presence will be greatly missed." Jo stepped back for a moment to let Penny come forward.

"To remember her, we'd like to have each of you throw a penny into our historic fountain and set an intention. As many of you know, my mother worked her whole life to preserve the character and integrity of this town and its surrounding region. She was grounded in the beauty of the mountains and wise with the knowledge of her ancestors. And so, with each penny, we'll bring energy to what she held most dear, our town's endurance and the wisdom within our hearts." Penelope grabbed a wooden box sitting on the fountain and opened it to reveal a mound of pennies inside.

"Please come forward one by one to throw a coin in and set your intention." Jo waved the front row of people closest to the fountain forward.

As a line formed, Jo signaled to a small group carrying large handbells to come forward. They stood to the side of the fountain, having one person in front to conduct the group. With a wave of the conductor's hand, they played the bells and made long, sweeping motions with their arms. The sound of the chimes rang through the air, and Autumn remembered the wind chimes Gran helped her make for the cottage porch. Now, the chimes brought everything full circle. They transitioned Gran's time to pass and called on Autumn's energy to come forward.

She stepped out of James's arms, giving him a warm smile as she made her way to the fountain. Autumn hugged her cousin and then her mother. She felt the glow of her necklace beginning to warm her chest as she stood there. Autumn stood silently for a moment to understand what it might be, and then she let her eyes wander through the crowd. She looked at each person as they stepped forward to receive a penny, and her gaze wandered out to the perimeter of the downtown park.

A girl about Autumn's age with deep brown hair flowing down over her shoulders stood in the tree line at the top of the hill by the parked cars. When she noticed Autumn staring at her, she worked her way down toward everyone. Autumn went around the backside of the fountain to meet up with her. As the two of them came together, Autumn squinted as she looked at the girl's face.

"Are you... Lainy?" Autumn remembered seeing the girl arguing with Kennedy on the side street after the preservation meeting.

The girl pursed her lips together as if unsure of what to say. She raised her chin again and met Autumn's eyes. "Yes, I'm Kennedy's sister." She swallowed hard before continuing, not knowing how Autumn would react.

"I wanted to say I'm so sorry for my sister's actions. I didn't know she would hurt anyone like that. Kennedy felt like an outcast her whole life, and nothing I ever said or did changed that. It's no excuse, but at least you know why she may have done it."

"I heard you went to the police and notified them about your sister. Thank you for doing that. It helped them get to us when we needed them most."

"I'm just glad no one else got hurt. I feel terrible about your grandmother, and I don't know how to make things right, not that it ever really can be right."

Autumn stood back for a moment and let the ancestors speak to her thoughts. She instantly knew Lainy had a warmth to her, something that was strong but reasonable and kind at the same time.

"The past is the past, but it's never too late to make things right. Someone very special taught me that, and I'd like to think there's truth to it." Autumn raised her eyebrows at Lainy as she continued. "In fact, I know some people who would like to meet you, if you'd be willing."

"All right... if you think it's a good idea."

Autumn looked back down the hill toward her family at the fountain. "Yeah, I do. It's the best way for us all to move forward. Come on."

Lainy followed Autumn toward the fountain and waited behind her as Autumn tapped Aunt Jo on the shoulder.

"Aunt Jo, there's someone I'd like you to meet. A long-lost relative, Lainy." Autumn stepped aside to show Lainy off behind her.

Jo gasped and then threw her arms around Lainy. "Oh, dear child, what you must have gone through all these years! Well, that's all done now. You're with family now."

Penny stepped up to face Lainy next. She looked her up and down and then embraced her just as her sister had. "Thank you for going to the police and helping to put a stop to all of this. You've allowed us to start healing, and for that I'm very grateful."

Simone came around the side and pulled the round shades down from her eyes. "So, you're Lainy? The twin sister."

"Fraternal twin, but yes. We're quite different, though. Always have been." Lainy looked directly into Simone's eyes, as if ready to receive whatever verbal chastising she was going to give.

Simone followed a line around Lainy, reading her aura before she spoke. She saw a bright yellow line bursting directly around her body and then tapering off to a pale yellow at the edges.

"You're a confident one, I can tell." Simone paused for a moment as they stared at each other. "I like that. And I like that you're not afraid to do what you feel you need to do. I'm pretty sure you'll fit in just fine around here. Welcome to the family." Simone said as she pushed her shades back up and turned to face the easing crowd.

"All right, everyone, thank you so much for coming. Please take a tea tin with you from the basket before you go to remember Lorna's soothing energy, and stay and chat for as long as you'd like." Jo wrapped up the memorial and stretched her arms out to gather Autumn and Simone in them.

"Girls, we got through it together. I'm so proud of us all." Jo squeezed them tighter.

"Now, onto the next chapter," Simone replied.

"Yeah, and if the New Year fortunes I prepped up for our upcoming Yule cracker collection are any indication, I'd say it's going to be a pretty busy next chapter." Autumn gave them all a wide-eyed look, and a burst of laughter filled the air, just as Gran would have wanted it.

CHAPTER 32

Tavish wandered out of the hearth room and stretched his front legs long in front of him. He gave a giant yawn as Autumn came by.

"Hey there, Tav. Have a good nap, did you?" She scratched the inside of his ear, and he purred and leaned into her hand. "Good boy."

"Hey Autumn, I'm about to finish up the last of these gift box designs, and then I'll send them to the laser cutter in the back, okay?" Simone peeked out from behind the computer on the shop counter.

"Yeah, that sounds great. I'd like to get them all cut out and ready for the display in the next week. I know we'll have some early holiday shoppers looking around soon, so I wanna be prepared."

Autumn walked to the front window with a few tall black metal candle holders and dark green tapers. She stood them up on a wooden crate in the window display and laid some spruce branches and a few paper pumpkins underneath them. Then, she stacked a pile of cable-knit throw pillows inside the crate.

She stepped back to check her work. "Nice. I think our window display totally says snuggle up and get ready for the colder months. I love it." Autumn fluffed up the throw pillows and looked out the front window to see James approaching the door.

"Oh, this is a surprise." Autumn went over to welcome him inside.

"Hey, Autumn," he said as he stomped his boots on the welcome mat and stepped aside to reveal his mother behind him.

"Oh, Mrs. Allan, hello. What brings you both in?" Autumn took his mother's coat and placed it on the wall hooks beside the door as Simone made her way to the front of the store.

"Hello, dears. Lovely to see you both again after the memorial. I wish it were under better circumstances that I've come on this Thursday afternoon, but it seems I'm in a predicament." They all ushered her toward the back of the shop and away from the door.

"I would have gone straight to Josephine, but James tells me you girls may be a better place to start. I've had a dream, and well," she hesitated to continue.

"It's all right, Mom. Tell them." James put his hand on his mother's shoulder and encouraged her to keep going.

"I'm afraid, I saw someone drown. I couldn't make out the details, but I just know they were lying lifeless face down in the river." She had a grave expression on her face as her chin dropped toward the floor.

"Mrs. Allan, why don't you come sit by the fire with us? I'll get you a nice cup of tea, and you can chat with Autumn for a few moments, all right?" Simone put her hand on Sorcha Allan's back and guided her toward the hearth room.

Autumn and James followed, adjusted the two wingback chairs, and stoked the fire.

"Just sit down here, Mrs. Allan, and tell me as much as you can." Autumn brought her to a chair and made her comfortable as Tavish circled her feet in support. James motioned for Autumn to take the other wingback chair while he stood.

"Thanks," she said, sitting on the edge of the chair and leaning toward Sorcha. "Now, let's start from the beginning."

Simone headed out of the hearth room, pulling the heavy curtains to a close on either side of the archway. She stopped for a moment and put her hands on her hips. As goosebumps rose on her arms, she immediately felt a rush of intense energy. The next chapter was about to be written.

Will the girls help Mrs. Allan discover who she dreamt about before it's too late? Find out in the next installment of the Hollow's Glenn Coven Mystery Series, *A River Of Resentment*.

Next In Series

Get the next book in the Hollow's Glenn Coven Mystery Series!

A River of Resentment, book 2 in the series, is available at the link below. Black magic looms through the waters in Hollow's Glenn, leaving a prominent community member dead and lots of questions mounting around who may be next. Discover how the founding families bring their magic together and whether Autumn and her newly forming coven can restore the energy balance once again.

Don't miss another great story with your favorite characters from Hollow's Glenn!

Grab your copy now!

https://kristenkingwrites.com/hollowsglennseries

Download your FREE Prequel Novella

to the

Hollow's Glenn Coven Mystery Series,

A Land Of Consequence.

Find out Autumn's origin story and what kept her mother, Penny, in the
mountain region for so many years.

Go to:

https://dl.bookfunnel.com/azstlfr1se

To get your copy now!

A Note From The Author

Thank you so much for reading my cozy paranormal mystery, *An Air of Deceit*. I hope the characters spoke to you and that you fell in love with the inviting mountain town of Hollow's Glenn. If you'd like to share the enjoyment with fellow readers, then leaving an online book review would support those interested in cozy reads as well. That way, we can create a movement of magical readers in love with the worlds and possibilities in each story.

Now, this is the first in the Hollow's Glenn coven mystery series, so there will be more opportunities to get immersed in the world of the MacKinnon girls and the founding families. Plus, with each book, I'll share some practical magic such as Gran's tea recipes, Autumn's seasonal journaling prompts, and Eve's pastry recipes.

You can also hop onto my newsletter list to get the prequel with Penny's story of how she left for the mountain region and why she stayed so long. You may even find out how Autumn's gifts started.

To read the free prequel novella, *A Land of Consequence*, and hear about the latest releases and other goodies, scan here:

Acknowledgments

To my twin flame, thank you for all the years you encouraged my creativity and always knew something inspired would materialize. I love you to the moon and back, infinity times around.

Along with my other favorite alpha reader, you gave me an outside view of the story every night before bedtime. I got to see Hollow's Glenn through your eyes and enjoy our own cozy nights all at the same time. I couldn't think of a better way to share my first draft.

About The Author

Kristen is an Amazon bestselling author, spiritual life coach, and creative. After many years blending project management, design, and coaching, she now lets her water energy lead the way through creative fiction writing. She finds that a good dose of magic sets the coziest tone for any day.

When not channeling her inner writing muse, Kristen enjoys baking for her family, creating herbal concoctions, and tapping into all things metaphysical. She spends time snuggling in her mountain home next to a cozy fire and her calico cat, with plenty of candles and jazz playing softly in the background. She loves to lose herself taking photos, pulling tarot cards, or charging crystals by the light of the moon.

For more from the author and to find her books and offerings, go to: https://www.kristenkingwrites.com